MOMMY
and the
MURDER

MOMMY
and the
MURDER

A NOVEL

Nancy Goldstone

HarperCollins*Publishers*

HarperCollins books may be purchased for educational, business, or sales promotional use. For information please write: Special Markets Department, HarperCollins Publishers, Inc., 10 East 53rd Street, New York, NY 10022.

FIRST EDITION

Designed by Alma Hochhauser Orenstein

ISBN 0-06-017660-1

95 96 97 98 99 ❖/HC 10 9 8 7 6 5 4 3 2 1

for *my* Emily

Prologue

"Elizabeth! I was going to call you but I didn't want to wake you up. You'll never guess what happened last night after you left!"

"Yes, Didi," I replied. "That's why I'm calling. I—"

"A man was *murdered*. Can you believe it? Right here in Lenox!"

"Yes," I tried again. "That's why I'm calling, I—"

"Elizabeth, it was so *awful*. He was *shot*. In the *head*. There was blood *everywhere*. It was so—no, Samantha, you may not just lick the maple syrup off your pancakes and then throw them on the floor. Because I said so, that's why. Oh, it was terrible, just terrible. He was *naked*, you know," she added in a whisper.

"No, I—"

"The police think it's some kind of love scandal. There was a note. A strange poem. Something about a garden. With priests and gravestones. Very creepy."

"What—"

"The thing is, it had to be somebody at the party, didn't it? John thinks so. Oh, you don't know John, do you? He's my second—or is it my third?—no, my second cousin. He's on the police force. He was there last night. Everybody was there.

They called in everybody in the county. The *DA* was there. Boy, did he look grumpy—what, sweetheart? Well, because he didn't get enough sleep, I guess. Because they woke him up in the middle of the night. Because that's his job. He catches bad guys. Yes, just like on TV. No, there aren't any bad guys here right now. Because I said there aren't. Because—"

"Didi," I cut in, rather desperately.

"What? Oh, yes. Where was I? Oh, yes, the police came. Margaux called them. She found the body. She's really something, isn't she? That house, the food—say, what did you think of her costume?"

Chapter

1

"So, listen, Em, if you don't like this play group, just tell me, huh?" I said.

We were driving along in the Jeep, just Emily and I. The instruction manual says to put the car seat in the back, but I never do. It's just not the same watching her through the rearview mirror.

"Because I don't want to be one of those mothers who says 'Isn't this terrific' and then find out later you had a terrible time," I continued. "Then again," laying my hand on the armrest of her car seat and hooking my little finger around all five of hers, "we can't just hide out in the house forever. We've got to get out there and meet people, right?"

At that moment we turned into the driveway of a large, split-level yellow house. It was the Friday before Halloween and the entire facade, from the garage to the bay window at the far corner, had been hung with Indian corn and dried flowers tied with orange and black ribbons and spaced at regular intervals. It looked like a funeral home for the Great Pumpkin.

"On the other hand," I conceded, "there's a lot to be said for seclusion . . ."

It didn't help any to remember that the whole idea of this play group had been mine. My sister Susan in LA not only had a play group for Brittany (who was two months younger than Emily), but also took her to Mommy-and-Me and Jamboree classes. Brittany, Susan reported, had already learned to clap her hands to music.

Here in the Berkshires there are no Mommy-and-Me or Jamboree classes. There are rolling hills, striking vistas, brilliant autumn hues, and impossibly clear blue skies, but if you want your child to have playmates, you have to find them yourself, which is how Emily and I came to be in front of the beribboned house.

As we pulled up, the front door opened and a dark-haired woman in her early thirties wearing black leggings and a sequined sweatshirt came out accompanied by two children. She carried a large black hat that she evidently intended as the finishing touch on an enormous scarecrow made of cornstalks that barricaded the walkway. Seeing us, the woman turned and gave us a hearty wave. It was Didi, of course. Didi Romeo.

I had met Didi through a cold call, like a broker. There are Romeos all over the Berkshires. There is a Romeo car dealer, a Romeo dry cleaner and a Romeo rug merchant. There are Romeo attorneys-at-law, Romeo dentists and a Romeo exterminator. A Romeo manages the cinema center and another the ice cream parlor. I got Didi's name by asking every merchant in Lenox if they knew someone with a child Emily's age. At the time, I was very proud of my sleuthing, although I see now that it was inevitable that I would have been referred to a Romeo.

This being New England, Didi had been startled at receiving a phone call from someone she hadn't already known for fifteen years. However, after duly establishing my credentials as a mother and full-time resident of town, she had been willing to admit that she had two children, Samantha, three and a half, and Sean, eleven months, just Emily's age.

Then, within the space of ten minutes, Didi had confided that she was a member of Overeaters Anonymous and given to manic-depressive behavior; that she and her husband, who sold insurance, were seeing a marriage counselor; that they were so overextended they couldn't afford the mortgage payments on the house; that she had breast-fed Samantha until the age of thirty-six months; and that she planned to pursue a career as a lingerie specialist as soon as the children were older. She then offered to help me meet some of her other friends and set up a regular play group.

I accepted immediately.

Didi told me about her sister-in-law, Pat, a part-time attorney at Kellerman & Merritt. Even I, new as I was to the area, knew that Kellerman & Merritt was notorious for representing developers over environmentalists, landlords over tenants and second-home owners over local tradespeople. Pat's son, Oliver, Didi reported, was two months older than Emily.

"You'll love Pat," Didi assured me. "She's so organized." She went on to say that Pat kept a changing table and a diaper pail in the dining room as well as the nursery, "just in case," and that she sorted Oliver's toys into categories. "Let's see if I can remember," Didi mused. "There's interactive, developmental, language stimulation—I love language stimulation—and one more, let's see, oh, yes, hand–eye coordination.

"She's a little strange, though," Didi continued hesitantly. "She eats all this microbiotic food. That doesn't bother you, does it?"

I assured her it didn't.

"Then why don't we set up a date for next Friday?" Didi suggested.

Two days later I met Astrid at the supermarket all by

myself. I first noticed her in Produce and trailed her to the deli. She was round-faced, blonde and blue-eyed and was wheeling around a gorgeous round-faced, blond, blue-eyed boy of about Emily's age. He wielded his bottle with one hand, as though it were a cigar.

Astrid's full name was Astrid Van Boonstraden. She was new, too, having arrived in Lenox only a few months before when her husband, Jann, a software engineer, had been transferred here. But I had only come from Manhattan. Astrid was from Holland. "You know, the place with all the tulips," she explained helpfully.

Astrid beamed when I asked if she and her son ("M-A-U-R-I-T-S," she spelled carefully. "You say it Morris, *ja?*") would join our play group. "Only in America would Maurits and I make new friends while buying bagels!" We exchanged phone numbers and I gave her the time and place of our first meeting.

Now Astrid's Subaru pulled in behind us.

"Hi!" I chirped.

"Hi, good morning." Astrid bobbed her head and smiled. She had obviously had her hair cut. It made her look like she just stepped off a paint can. She shifted her hip under Maurits, who eyed us suspiciously before returning his full attention to his bottle. "What a beautiful morning, *ja?*"

Didi carefully placed the witch's hat on top of the cornstalk scarecrow as Samantha tugged at her sweatshirt. "Who dat?" she demanded, pointing at Emily.

"That's Emily," I answered proudly, bending down so that Samantha and Emily could be eye-to-eye. Emily cocked her head to one side and regarded Samantha gravely. Her forehead wrinkled slightly as she concentrated, in a way I find irresistible.

"HI, EMILY!" Samantha shouted in her face.

Emily transferred the look of concentration to the scarecrow.

"HEY, EMILY!" Samantha persisted, pulling on Emily's skirt.

Didi intervened. "Samantha, sweetheart, she can't answer you."

"Why not?"

"She can't talk yet. She's too little."

"Oh." Samantha turned to Astrid without missing a beat. "Who dat?" she asked, pointing at Maurits.

"That's Maurice, honey," said Didi.

"Actually, it's Maurits," said Astrid. "You spell it M-A-U-R-I-T-S, but you say it Morris, *ja?*"

"That's what I said. Maurice," Didi replied pleasantly.

Samantha squinted up at Astrid. "You talk funny," she said.

Pat pulled up behind Astrid in a black Pathfinder. She was a rather short, rather thin brown-haired woman wearing a boxy blue suit with a knockoff Gucci silk scarf and high-heeled pumps. We all watched as she pulled Oliver, a briefcase and several neatly stacked Tupperware containers out of the car. As she tap-tap-tapped her way up the driveway to the front door I could see that each plastic bowl was labeled with a different-colored tape. The one on top read "Pureed Turnips." She reminded me of a Girl Scout determined to win the cookie sale.

Pat just had time to hand over these goodies to Didi when a hush fell over our little party.

"What is it?" I asked, turning just in time to see a sleek midnight-blue Jaguar glide to a stop beside the curb.

"That must be the woman who answered my advertisement," Pat murmured, squinting into the sun.

"What advertisement?" I asked.

"I just thought it would be a good idea to get as many children as possible," Pat explained, "so I ran an ad in *The Penny Saver*."

A boy of perhaps five let himself out of the back of the Jag, slamming the door behind him. Moments later a tall, stunning woman emerged from the front seat holding a three-year-old in her arms, her soft blonde hair gleaming in the sun.

She was dressed in a pair of dark blue jeans made of a rich brushed material. The color matched the car. Even from a distance I could tell that her scarf, which was coiled carelessly around her neck, was cashmere and her cowboy boots hand-tooled leather. As she sauntered up the walk to the house, I stole a look at my companions. They stood frozen, a mixture of awe and shock on their faces, as though they were about to meet an apparition with a penchant for Ralph Lauren. So imposing was her presence that even Samantha was quiet.

Finally, Astrid broke the silence. "Poof, that's what I call a car," she said.

It was Margaux.

I could tell that she noticed me while she was pulling the three-year-old out of the car, but instead of acknowledging my presence she strolled up to the other women on the lawn and introduced herself. Then she got to me.

"Hello, Elizabeth."

"Hello, Margaux."

"Ooh!" said Didi brightly. "You two know each other?"

"We're old friends," said Margaux.

Didi clasped her hands together hospitably. "Why doesn't everyone come in?" she said.

In honor of the first official meeting of the play group, Didi had dragged out boxes and boxes of toys—more toys than I had ever seen in any one place that wasn't selling them retail. There were scooters and tricycles, two rocking horses, blocks, dolls, doll carriages, doll clothes, doll accessories, stuffed animals, a toy kitchen, a toy workbench, a toy truck stop, a farm with movable sheep, horses, pigs and chickens, a toy doctor's kit, a toy nurse's kit, a toy cosmetics kit and a miniature drum set. Rising above this carnage like the obelisk in *2001: A Space Odyssey* was a forty-two-inch color television playing *The Little Mermaid* with the sound turned off, while the speakers attached to an incredibly complex-looking CD unit blared "Zip-A-Dee-Doo-Dah."

"We went a little overboard at Christmas," Didi murmured.

We put our children down in the midst of all this treasure and ringed them expectantly. They seemed dazed. Emily picked up a block, stuck it in her mouth and put it down. Maurits poked his finger at one of the cows. Oliver, who was walking, toddled over to one of the scooters, climbed onto it and then cried because he couldn't figure out how to get off. Sean hid in the corner behind the television. Alden, Margaux's youngest, clung to his mother. Samantha waited until Tolin, Margaux's oldest, sat down on a tricycle and then screamed that she wanted it.

"Well, isn't this nice," said Didi as she yanked Samantha and Tolin apart.

Pat established herself on the sofa, donned a pair of formidable horn-rimmed glasses and opened her briefcase. She emerged with a fistful of papers that she proceeded to distribute. "While the children are playing, why don't we get this over with?" she suggested.

I glanced down at the pages. They were typewritten forms, not unlike job applications. "Name," "Address," "Phone Number," "Date of Birth," "Child's Name," "Child's Address (if different from your own)," "Date of Birth," "Favorite Color," "Child's Favorite Color (if different from your own)," et cetera, et cetera.

Astrid squinted at hers. "What's this?" she asked.

"I just thought it would be nice for all of us to have some information about each other," Pat explained. "Once they're filled out I'll have them mimeographed and I'll send each one of you copies for your files."

"Oh, of course," said Astrid blankly, nonetheless beginning gamely on hers.

We all took her cue and got to work, except Margaux. Pat eyed her for a moment. "Is something the matter?" she asked finally.

Margaux bounced Alden on her lap. "I'm afraid I don't have anything to write with," she replied coolly, even though a Cross pen-and-pencil set was visible in her open Fendi knapsack.

"So, Margaux," said Didi, putting down her pencil and smiling encouragingly, "Pat tells me that you are a writer."

"Yes, I am."

"Really!" Astrid exclaimed. "You mean you write books and things?"

"Yes."

"*Ja?* That is really exciting! What are your books about, please?"

"Well, it's a little difficult to explain . . ."

"Oh, please," Pat chimed in. "After all, it's not often you get to meet an author face-to-face."

"Well," said Margaux, sitting up a little straighter and brushing a strand of expertly cut golden hair off her forehead with her right hand, revealing the presence of an enormous sapphire-and-diamond bracelet, "my work focuses around two main themes: the victimization of women by men throughout the ages and the personal struggle for passionate self-determination. It is my intention, through my work, to identify and highlight instances of erotic subjugation in order that women will at last achieve their rightful place in the universal order of sensuality. History demonstrates that traditional relationships between men and women are inherently unequal and unfair—I am speaking particularly of *orgasmic* relationships, which I have defined as the ability of the female partner to achieve a climax of equal proportion and intensity to that of the male partner. It is only through addressing these grievances—either through writing, as I do, or by general outpouring of sentiment—that women can at last throw off the yoke of male dominance."

The room momentarily fell silent. Then Didi spoke.

"Is it a mystery?" she asked. "I just love mysteries."

Pat's beeper went off.

"Didi, I have to call the office."

"Of course," said Didi. "I'll go with you."

As they walked off, Astrid leaned over and sniffed at Maurits. "Mauu-rits," she crooned, "is that a poopie-doopie I smell? I think so." Maurits gurgled happily. "Maybe we go upstairs and change your diaper now?"

Margaux and I were left alone.

I had first met Margaux when Howard and I came up from the city for a long weekend to look for a place for him to finish his novel. I remember walking down Main Street in Lenox thinking how absolutely perfect everything was. The sky was perfect. The snow was perfect. The town was perfect. Being married was perfect. But mostly, walking next to Howard was perfect.

It wasn't just his looks, good as those were, that made people turn and stare after him when we passed, I decided as we strolled along holding hands and looking in shop windows. It was the way he carried himself. The angle at which he set his head. The way his clothes hung. The expression in his dark eyes. The entire picture said: ARTIST. WRITER. LOVER of BEAUTY and CULTURE. Just plain LOVER. In other words, everything I, who spent my time staring into computers at little green numbers for money, admired in the world and wasn't. Special.

But if Howard was special, I reasoned, then the person walking next to him holding his arm must be special, too. In fact, I was still just getting used to being the person walking next to him holding his arm. It seemed slightly unreal, as though any moment something would come along and . . . that's when we strolled around a corner and came upon a quaint little bookstore.

I love books. I've always loved books. I love the way they feel and the sound they make when you turn the pages. I love their smell. I love books about romance, books about history, books about nineteenth-century British parliamentary intrigues. Before I met Howard, there was nothing I liked better than to browse through a quaint little bookstore in a quaint little town like Lenox.

But Howard didn't like quaint little bookstores in quaint little towns because they almost never carried copies of either of his books. And if Howard walked into a bookstore and did not find himself tucked in between Graham Greene and Thomas Hardy, he made it a point to stride up to the owner and, in a voice loud enough for everyone in the shop to hear, ask if there were copies in the back. If there were not (and there almost never were, Howard's novels having been published by a small press in Berkeley which had, as of then, sold a total of 279 copies), Howard would grab a copy of Danielle Steel or Judith Krantz or whoever else happened to have a bestseller (there was nothing Howard loathed more than a bestseller) and, in the same strident tone, lecture the proprietor on his or her lack of taste and general ignorance of serious American fiction. Then he would slam the book down on the owner's desk, march out of the store and promptly complain of a headache which would cause him to walk down the street holding his hands to his temples and muttering.

In this case, it didn't matter, since I wouldn't have gone into this bookstore anyway. Some woman was going to read from her new book, *Aphrodite Aflutter: The Search for Orgasm in Women's Literature*, and it's impolite to browse while someone is reading, even something like that. But Howard suddenly wheeled around and ducked into the store.

I hesitated a moment and then followed him inside. Folding chairs had been set up in rows and I found Howard sitting near the front on the right. I took a seat beside him. At that moment, a beautiful statuesque blonde in her mid-thirties rose from a chair on the side to address the audience.

Her dress was expensive, clingy and sexy. Her voice was soft and sexy. Her eyes were blue and sexy. Her figure was slim and—well, you get the picture.

Guess who.

The reading lasted almost an hour. I don't remember much about it, except that she spent fifteen minutes describing having an orgasm while peeling a grapefruit. After she finished there was sporadic but enthusiastic applause, and then the audience slowly began to disperse. A handful of people gathered around the author, but most straggled out the door.

Howard and I got up and made our way to the aisle. I was turning toward the exit when he put his arm around me.

"I quite enjoyed that, didn't you?" he asked.

I didn't know what to say. Howard didn't generally enjoy anyone else's work. In fact, if Howard praised another author's work, you could pretty much assume that that person was dead.

"Let's go tell her," he said, taking my arm and steering me to the front.

We joined a circle of perhaps five people who had gathered

around the blonde woman, Howard standing a little off to the side and me standing a little off to the side of Howard.

"Excuse me," said Howard, interrupting a man of about eighty in a tweed sport jacket. "I just wanted to tell you how much I enjoyed your reading."

"Why, thank you so much," the blonde replied.

"Perhaps you've heard of me. My name is Howard Hack . . ."

"Howard Hack! Of course I've heard of you! I adored *The St. Paul Duet!*" She stuck out her hand. "Hi, I'm Margaux Chase."

"A pleasure," he replied, letting go of my hand to take hers.

"You know Ann Wheat, don't you? She's a very close friend of mine and she also loves your work."

Ann Wheat was the author of *Witches' Brew*, which had been on top of the *New York Times* bestseller list for the past five months.

"Ann Wheat? I love her work. She's marvelously talented," exclaimed Howard.

"Oh yes," I agreed. "We keep a copy by the bedside."

"This is my wife, Elizabeth," he said, putting his arm around me a little stiffly.

Margaux smiled pleasantly. "Oh. Do you write, too?"

"I'm on Wall Street," I replied, feeling like I had just confessed that I worked in a landfill.

Margaux reached out and touched one finger to Howard's shoulder. "You know, I'm having a few people over to my place this afternoon. Why don't you join us?"

Margaux's "place" was a seven-bedroom nineteenth-century farmhouse set on fourteen acres with a long winding driveway guarded by a row of ancient, magnificent cedars. Her barn doubled as a garage, and there was a stable for her horse and a pond in the back, tucked just out of sight of the house.

The first thing I noticed when I walked into the entranceway was that the wall on the right was dominated by a huge lithograph of a family tree that dated back to Richard the Lionhearted. Margaux's name appeared in the lower right-hand corner.

"A few" people turned out to be about fifty. Three uniformed waiters passed out little canapes from doily-adorned silver trays. Margaux stood in the foyer next to a tall, silverhaired man. Maybe it's her husband, I thought hopefully.

"Howard. I'm so glad you could come. This is a friend of mine, Vincent Marchione. Vincent is in charge of narcotics for all of Brooklyn."

"Sounds like an extremely responsible position," I said.

Vincent laughed. "I'm with the district attorney's office."

"Oh, yes, this is my wife, Elizabeth," said Howard, once again putting his arm around me stiffly.

"Elizabeth's on Wall Street," Margaux added.

"Really," said Vincent. "What do you do, exactly?"

"I trade commodities," I replied.

"Oh!" said Vincent, brightening visibly. He took me by the elbow and led me over to get me a drink where, for the next fifteen minutes, he cross-examined me on the commodity markets while I cross-examined him on Margaux. He learned that assistant district attorneys making $68,000 a year should never go anywhere near the commodity markets. I learned that Margaux had been married to an avant-garde poet with whom she'd had one child, had left him for a violinist with the Boston Symphony Orchestra with whom she'd had a second child, had left *him* for a retired Marine colonel who had had some curious involvement in Nicaragua, and had left *him* for Vincent. I also learned that Margaux came from one of the 500 wealthiest families in America.

At this point I happened to glance over my shoulder and saw Howard and Margaux engaged in an animated conversation. Vincent did too and, without further discussion, we both hurried back to join them.

Now Margaux got off the couch and crouched down next to Emily.

"She's so beautiful," said Margaux.

I looked over at my daughter, who, at that moment, was bending intently over the pages of a picture book. She'd never had the chubby cheeks, dimpled chins and startled faces of the babies selected for tire commercials. Her body was slender and graceful, the curve of her neck delicate. Her light brown hair, even at eleven months, was already curling into ringlets. Her eyes were large and blue, and she had a little Cupid's bow mouth. I turned back to Margaux.

"I know," I said.

Margaux forced a smile. "How have you been doing?" she asked.

"Fine."

"I know how hard it is, being a single mother."

"Oh," I replied, "*are* you ever single?"

Margaux hesitated and I thought for a moment she would retreat to the couch. But then she said, "You know, Elizabeth, one of the first things that Howard said to me was that you two were finished and it was only a question of the formalities until you broke up."

"We'd been married *three weeks*," I pointed out.

"He never mentioned that part."

"Look, Margaux," I said impatiently, "what do you want?"

"I just thought, since we're both in the same boat and it's hard enough to find somebody to talk to up here, that we should try to forget it."

"That's easy for you to say. I never slept with any of *your* husbands."

"Look, Elizabeth. I don't know why you're singling me out. If you stay mad at everyone that Howard slept with, you're not going to have very many women left to talk to."

This time *I* almost got up. But it was true. I should not, in fact, keep blaming everyone else because I had been silly enough to marry a man who was just using me as a financial way station while he worked his way up the literary ladder.

Margaux sensed the tension easing. "Look, Elizabeth," she said, softly, again, "I give a little costume party every Halloween. Why don't you come?"

"A Halloween party!"

Margaux and I both jumped and turned around. There were Didi, Pat and Astrid grouped behind us, Didi holding a pot of coffee. How long they had been standing there, God only knows.

"A Halloween party!" Didi repeated. "What a nice idea. Milk and sugar?"

Chapter

2

I had met Howard three years earlier at a fundraiser. One of the first things you learn when you work on Wall Street is that every member of every organization that wants to raise money for anything targets you as a benefactor. So when the invitations to the Quill Literary Society's annual gala came in, everybody in the trading room did what they always do—they ceremoniously marched up and dumped the little white linen envelopes into the big green garbage pail in the center of the room. I had to wait until eight o'clock, pretending to catch up on some paperwork, before I was alone and could quietly roll up my sleeve and fish mine out.

Even then, I hadn't actually decided to go. I had just decided not to rule out the possibility of going.

What I was doing working on Wall Street—trading commodities, of all things—I couldn't honestly say. I certainly hadn't arrived in front of my bank of computers and tangles of telephone wires by design. Numbers were easy for me, true, and I enjoyed the split-second decision-making, the feeling of being in the middle of something important (even if it was only the cattle market sometimes), the money, the power, the attitude. But I was probably the only person in the room—in the whole Street—with a copy of *Pride and Prejudice* in her desk, and definitely the only one whose attention could be diverted away from a lucrative trade by the trials and tribulations of a fictitious community of clergymen as set down in the Chronicles of Barsetshire.

If anyone had pointed out to me that this was probably a sign that I was in the wrong place, that I was denying what I really wanted to do, I would have dismissed it. I knew I was different, of course, but I never made the connection to anything deeper. I guess there are some dreams that are too important to admit, even to yourself.

In the end, I went.

For the event, the Quill Society had rented the Hall of Fishes at the Museum of Natural History (the one with the big whale suspended from the ceiling). By the time I got there, still in my blue suit, carrying my briefcase, there were some 200 people in the room. But only one Howard.

He was on the other side of the hall, standing in front of the polar bears. He was wearing a black bow tie, a black leather motorcycle jacket over a black fancy dress shirt, black cummerbund, black jeans, black boots and black sunglasses. He looked like Zorro.

Even from fifty feet away he caught me looking at him and raised his glass with a grin. It was the grin that got me. It was a dangerous grin, half-pirate, half-knight.

I just stood there, frozen. My mouth dropped open, as it always does when I'm nervous, so I'm sure that I looked like one of the fish.

Then he began to saunter over in my direction.

I glanced around reflexively and could not help but notice that every other woman in the room looked better than I did.

Zorro got closer.

I tried to pretend I was looking over his shoulder for someone I knew.

He looked straight at me. I expected him to swoop me into his arms at any moment and kiss me passionately.

I caught myself looking like the fish again.

"Hello," he said. His voice was deep and rich.

I nodded.

He looked down at me searchingly. "Your eyes are the most fabulous blue," he said. "I think it's those tiny flecks of violet that make them so arresting." He flashed me that grin again. "And your hair is dark. I love dark women. It's the allure of Madame Bovary over Hedda Gabler. Blonde is so tedious as an ideal of beauty, don't you think?"

I nodded.

"But I confess that, as lovely as you look up close, it was your long splendiferous legs that I first noticed when you entered what was, before, a rather dull room. But I'm sure everyone tells you this. Would you like a glass of wine?"

"Uh, sure," I said.

He took my arm and started to lead me in the direction of the bar. "Perhaps you've heard of me. My name is Howard Hack . . ."

Maybe I was just ready to fall in love, I don't know. I was nearly thirty, which may have had something to do with it. But I think it was more than that. I'd always had plenty of dates and, since I started on Wall Street, I went to the best restaurants, drank the best champagne and went to openings in limousines. But somehow it was never interesting. There was an emptiness about doing wonderful things with people who could just buy them and didn't really appreciate them. Besides, I always ended up talking about the market. I was in a box at the Met once, watching Kiri Te Kanawa sing Madame Butterfly, and I had to field whispered questions on cattle arbitrage during "Un Bel Di."

Still, I had always just assumed that when I got married it would be to someone like me: ambitious, always working, only probably much richer. I don't know, I suppose I thought we'd have his-and-her Reuters screens on either side of the bed.

Suddenly I found myself completely, certifiably crazy for a man whose wardrobe boasted not a single monogram, whose depressing little efficiency apartment contained so many books that it resembled a storage room at the 42nd Street Library and whose vocabulary was laced with quotes that had nothing whatsoever to do with the price of frozen orange juice. It was like being introduced to an impossibly rich, delectable *crème caramel* after spending your whole life eating Jell-O Instant Pudding.

Those first months were enchanted. Although the money he earned from teaching and translating other people's work barely pushed him over the poverty line, Howard nonetheless attempted to squire me around Manhattan in a touchingly chivalrous manner. We went to chic little cafes and downtown taverns where artists congregate. He took me to galleries, museums, lectures, concerts, readings and libraries. We wandered through curious little bookstores (without incident, in those days) and into smoky jazz clubs.

I'd never met anyone like him. Where others were solid, earnest, plodding, Howard was mercurial. He could change from passionate lover to best friend to tortured artist and back to passionate lover again during the course of eating a pizza.

Where other women I knew at work occasionally received flowers or candy at the office, I received, in order of appearance, a blue balloon, a pair of long white pearl-button evening gloves, a book of romantic poetry and a pair of cat's-eye sunglasses. He introduced me to B. Traven, hot fudge sundaes at three in the morning at the Empire Diner and sex.

Sex. Howard was to sex what Frank Perdue was to chickens. He made love to me everywhere. On the bed, on the floor, in the bath (no mean feat), on the kitchen counter, under the dining-room table. He was a genius at finding places where we could snatch a few minutes' privacy. Outside, in the little, out-of-the-way (at least, I hope they were out-of-the-way) upstate parks we drove to on Sunday afternoons. In a hansom cab we'd hired one night to take us around Central Park. At parties, at concerts, at readings. He said it had never happened to him before like this. That he just couldn't keep his hands off me.

On the day we became engaged, Howard rented a subcompact and we drove 150 miles in the dead of winter to the Berkshires so that he could propose to me by candlelight in Edith Wharton's drawing room. The mansion had been closed for the season, so we had to sneak in by wading through a foot of snow to a side window on the wraparound terrace. Our noses were running so badly that anyone would have thought we were attending a funeral. But when we finally made it inside and Howard lit the candles, produced a little hammered-silver ring that a sculptor friend had fashioned for him, took me in his arms and murmured whole passages from Keats's *Endymion: A Poetic Romance*, I worshipped him.

Howard and I were married a month later. Although Wall Street itself was in the midst of a severe downturn, with even the most prestigious firms laying off people right and left, my desk was still making money, quite a lot of money, actually.

Nineteen eighty-nine was one of my best years, and I was already ahead of schedule for 1990. Accordingly, Howard gave up the dreary little downtown efficiency and we moved into a two-bedroom apartment just off Park Avenue in the mid-Eighties. I used the proceeds of my bonus for the down payment.

It was then that Howard, at my urging, gave up the myriad of small projects that had supported him in the past in order to devote his full attention to his next novel. It was to be his breakthrough book.

To be honest, I have to admit that even at that early date in our relationship when I was most susceptible to his charm, when I loved and admired him and wanted him desperately to succeed, I thought the likelihood of Howard's writing such a book improbable. I had read both of Howard's previous efforts and found them, well, difficult. In fact, it was only with great effort that I finished them at all. Despite long eloquent passages, nothing ever seemed to happen in one of Howard's books. Characters came and went for no particular reason, situations changed without explanation and conflicts went unresolved. You got the feeling that you could put the book down, lose your place, then pick up the narrative at random and it would make absolutely no difference.

Of course, I understood that I was far from being a sophisticated literary critic. It was quite possible that I was simply ignorant of what comprised greatness in contemporary literature and therefore incapable of appreciating someone of Howard's talents. Certainly his language skills were impressive. Accordingly, I put aside my personal feelings and did all I could to encourage his efforts. Still, I couldn't shake the nagging suspicion that if I, who loved him so, found his work, well, boring, then it was unlikely that Howard's style would appeal to a mass audience.

Perhaps it was out of a sense of guilt for this very misgiving that led me at every turn to put consideration for Howard's career ahead of my own. For it is certain that, bit by bit, our lives began to revolve around Howard and his breakthrough book.

One of the first steps in this direction was to get Howard out of the city. He felt sure that a prolonged stay in the country would give him the peace and tranquillity he needed to finish his novel. We looked at the Hamptons first but finally settled on a small house in the Berkshires. Not only did it have stunning scenery and a great literary tradition, but it was cheaper.

Margaux, who, by the time we had settled in, had broken it off with Vincent and was engaged in a torrid love affair with the contractor who redid her bathroom, introduced Howard to a number of people in the business who had second homes in the Berkshires. She even invited her agent up for a weekend specifically to meet him. Howard, in turn, began to work feverishly, often spending entire weeks in the house in front of his word processor. Every Friday night, when I arrived, the neatly stacked pile of printed pages on the side of his desk was measurably larger.

I was aware, of course, that Margaux seemed to have no scruples about fooling around with other people's husbands. I was also aware that, with Howard alone in the country on weekdays, he could do whatever he wanted. But I married the man I believed in and you either trust somebody or you don't.

Then, in March, I discovered that I was pregnant.

Since I'd always wanted a child, I was naturally thrilled to find out I was going to have one. I remember spending a lot of time poring over lists of names. What I did not spend much time considering were the changes a child would make in my life. Oh, yes, I conceded, when questioned by friends, family or co-workers, I might not be able to do *everything* I'd done in the past, but I didn't really mean it. It was simply, I thought, a matter of organization. After all, this was the 1990s. Lots of women had careers and children. That was what the feminist movement had been all about—being able to work it all out.

But what I discovered after I had my baby was, it was not a question of working it all out. I didn't *want* to work it all out. I wanted to stay home with my baby. I couldn't get enough of her. The tiny hands and feet, the incredible smoothness of her skin, the pink lips, the droll expressions that would appear without warning as she became aware of and then began to test her facial muscles that made me want to laugh and hug her at the same time. I wanted to experience every second of her growth, catch every smile, every caress. What would I feel like, I wondered, if I were sitting at my desk trying to figure out how to squeeze ten more points out of a four-sided soybean arbitrage at the very moment my child was reaching out on her own for the very first time to touch—someone else's face?

"What do you mean you're not going back to work?" demanded Howard.

We were in the kitchen in the house in the Berkshires, where we had come to spend my maternity leave. Although it was not a large house, it was larger than our apartment in the city. And I'd loved it right from the beginning. It was a white clapboard, black-shuttered colonial with a red door, just like I'd always dreamed about while I was growing up in the pink stucco bungalows of suburban L.A. I remember it was a clear, very cold day in early February and the sun shining on the snow made everything so beautifully bright that it was difficult to look at.

To say that Howard had not taken to fatherhood with the enthusiasm I had hoped for and expected was something of an understatement. In fact, Howard had not taken to fatherhood at all. Every time Emily cried, Howard got one of his headaches. He refused to change her diaper or to bathe her. He said I was better at it. He complained that every time he picked her up she cried, so eventually he refused to pick her up at all. "Why would I voluntarily subject myself to abuse from my own child?" he asked.

"What do you mean you're not going back to work?" he repeated now.

"We can do it," I assured him quickly. "I've got it all figured out. We've still got some of last year's bonus and if we rent the apartment—just for a while, you understand—"

"Rent the apartment?" Howard echoed. "You mean, live here in the country? Full-time?"

"Yes. You know, not forever, just until I'm ready again . . . We can do it. Of course, we'll have to live more simply—not spend too much money—for a little while—just until . . ." I swallowed.

"Elizabeth." Howard allowed a look of hurt to settle on his face. "Surely, after all this time, you know me better than that. I've never cared about money. Who knows better than I how corrupting to art money can be? Look at Hemingway."

"What about Hemingway?"

"He was never the same once he started making money."

"How do you know that? I never heard that—"

"Money can be a terrible trap for a writer," Howard continued. "It's something that I've always carefully guarded against."

"Well, yes, of course—"

"So it obviously isn't money I'm thinking of, Elizabeth. It's you. Your happiness."

"Well, yes, of course—"

"Elizabeth. I understand how you feel," he said, putting his arms around me. "I really do. But you have to get beyond the feeling of the moment. You have to ask yourself, are you sure this is what you really want?"

"What do you mean?" I asked.

"You've worked so hard, put in so many years. Do you really want to throw it all away? Just like that? Because that's what you'll be doing, you know."

Was it? I wondered.

"Elizabeth. I know you. You're not happy unless you're working. You'd miss your job. You'd miss the city. I know some people here, but all your friends are in New York."

"That's okay," I said slowly. "It's not like we're moving to Alaska."

He frowned then and allowed his arms to drop to his sides. "Of course, it's up to you," he shrugged. "But to tell the truth, I should think after about two weeks you'd be climbing the walls." He turned away. "I have to work now," he announced over his shoulder.

I sat at the kitchen table for a long time after he left. Every other time Howard and I had had one of these discussions, I had always let him persuade me. This time, too, his arguments rang true.

Then I got up from the table, walked over to the phone, picked up the receiver, dialed my office in New York and quit.

Things disintegrated pretty quickly after that. There were many arguments. Howard didn't like having Emily around all the time. He wanted to hire an *au pair*. I refused to consider it. I was worried about money and wanted to sell the apartment in New York. Howard refused to consider it. The atmosphere in the house became strained and Howard started spending more and more time away from home.

Finally, one sunny morning I woke up to the sound of Emily cooing, the smell of fresh coffee perking considerately in its machine and a three-page single-spaced typed letter, replete with obscure literary references and long, involved quotations in French (I don't read French), the essence of which was that Howard felt it would be best for all concerned if he left and took the car with him.

I later found out he took Margaux as well.

About a month after that I was notified that Howard had filed for a divorce.

And it was just two weeks after that that I read, in the "Book Notes" section of the *New York Times*, that the agent who represented Margaux was now also representing Howard and that she had arranged for him to receive an advance of $1 million on his novel. The article went on to say that this was only the first leg of a three-book, $3 million contract, the additional $2 million payable upon delivery of the subsequent manuscripts.

Chapter

3

What to wear to Margaux's Halloween party prompted a spirited debate between Emily and myself.

"Here's the thing, Em," I argued as we pulled out of our driveway early Saturday morning, the day of the party, "it's got to be terrific. Absolutely terrific. Because you know that Margaux's costume will be terrific. In fact, I wouldn't put it past her to have invited me at the last minute just to make sure I wouldn't look right."

That look of intense concentration crossed Emily's face again.

"Oh, you don't think so, huh? Well, I think I've had just a little more experience in this area than you have, Em. And, let's face it, you always tend to give people the benefit of the doubt. That's a lovely trait and all," I added hastily, "but, sometimes you need to . . . never mind. The point is, Margaux's had months and months to come up with an idea for a costume and she probably spent hundreds—maybe even thousands—of dollars on it.

"But, hey, no sweat," I continued. "All we have to do is make sure that our outfit is every bit as terrific as hers without spending more than fifteen dollars on it."

Emily inclined her head in a thoughtful way and looked out the window.

"No, Emily, it's more than just a costume," I reasoned. "This is a big party for me. You may not realize it, but I haven't been out for some time now and I'm a little nervous. There'll be all kinds of people at this party. People from New York.

"It's even possible, Em," I continued, turning right on the main road and heading toward town, "that your—your father himself will be there. Now, I know you're going to say that that shouldn't matter, and you're absolutely right, it shouldn't. It's our opinion that counts, not his. Not that I want to prejudice you against your father, Em," I cut in hastily. "I know you're going to have an absolutely wonderful relationship with him. As soon as you see him again, I mean."

Emily coughed.

"Ah, here we are," I announced, quickly changing the subject. "This is where we are going to look for costume inspiration. It's called a video store."

I undid her safety strap, then caught sight of myself in the rearview mirror for a moment and stopped. "So, what do you think?" I asked softly. "Think there's hope?"

Emily turned to look at me. Her eyes were astonishingly blue in the sunlight. "Mmmbbddd," she said.

"Thanks, honey," I whispered, giving her a big hug. "You always know just the right thing to say."

We were in the video store a pretty long time. You'd be surprised how tough it is to find just the right look to impress a roomful of strangers. I picked up one box after another.

"So, what do you think, Em?" I wanted to know. "A vampire? No, too stock. A cheerleader? Too prim. A go-go dancer? Blech," I said.

"How about *Fatal Attraction*? You're right, I don't look good in ringlets. *Buffy the Vampire Slayer*? A little too young. *Basic Instinct*? A little too basic . . . hey, what're you doing, hon?" I asked as Emily reached out for a box. "No, no, sweetheart, let Mommy hold the boxes. What do you have there?" I asked, finally prying it out of her hand. "Oh, *Cabaret*," I said. "I *love Cabaret*. Wait a minute . . ."

By the time I had second thoughts about this costume I was already in Margaux's foyer.

Margaux's annual costume party had a guest list of 150. Having been invited impromptu, I was one of the few not to have received an invitation printed in orange lettering on black stationery. Flashlight-bearing teenage boys, looking as though they were responsible for landing incoming F-16s, directed cars to the parking area set off behind the stables. The walk to the front door was lined with dozens of jack-o'-lanterns in various states of grimace, their candlelit faces flickering eerily in the wind, like ghostly spirits with a bad electrical connection. As I stepped inside the front door, I saw waiters dressed as gangsters bearing trays of black-and-orange appetizers shouldering their way through pockets of lime-green monsters and wicked witches and overweight Cat Women. Three enormous tables ladened with food were against the far wall, and two bars had been set up, both of which were already doing a very brisk business. It was just what I had expected Margaux's party to be.

I stood there, clutching my coat around me, looking at all the people. Whatever could have possessed me, I wondered, to wear something so obvious? What was I doing in little black shorts and fishnet stockings? This wasn't me. Maybe I should wear my coat. Maybe I should just go home. Maybe . . .

"Elizabeth. You came. How nice."

It was Margaux. She was wearing a real honest-to-God hoopskirt overlaid with yards and yards of sprigged muslin, her blonde curls framed by a delicate lace-edged bonnet. The dress had little puffed sleeves, slightly off the shoulder, and with it Margaux carried a crook adorned with pink ribbons.

Oh my God, she's Little Bo-Peep, I thought and shrugged out of my coat without thinking.

Margaux surveyed my costume up and down as a servant came and took my coat away. "Oh," she said. "You came as Sally Bowles."

"Yes."

At that moment Louis XVI and Marie Antoinette came in behind me and Margaux pivoted abruptly. "Excuse me, Elizabeth," she said without turning back to me. "Fran-*cine*," I heard her gush.

Rather than stand alone in the middle of the room, I walked over to get a drink. The bartender had just finished pouring a beer for Rasputin when a big, fat California Raisin grabbed at my elbow.

"Hot pants, huh?" he leered.

"Sally Bowles," I replied coldly.

"Nice Bowles," smirked the Raisin.

I shook off his arm and spun away. In the process of doing so, my left elbow hit Rasputin's freshly poured beer. It was a perfect shot. No one got a drop of beer on them. Except Rasputin. Rasputin got drenched.

As anyone who has ever dropped, say, a carton of eggs or a full cat-litter box knows, there is that split second when time stops and you almost believe that you can will the mess back into its carton. That's what happened with Rasputin and me.

The only difference was that the mess doesn't usually speak up.

"I'm Adam Rothstein. I don't believe we've met," he said, in a completely deadpan voice, beer dripping from his fake bushy black eyebrows.

Whoever he was, Rasputin was the perfect choice. This guy had the most mesmerizing eyes I'd ever seen. Other than that, between the long black wig and false beard, it was kind of hard to tell what he looked like.

"Elizabeth Halperin," I croaked.

He nodded and raised his left hand to wipe the beer from his face.

"Uh, uh, here, let me—" I looked around frantically, caught sight of a pile of tiny cocktail napkins, grabbed the one on top and started to blot his cassock.

"Thank you," he said.

I stopped. "Would you rather do it yourself?" I asked.

"Actually, I was kind of enjoying your doing it."

"Oh."

"Does that mean you're going to stop?"

"Yes," I replied.

"Well," he said, "in that case, you leave me no choice but to go to the bathroom." He paused. "You wouldn't happen to know where the bathroom is, would you?"

"Down the hall, second door to the left."

He turned and moved across the floor. I remained rooted to the same spot, watching him go. I even craned my head a little as he turned the corner.

Wait a minute, I thought. What had he said his name was? Adam Rothstein? I'd heard that name before, recently. But from where? Maybe it's not too late to apologize, I thought hopefully. Maybe I can still—

"You certainly made a big splash at my party," commented an amused voice next to me.

I turned to confront Little Bo Peep.

"And just who was it I baptized?" I inquired.

"Adam Rothstein?"

But, suddenly, I wasn't paying attention to her. Because, suddenly, over Margaux's shoulder, I had caught a glimpse of . . .

Howard.

He was off in a corner, in conversation with a very young, very pretty woman dressed as a flapper. He was wearing cowboy boots, a black cowboy hat, a brocaded vest, and a pair of six-shooters in a leather belt over his jeans. On anyone else, this outfit would look preposterous. On him, it looked like Tom Cruise filming a western. As I watched, he gave his companion the long, slow, half-lidded look I knew so well, and I felt as though I'd just been forced to swallow some of that horrible pink bubblegum penicillin Emily takes for her ear infections. At that very moment he lifted his glass to take a drink and caught me staring at him. With utter composure, Howard flashed his grin and tipped his hat in my direction.

"Who's that?" I saw the flapper ask.

Who's *that*? I thought, furious at having been caught staring, even angrier that he'd had the nerve to smile at me as though this were a book signing and I'd just asked for his autograph.

Margaux, aware that she was no longer the focus of my attention, turned just in time to see Howard and his beautiful young date approaching.

"Mind if we join you?" he asked.

I grasped my wine glass more firmly, determined not to show my discomfiture. Out of the corner of my eye I saw Rasputin return to the room and then lean up against the far wall, watching me. I guess he was trying to decide if it was safe to get another beer.

"Of course not." Margaux's tone went arctic. "In fact, we were just on our way over to you. Really, Howard, what terrible manners you have. Bringing somebody new over and not even bothering to introduce her." She stuck out her hand. "You really must excuse him. I'm Margaux Chase."

The flapper took her hand coolly. Although she barely looked old enough to drink, she had the outward composure of a woman of fifty. It was very disconcerting. "Holly Ivy," she replied, meeting Margaux's gaze head-on.

For a split second Margaux's face registered shock, even fear. Then it passed.

"So nice to meet you," she said, straightening regally. "I've heard so much about you."

So had I. Actually, so had everyone. Holly Ivy was a graduate student at Smith College who had had an affair with a noted novelist, and who had subsequently written a novel about a graduate student at a prestigious women's college who had had an affair with a noted novelist. The novel, entitled *Sleeping with the Competition*, had come out to rave reviews and was currently on the bestseller list. Holly herself had been pictured in many publications, including *Time* magazine, which is where I had seen her. She had been photographed on campus at Smith wearing a sleek black suit with a white silk scarf, flanked by a pair of enormous sheepdogs. I remembered admiring the dogs.

Howard smiled. "Holly's doing a new book."

"Of course she is," Margaux responded evenly.

"I thought she should meet Francine. Perhaps Phillip."

"What a good idea," Margaux agreed, utterly without enthusiasm.

Silence.

"Well, I'm sure you three have a lot to talk about." Margaux waved her crook vaguely. "So if you'll excuse me . . ."

The three of us were left staring at each other. Only Howard seemed perfectly at ease.

"Holly, I'd like you to meet my ex-wife, Elizabeth—" he broke off. "What last name are you using these days?"

"Sap," I said under my breath.

"Pardon?"

"Never mind."

Holly turned her imperturbable gaze on me. She had deep, utterly beautiful violet eyes. Naturally. "Are you a writer, too?" she asked.

"No."

"An editor?" she suggested hopefully.

"A mother."

"Oh." She turned away and began to scan the room. "I think I see Peter over there," she said to Howard. "I really must say hello," and she glided away.

As soon as Holly was gone, Howard looked me up and down.

"What?" I demanded.

"Being single obviously agrees with you."

"What do you want, Howard?"

"I have to want something? I haven't seen you in a while. You know, just because we're not together anymore doesn't mean we can't speak to each other."

I didn't bother to reply.

"Sally Bowles, huh? Great fishnets."

"Thank you."

"The guy you gave a beer bath liked them, too."

"Go fuck yourself, Howard," I said.

"You two looked very chummy. Did you know that he's staring at you even as we speak? My, that was a clever way to break the ice."

"Praise from Caesar." I started to turn away, but Howard grabbed my arm.

"Wait a minute. I want to talk to you."

"You let go of me," I hissed.

"No, really . . ."

"Goodb—" I angrily shook my arm free.

"THERE SHE IS!"

We both turned on a dime. There, charging toward us like a herd of gigantic stampeding stuffed dolls, was—the play group.

Didi was in the lead, dressed as the Easter Bunny. She had at least a dozen boxes' worth of cotton balls stuck to a pink sweatsuit and she clung to a pastel basket stuffed with jellybeans and fake plastic grass. Pat, dressed as a drum majorette, wearing a very short skirt and the sort of knee-high white fashion boots that were all the rage in the sixties, was in hot pursuit. Astrid brought up the rear. She wore what looked to be an authentic Dutch costume, complete with a curved hat and wooden clogs. The clogs made a heavy thumping noise with each step and left marks on Margaux's highly polished wood floors.

Howard took a beat.

"Friends of yours?" he drawled, turning and walking away.

Yes, as it happens, they are friends of mine, I thought, as Howard sauntered back to Holly Ivy. They are certainly a whole lot more decent than anyone you run around with. And I made it a point to stand and talk to Didi, Astrid and Pat for the next fifteen minutes.

Then they suddenly dispersed, leaving me alone in the middle of the room.

It was the moment I'd been waiting for. I'd felt Rasputin's eyes on me the whole time. The feeling had produced an extremely pleasant tingling sensation up and down my spine. Now I deliberately waited alone in the center of the room to give Adam Rothstein the opportunity to approach me.

Nothing happened.

I waited a little longer. This time, I discreetly scanned the crowd for his presence. After all, it was I who had embarrassed him. Maybe I should seek him out.

Nothing. He seemed to have disappeared into thin air.

Give him another minute, I urged myself, even though I was beginning to feel (ridiculously) as though I were being deliberately stood up.

A full fifteen minutes later I walked to the bar, chin up, secured myself a very large glass of wine and fled.

I ended up at the far side of the house, where Margaux had added a glassed-in conservatory. I peeped in and saw that there was no one there, took myself and my wine inside and stood between the dill and the basil looking out at my own reflection in the glass, thinking unpleasant thoughts about Howard, Adam Rothstein, Margaux, Holly Ivy and the whole damn crew.

"Isherwood was a friend of mine, you know."

I turned around. There was Louis XVI.

"The movie was all right, of course, but I never felt it did justice to the stories."

"Neither did I," I said.

"I think the expatriate movement produced some of the strongest literature of the twentieth century."

"I'm afraid I'm more of a nineteenth-century person."

"Ah!" he brightened. "I adore the nineteenth century. Who are your favorites?"

"Oh, Dickens, of course, Trollope . . ."

"Yes, Trollope is marvelous. And highly underrated in this country," he added.

"I just finished *Barchester Towers*," I confessed.

"Ah! Mrs. Proudie," he laughed. "Are you visiting from New York?"

"No, I live here," I replied.

He put out his hand. "I'm Phillip Laramee," he said.

"Elizabeth . . . Halperin," I replied.

"Are you a writer?" he asked.

"Uh, no. Just a reader."

"Good," he said heartily. "We certainly need those."

Well, *he* did, at any rate. He was a publisher. Howard's publisher. Margaux's too, but who was counting. We had never met, but his name had been mentioned so often at the kitchen table during the last three months of my marriage that I often thought I should set him a place.

It was Phillip Laramee, I realized, who was personally responsible for Howard's three-book contract, with its tangential millions, and therefore, indirectly, personally responsible for my divorce.

"You know, Elizabeth, this may sound odd when I tell you that I am a publisher, but I don't get to talk about literature very much. This has been very refreshing. Do you ever get into New York?"

"Occasionally."

"Well, the next time you plan to visit, please give me a ring. I'm in the book. Laramee, Buford & Young. I'd love to take you to lunch."

"Thank you," I said. "That sounds nice."

"*Philll*-ipp. Are you in here?"

Phillip smiled at me. "I think I'm being paged." He turned toward the door. "Over here, Francine."

Marie Antoinette swept around the corner. "Phillip, what do you mean by sneaking off and leaving me alone to . . ." She pulled up short. "Oh, I didn't know you had company." Then she squinted in my direction. "I know you."

I knew her, too. It was Francine Weezle, Howard's agent. Margaux's too, but who's counting.

"Oh, I'm sorry," said Phillip. "Elizabeth, this is Francine Weezle. Francine, this is Elizabeth Halperin."

Francine looked me in the eye. "You mean Elizabeth Hack."

"I use my maiden name now," I said quickly.

Phillip turned to me. "As in Howard Hack?"

"He's my ex-husband," I said.

"Ah," said Phillip.

"Speaking of Howard," said Francine with a frown, "I think you'd better come along. Some smoothing over is in order. Our favorite author couldn't leave well enough alone by just tagging along with us. He *had* to bring Holly. Every time I pass her, Margaux looks like she's ready to throw a drink in my face."

Phillip sighed. "Very well." As he followed Francine out the door, he turned back to me.

"This is why I never get to talk about literature," he said.

After my conversation with Phillip, I decided to stick around a little more and followed them back to the main room. Maybe Margaux really would throw a drink in Francine's face. Or better yet, Howard's.

But neither Margaux nor Howard were there. The play group was, though. They had evidently had something to drink, because Pat was leading Didi and Astrid through what looked to be an old cheerleading routine.

I think I'll give Rose a call, I thought, and ducked up the stairs to find a phone.

Rose was Emily's baby-sitter. She was a seventy-two-year-old great-grandmother who drove an old pickup truck with a ram's head on the front and a shotgun on the floor of the passenger's side. She lived alone, hauled her own firewood and grew her own tomatoes. She had five children, eighteen grandchildren and twelve great-grandchildren. When I had inquired about her husband, she'd told me she'd been married to an abusive alcoholic who was now dead. Something had told me not to pursue the matter. Now, ordinarily, I would not retain someone to watch my child whom I suspected of hacking her husband into hamburger, but Emily loved Rose and Rose loved Emily. Besides, I never had to worry about anybody breaking in.

I got to the top of the stairs and looked around for an open room. About three doors down I found a small guest room with a phone by the bedside. Margaux had two lines. One was busy, so I hit the button for the other line, picked up the receiver and dialed home.

Ring. Ring. She'll pick it up now, I thought.

Rose picked up the phone. "Hello?" she demanded. I could hear the television playing loudly in the background. Something horrible was clearly happening in whatever show she was watching, because a woman was screaming in agony.

"Hello, Rose. It's just me . . . Elizabeth . . . calling to check up on things."

"Oh, yes," said Rose, obviously anxious to get back to the screaming woman.

"Uh—is everything okay?" I asked. She'll say everything is fine, I thought.

"Everything is fine," said Rose.

"Is Emily asleep?" Oh, yes.

"Oh, yes," said Rose.

"What time did she go to bed?" About eight-thirty.

"About eight-thirty," said Rose.

"Thanks. I'll be home soon." Take your time.

"Take your time," said Rose.

I hung up the phone with the distinct feeling that Rose felt she was dealing with not one but two children.

I had just put down the receiver when I heard a noise through the wall. Startled, I bent a little closer.

"Ughhh," said the noise.

I bent still closer.

"Urgghh," said the noise.

I put my ear to the wall.

"ERhgh—ERhgh—"

It was the unmistakable sound of Howard, having an orgasm.

I don't know why I was surprised. I think I mentioned that sneaking off to make love in public places—parties, restaurants, political rallies—was a specialty of Howard's. We'd done it ourselves at other people's houses while we were engaged. Then it had seemed romantic, exciting. Discovering it here in Margaux's guest room was neither.

The noise stopped.

I waited a few minutes and then turned around to leave the room and sneak back to the party. I was in the doorway when the door to the next room opened. There was no time to move out of the way.

There was Holly Ivy rearranging something in her purse. She looked up at me coolly and I could see that her makeup was smudged. I felt my cheeks get hot, as though it was I who had been caught instead of the other way around. Then, without a word, she turned away and continued on to the landing.

After that I really did leave. I didn't even try to find Margaux to pay my respects. I grabbed my coat from the rack, described my Jeep to one of the car parkers and sped out of there so fast I'm afraid I kicked gravel up on the people coming up behind me. I remember pulling up into my own driveway, digging through my purse for thirty dollars for Rose, cutting off her attempts at conversation and basically throwing her out of the house in order to get to bed.

There are some things you learn very quickly when you're a parent. One is that it is precisely on those occasions when you have let down your guard, when you're not on your game, when you've thought "what the hell" and downed that third glass of wine or stayed up the extra hour and a half to finish your book . . . it is precisely on those occasions that your child will fall ill.

In my case, reality settled in at 5:37 Sunday morning with the advent of Emily's ear infection. Of course, there is no way to tell an ear infection *for sure* without a trip to the doctor, which brings us to another thing you learn very quickly about parenthood: that is, when your child does become ill, he or she will be sure to do it on a weekend when there's nobody at the pediatrician's.

All the signs were there, however. Emily was crying, unable to sleep, pulling on her ear—all the while trying to suck on her blanket, which only caused more crying and ear-pulling. On such occasions a mother has a job to do, and whether she has to do it on four hours' sleep and a violent hangover is immaterial.

The job involves three separate tasks. First, to ensure that this is a *run-of-the-mill* ear infection and not an ear infection that is a symptom of a truly alarming virus, the child's temperature must be taken. A child's temperature is taken rectally. No one especially likes to have their temperature taken rectally. Add in that this is the wee hours of the morning and your child, who does not see the need for the procedure in the first place, is already overtired and miserable. The invariable upshot is kicking, squirming and long, anguished, infuriated, heartbreaking wails capable of rousing sleeping neighbors at one thousand feet, each of whom will believe that you are beating your child.

The second task is administering Tylenol. This is largely a repeat of the first. There will be more howling and struggling. Orange-flavored (and -colored) Tylenol will land on the child's pajamas, on your pajamas, on the wallpaper. After some minutes of this, however, you will be able to take advantage of a particularly maddened, open-mouthed wail to sneak in a dropperful of medicine.

The final task is the soothing. As it takes anywhere from half an hour to forty-five minutes for the medicine to bring relief, during the intervening period your child must be rocked, patted and stroked. It is helpful, in such circumstances, to turn on some quiet music.

And so it was that, half-asleep, with a pounding ache in my head and a sick, miserable child in my arms, I switched on the radio to the local easy-listening station just in time to hear a newscaster announce that Howard had been murdered.

Chapter

4

That's all there was. No follow-up, no commentary, no interviews. Just a statement on the radio that a man identified as Howard Hack had been killed at a costume ball on Underhill Mountain Drive late last night and that the police were investigating.

I stopped rocking and just sat there, stunned. Emily shifted against my shoulder and uttered a little, halfhearted protest. The Tylenol was beginning to take effect. I started rocking again automatically.

"Did you hear that, Em?"

Emily nestled closer and laid her cheek against mine exactly as though it were she who was doing the comforting. I held her tightly.

"I thought I heard—I thought I heard—" I realized I was shaking and with an effort I controlled myself. From emptiness a jumble of emotions rose up and possessed me. Horror. Fear.

Sadness. Regret. Loneliness. And—what was that last one? Relief?

"But maybe they got it wrong. Maybe it's someone else. Maybe it's not true—" and I half-started out of my chair.

It is impossible to describe my sudden, overwhelming, uncontrollable urge for more information. I think it was much worse for me, having worked as a trader, than for an ordinary person. I took for granted that whenever a piece of news broke, I could count on information pounding at me from every angle and crevice—screens flashing, numbers being shouted across the floor and updates coming in on the ticker from every available news service. Telephone and telex lines linked me around the world and economists' reports, government reports, analysts' reports, five or six newspapers and a dozen journals piled each day upon my desk provided almost unlimited background information. Accordingly, I had gotten into the habit of culling and assimilating data almost instantaneously.

But this—this was an almost complete absence of information. It was like not having enough air to breathe.

I rushed outside to the porch and grabbed the copy of the local Sunday paper, which I have delivered. I tore through the front section, City & Town, even the book page—nothing. The story had broken too late to make the paper.

I stood in the middle of the kitchen floor, still in my pajamas, Emily asleep on my shoulder, surrounded by comics, television listings and pumpkin recipes. What to do? Call someone. Who? Margaux? Not Margaux. The police? Not the police. Then it came to me.

That's when I called Didi.

"Elizabeth! Can you believe it! Right here in Lenox!" she hurried along after the brief digression about Margaux's dress.

It was true, then. "What happened, Didi?" I asked tensely.

"What do you mean, what happened? A man was murdered! Right here in Lenox! At a party!" She was so excited she'd begun to repeat herself.

"I know he was—"

"And I was there!"

"Didi, just—"

"Right here in Lenox!"

"Try to—"

"Did I tell you he was shot? In an upstairs bedroom?"

"No, I—"

"He was shot in an upstairs bedroom! Right here—"

"—in Lenox," I finished for her.

"Yes! Can you believe it? I just can't—"

"STOP!"

Didi stopped.

"I want to hear everything," I told her. "Everything. But from the beginning. And *slowly*."

"Well—" and Didi began to tell the following story:

Just before one o'clock—that being the time Didi, Astrid and Pat had predetermined to leave—the three were assembled, like most of the rest of the party, around the dessert table, having a last sweet as fortification for the drive home. Suddenly they became aware of a commotion at the head of the stairs and, like several of those around them, went to investigate.

They found quite a crowd of people around the door to one of the upstairs bedrooms. The door was open but it was impossible to get close enough to see what was inside, so they had to ask those around them what was going on.

Someone had been shot, they were told.

No! Who?

A man—one of the guests—a friend of Margaux's.

Someone from town?

No. A weekend guest. A New Yorker.

Shot, did you say? Where? Was he hurt badly?

Hard to say. Looks bad. Blood everywhere. He was naked, someone else whispered.

No!

Well, he was a New Yorker.

At this point, the police arrived. People were politely but firmly pointed away from the bedroom door and in the direction of the downstairs living area. There they were divided into three lines for questioning. At the head of each line was a police officer. Didi got into her cousin John's line.

Oh, hi, Didi. Nice rabbit. Where's Tom? Wouldn't wear a costume, huh? Can't say that I blame him.

Didi told him about Margaux and the play group. Then she asked him what had happened.

Guy name of Howard Hack ate it upstairs, her cousin reported. Found naked in front of some portable computer. Guy was apparently some kind of a writer. Found a note with him, too. Perfumed envelope. Some kind of weird poem inside. Creepy. Graves and priests. Did you know this guy?

Didi didn't think so. What did he look like?

Dark hair. Would have been wearing a cowboy outfit earlier. Black hat, black shirt, black jeans—

Oh! Yes! Didi remembered him. Very handsome.

Not anymore, noted the cousin. Head wound. Very messy.

Yu-uck, Didi responded.

Had she spoken with this guy?

Didi shook her head.

Remember seeing him at all?

Yes.

When was the last time she saw him? About what time?

Early. Before dinner. He was speaking to—she stopped.

C'mon, Didi. If you know something, you gotta spill it.

Nothing. Just that he seemed to be arguing with a friend of hers.

Who?

Didi told her cousin about me.

("I hope you don't mind," she said.

"Of course not," I replied. "Go on."

"*Did* you know him?" Didi asked.

"Yes."

"Was he—were you—"

"He was my ex-husband," I explained flatly.

"No!"

"Yes!" I said. "Go on.")

Then Didi said her cousin flipped out a little pad and wrote down my name. Know what they were arguing about? he asked.

No, said Didi.

Then how did she know they were arguing?

He was holding my friend by the arm and she was trying to shake him off, Didi reported.

("I hope you don't mind," she said again.

"Of course not," I replied again. "Go on.")

Oh, said the cousin and wrote.

Who do they think did it? asked Didi.

Hard to say, replied the cousin. Probably somebody at the party. Poem indicates some weird New Yorker kind of sex thing. Murder weapon not found yet, however.

Weren't they going to search everybody? Didi asked, noticing that many people had left after questioning.

In *this* crowd? Cousin raised eyebrows. Just about every lawyer in town is here. Half the Board of Selectmen is here. Jeez, Joe Cobb is here.

"Who's Joe Cobb?" I broke in.

"Joe Cobb? He's the head of the board," Didi replied.

"Oh."

"Didn't you see him? He had this great costume. He was the California Raisin."

*　　　*　　　*

Two hours later, Emily and I found ourselves in the waiting room of Berkshire Pediatrics.

We had been in this waiting room many times before. We had been in it when it was so packed with sneezing, coughing, runny-nosed kids that it was obvious that if Emily were not sick before, she surely would be by the time we left. We had sat there when Emily had roseola, and waited to see curmudgeonly old Dr. Friske, who answered my questions with only the thinnest veneer of politeness, clearly demonstrating that I was wasting his time. We had sat there when Emily had the stomach flu, and waited to see rotund Dr. Adelman, pink-faced and slightly moist, given to alarming conjectures ("We'll just take this blood test and make sure it isn't leukemia"). We had sat there for Emily's well-baby checkup, to see Dr. Patarkin, whose cool efficiency was in sharp contrast to the Timberlands and two long hippie-like braids she always wore around the office.

But there was one thing we had never done before. We had never, ever sat in the waiting room on a Sunday.

It was like being in a ghost town. The whole building had been shut down for the weekend and the lights were on only in the elevators and this one room. The only way I knew for sure that I was in the right place was that even though Emily and I were the only patients in the room, they were still making us wait.

I got up and carried Emily over to the one woman sitting in the block of desks generally reserved for a small army of receptionists. I cleared my voice. "Excuse me," I began.

"The doctor will be with you in a moment," she said without bothering to look up.

I would have taken more comfort in this remark if it wasn't the very same thing she'd said ten minutes ago. "Look," I said, "I know it's Sunday and all, but Emily really isn't feeling well and I just wondered—"

"It shouldn't be more than a few minutes now," she said,

finally looking up. I noticed for the first time that she was young and rather pretty, if a bit overweight, but that she was so heavily made up that it was almost impossible to see this through her eyeliner. "You're lucky to be seeing a doctor at all," she informed me. "These aren't normal office hours."

"Then what are you doing here?" I asked, shifting Emily from my right shoulder to my left.

"Me? I'm just helping out," she replied. She raised an arm and indicated some piles of papers in front of her. As she did so, a waft of perfumed air hit me full in the face. Opium, I thought, sniffing. Who wears Opium at eleven o'clock Sunday morning?

I was just stepping back to take a seat again when a thought occurred to me. "Who is the doctor on call, by the way?" I asked. Please don't let it be Dr. Friske, I prayed. I don't think I can take another lecture on being overprotective.

"Dr. Rothstein."

I wet my lips. "Did you say—Rothstein?"

"Yes."

"*Who* Rothstein?"

She looked up at me. "Adam Rothstein." She frowned. "A flyer went out announcing that Dr. Rothstein had joined the group from—" At that moment, a light buzzed on the console in front of her. "Dr. Rothstein will see you now," she said primly, and, checking her hair in the hand mirror that lay on the side of the desk, got up to lead us into the inner office.

In the brief walk to the examining room, I just had time to settle on a plan of action. Well, not a plan, exactly. More like an attitude. And the attitude was—dignity. I would treat Adam Rothstein with dignity. The Queen of England herself would not treat Adam Rothstein with more dignity than I intended to. You can't go wrong with dignity, I reasoned.

I just had time to draw myself up to my full height when there was a discreet knock followed almost immediately by an opening door and Adam Rothstein strode into the examining room.

Without the beard, the wig, the cloak and the bushy eyebrows, Adam Rothstein was a tall, lean, extremely athletic-looking man. He wasn't movie-star handsome, exactly—his nose was a little crooked and his jaw slightly too long—but there was so much going on in his face that he was every bit as arresting in a lab coat as he had been as a crazed Russian Orthodox monk. He was by far the most attractive man I had met since—since Howard.

Well, I thought, that explains the Opium.

I caught myself kind of gaping at him and tucked in my lower lip abruptly. Dignity, Elizabeth, I cautioned.

He made straight for Emily. "What seems to be the trouble?" he asked.

"Uh, uh, her ear hurts."

"Which ear?"

"The, uh, left . . . no, no, the right. No, the left."

"That's all right," he said. "I'll check both."

Emily, who usually twists, screams and kicks at the very sight of Drs. Friske, Adelman and Patarkin, sat perfectly still, almost cooing while Adam Rothstein stuck the whatever-you-call-it in her ears and peered in. She broke into her first smile of the day when he felt for swollen glands.

Traitor, I thought.

"Yup, right ear's inflamed, all right," he said. "Or is it the left? Doesn't matter in any event. Couple of doses of pink stuff'll fix her right up."

"Pink stuff?" I repeated.

"Bactrim," he said, writing out a prescription on a pad. "I see from Emily's chart that she didn't respond well to Amoxicillin." He tore off the sheet and handed it to me. "Two teaspoons a day, one in the evening, one in the morning, with plenty of water. Make sure she finishes the whole bottle. If she doesn't seem better in a few days, call me."

We stood facing each other. Those eyes again, I thought, weakly. Those eyes . . .

"Uh, yes. Right," I blathered on. "Well, thank you for seeing me. I mean, us."

"No problem. I was coming in anyway to do some paperwork."

"Well, thanks again," I said, expecting him to turn and leave the room.

"Oh, yes," he said, "there is one more thing."

"What?"

He took a step forward, placed one hand courteously over Emily's eyes, drew me tightly to him with the other and kissed me.

It's a good thing that there isn't much traffic in the Berkshires on Sundays after leaf season, because I'm not sure I would have noticed if there was another car on the road. What I did notice was righteous indignation (How dare he! I'd write a letter to the AMA, the Board of Health and *Parents* magazine!). That shifted almost immediately into guilty satisfaction (But what a great kiss! I couldn't help kissing him back!). Then, finally, there was dreamy reverie (He follows me home. We have an intimate, candlelight dinner for two in front of the fire. I turn to him . . .). My cheeks started burning and I was right back at righteous indignation (The nerve of the guy! There ought to be a law! There probably was a law!).

In this way Emily and I made the journey to the pharmacy to have her prescription filled. It wasn't until we were driving home and almost hit the traffic cop who stands in front of the Lenox Shops on weekends that I finally stopped feeling and started to think. And what I thought was how odd it was that, on the very day that I had been released, so to speak, from Howard's presence, I should have been kissed for the first time since—well, since Howard. I wondered if Howard's death wasn't, in some perverse way, going to bring me luck. Maybe his ending was my beginning.

In any event, I reasoned, one thing was clear. I wouldn't be hearing anymore about Howard. No more late-night vitriolic phone calls. No more arguments in restaurants or at parties. No more dealing with lawyers and papers and child support. No more worrying about having to explain to Emily when she was older why her father didn't spend any time with her. Come to think of it, Howard dead would probably be a much better father than Howard alive.

I was still musing on this theme when I walked into my house and discovered the message light blinking on my answering machine.

It was the police, asking me to call.

I had always thought, from watching reruns of old movies I suppose, that witnesses were interviewed at police headquarters. But after I'd explained about Emily's ear infection, and how I'd had to take her to the pediatrician's already this morning, and how she was sleeping now and how I didn't really like to leave her with anyone when she was sick, and how I didn't like to take her out with me in case she got worse, and, even if I did bring her with me, how difficult it was to have a coherent conversation with a fretful baby on one's lap, whoever it was on the other end of the line said "Hold on" and when he came back said all right, they'd come to me then, which is how the chief of police of Lenox came to be standing at my front door.

"Elizabeth Hack?"

"Halperin," I replied. "I use my maiden name now."

"I'm Chief Rudge and this is Detective Fineburg of the state police. May we come in?"

"Certainly." I hurriedly threw open the door and they stepped inside the house.

Of course I knew it was Chief Rudge. For one thing, he was wearing his little badge that said "Rudge" on it. But anyway, everybody in town knew Ned Rudge. He was a very short, wiry man with almost no hair and oversized ears, a condition he liked to disguise by never taking off his cap.

Detective Fineburg was a tall, gangly man dressed in a hound's-tooth sport jacket with torn patches at the elbows, rumpled brown corduroy pants and work boots. His flowered tie was of such violent hues that it seemed somehow fluorescent. He had frizzy black hair with little squiggly lines of gray through it. He looked like something you'd see in a *New Yorker* cartoon.

"Can I—may I get you something?" I stammered, feeling unaccountably guilty.

"No, thank you," replied the chief as he and Detective Fineburg followed me into the living room. "We're just here to ask some questions." He spoke in a monotone, each word enunciated a little too clearly. "If you'll just sit down we can . . ."

"I'd love some tea, please."

The chief and I both turned to Detective Fineburg, who, with the comfortable familiarity of a bookseller in his own store, stood perusing my bookshelves.

"Tea," I repeated blankly. "Of course. I'll just put the kettle on. Any particular kind?"

"Got any herbal?"

"Uh, sure. Lemon Zinger, Mandarin Orange, Cinnamon Rose, Raspberry Patch—"

"I've never tried Raspberry Patch."

"It's very good," I assured him, "if you like raspberries."

During this little interchange, the chief stood in the middle of the room, his head swiveling back and forth like he was watching a tennis match. Detective Fineburg, however, seemed not to notice.

"Sounds great. Got any honey? I like my tea with honey."

"Of course," I said again, turning for the kitchen. A few minutes later I returned with a steaming mug and some cookies on a plate.

"You're right," said Detective Fineburg, tasting his tea. "It's terrific."

"Now that we've had our tea . . ." began Chief Rudge.

"Right," nodded Detective Fineburg, reaching for a cookie. He took a bite, raised an eyebrow at me. "What *are* these?"

"Peak Freen Fruit Creams," I replied.

". . . and our cookies," continued the chief.

"Right," nodded Detective Fineburg again.

"Mrs. Hack," the chief began again.

"Halperin, if you don't mind," I said.

"Halperin. We would like to ask you some questions about last night's party."

I nodded.

He brusquely flipped a pad out of his shirt pocket. "Now, for the record, you *are* Mrs. Howard Hack, widow of the deceased."

"I *was* Mrs. Howard Hack," I replied.

Detective Fineburg raised his other eyebrow. I'd never seen anyone ambidextrous with their eyebrows before. "Really. When did this happen?"

"Just last week."

Chief Rudge was scribbling on his pad. I saw him write the word "divorced."

"You have just the one child?" asked Detective Fineburg.

"Yes."

"Is it a he or a she?"

"She. Emily," I volunteered. The chief wrote down "Emily."

"And how old is Emily?" smiled Detective Fineburg.

"Eleven months."

"Ah. Great age, isn't it?" The detective was still smiling. "I've got two myself. Girls."

"How old are they?" I asked.

"Three and five. Best thing that ever happened to me."

I saw the chief write down "three and five" and then frown and scribble it out.

"And Emily is—was—Howard's child?"

"Yes."

"Did he see her often?"

"No."

"Really? Why not?" asked Detective Fineburg in a tone of surprise.

"He—he wasn't really that interested," I answered.

"Too bad. He didn't know what he was missing. Did he see you often?"

"No."

"When was the last time you saw him?" asked the detective.

"At Margaux's party."

"Right. We'll get to the party in a minute. I meant before that," he said. "When was the last time you saw him before that?"

I shrugged.

"That long ago, huh?" He nodded sympathetically. "You spoke to him on the phone, though?"

"Yes."

"Do you remember the last time you spoke to him?"

I thought. "About a week ago."

"Do you remember what you talked about?"

"The divorce."

"I see." Detective Fineburg nodded again. "Let's go back to the night of the party, okay?"

"Okay."

"You said you saw Howard at the party. Did you speak to him?"

"Yes."

"What did you talk about?"

"Oh, just the usual party chitchat," I replied airily. "How've you been, that sort of thing."

"I see." Detective Fineburg smiled again. "Do you remember about what time that was?"

"Early," I replied.

"Did you talk to him again that evening?" he asked.

"No," I answered. It was true. I had *heard* him, but I hadn't spoken to him.

"Very good." He set down his cup suddenly, jumped up and held out his hand for me to shake. "Thanks for the help."

I shook his hand. "No problem," I said.

The chief closed his pad with a snap. "Thank you for your cooperation." He strode to the door.

Detective Fineburg trailed behind. He stopped in the doorway and turned around.

"Oh, one last thing," he said. "Can you think of anyone who'd want to kill Howard? Someone with a motive?"

"No," I said.

"Think carefully. Any enemies? Any disgruntled girlfriends?"

"I have no idea. Keeping up with Howard's girlfriends was a full-time job."

"I see. Well, thanks again for your help."

I watched them from the window. Detective Fineburg waved and I waved back.

Well, I thought. That's that.

Chapter

5

Then again, maybe not.

My first inkling that even in death Howard was not just going to go away came at about 7:45 Monday morning. Seven-forty-five is when the *Today* show slots its first celebrity interview. Usually it's somebody from Hollywood—the latest sex symbol, the hottest director. Only rarely is it someone from the literary community, and then only an author of stratospheric stature, like Danielle Steel, for example. But this morning, in its 7:45 slot, *Today* had someone virtually unknown outside of the most exclusive literary circles.

This Monday morning, *Today* had Phillip Laramee.

I blinked as he came on the screen. Gone were the green tights, the velvet cape, the high, heavy, imperial headdress. The camera closed in on a distinguished, surprisingly handsome man of perhaps sixty, conservatively but impeccably attired in a dark gray European-cut suit and blue silk tie. He sat, erect but obviously at ease, hands folded quietly over a book in his lap.

The camera switched to a somber Gene Shalit and I immediately hit the volume button on the remote control.

"As some of you may know," Gene began, looking directly into the camera, "over the weekend, tragedy has struck the world of letters. Howard Hack, a brilliant young author, was murdered at a country home in western Massachusetts, on the eve of the publication of his most important book. With us today is Phillip Laramee, of Laramee, Buford & Young and publisher of Mr. Hack's book. Phillip, thank you for being with us on such short notice."

Phillip smiled tightly and inclined his head soberly.

"Phillip, you were Howard Hack's editor and publisher. Can you tell us something about him and about the effect his murder will have on the literary community?"

Phillip paused a moment to consider the question.

"You know, Gene," he began. "In the world of letters, in each generation there rises a voice—urgent, imperative—*demanding* to be heard. In the twenties, this voice was F. Scott Fitzgerald's. In the thirties, Ernest Hemingway's. In the sixties, Norman Mailer's.

"Gene, Howard Hack's was such a voice. As you know, I have dedicated my life to literature . . . I have immersed myself in its vitality and embraced its resonance . . . I spend my days reading and evaluating the great writers of our time . . . and I have yet to meet his equal, such promise did he intimate. Not just the literary community, but the world must mourn the loss of such a voice."

Gene nodded with sensitivity and understanding. "I hate to ask, but I understand that there is quite a mystery surrounding Howard Hack's death. Has anything more been learned?"

Phillip shook his head. "I only know what everyone else knows. He was killed at a friend's home in western Massachusetts. At the moment he was shot, he was typing what we believe to be the first chapter of his next novel."

Gene changed the subject. "Can you tell us something about Howard Hack's book? The one that's about to be published?"

"Howard's novel is rooted in that eternal truth for which so many novelists strive and yet so few attain. Primal, urgent, exigent truth."

"Can you tell us something about the story?"

"It is a love story." Phillip held up the book he'd been cradling in his lap. The camera zoomed in for a close-up. Red lettering flamed on a black background.

" '*Passion Palace*,' " Gene read off the cover. " 'A Novel of Seduction.' When will it be available to the public?"

"It should be in the stores by the end of the week."

Gene smiled, although it's always hard to tell behind the mustache. "I look forward to reading it. *Passion Palace*," he said again. "The legacy of a great writer. Published by Laramee, Buford & Young. Thank you again for your time, Mr. Laramee. When we return, Katie with a mother who may lose her child because she won't give up her pet."

The screen faded to a Campbell's Soup commercial.

Howard's book—a seductive love story? Rooted in truth—what did that mean? And when had the name been changed? What had happened to the original title, *Genius Tortured*, or the original book, for that matter, about (to quote Howard) "one man's descent into existential metaphysics?"

Well, at least it was Monday. Monday meant that it had been twenty-four hours since Howard's murder, which in turn meant that the newspapers had had time to cover the story. *That* meant that I could now read about the crime. I'm *good* at reading. I almost tripped over my own feet getting out onto the porch for the *Berkshire Eagle*.

There it was. Page one.

CELEBRATED AUTHOR FOUND DEAD AT FASHIONABLE COSTUME PARTY

A special eyewitness report by Agnes Myrtleton, Society Reporter

In all my years of covering the Berkshires' social scene—which will be thirty-three this Christmas—I can safely say that I've never attended a party quite like the Halloween costume ball given by Margaux Chase this past Saturday night. Howard Hack, the world-renowned writer, was found dead in an upstairs bedroom at approximately 12:45 A.M. He had been shot while sitting at a portable computer, at work on his next epic.

It was a bleak ending to an otherwise inspired evening. Margaux's lovely home on Underhill Mountain Drive, decorated in the spirit of the holiday, had surpassed even my wildest expectations. The guest list included the Berkshires' most prominent citizens and many visiting New York literati. Margaux herself, dressed in an exquisite reproduction of a children's fairy tale, was cool and poised throughout what any hostess would consider trying circumstances.

(Continued on page six.)

No arguing with that, I agreed, and turned to page six.

Page six, luckily, contained a number of articles devoted to the subject of Howard's murder. In general, the paper supported Didi's account, with the addition of some salient facts and some significant differences.

According to the *Eagle*, somewhere around 12:45 A.M., just a little while after I'd left, one of the waiters was summoned and told to bring a sandwich up to a guest in one of the upstairs bedrooms. Despite intensive questioning by the authorities, the waiter could not recall who had given him this order, having concentrated instead on the order itself—filet mignon on rye with lettuce and tomato, hold the mayo, and a side order of asparagus vinaigrette. The waiter assembled the food on a tray, hoisted it to one shoulder and trooped up the stairs. He knocked discreetly on the door of the bedroom at the top of the stairs. When there was no reply, he tried the doorknob and, finding it unlocked, peeked in. It was then that he encountered Howard.

Howard was sitting in front of a laptop computer, where he had apparently been typing something, naked except for a set of earphones and a pair of black stretch socks. The earphones were attached to a portable CD recorder, which was playing the Grateful Dead on autoreverse. Subsequent results of the autopsy revealed that death had been administered by a single bullet, fired at close range at one o'clock to his left earlobe. Traces of semen, vaginal discharge and crabmeat cocktail were discovered on his genitals.

The force of the shot had knocked Howard's head down on the keyboard. The computer had not been disturbed, so that visible on the screen was the following:

Chapter One

Sitting in recumbency, with his battered behemoth's head protuberating from the furrows of his Cyclopean shoulders, there was a legerdemain quality about him, a thing that struck me as both lubricious and lamentable, he was an hereditary misprint, an apostate issue that had run amok, flowering beyond all touchstonesgggggggggggggggggggggggggggggggggggg gggggggggggggggggggggggggggggggggggggggggggggggggggg gggggggggggggggggggggggggggggggggggggggggggggggggggg gggggggggggggggggggggggggggggggggggggggggggggggggggg gggggggggggggggggggggggggggggggggggggggggggggggggggg ggggggggggggggggggggggg

The murder weapon, a .25-caliber handgun, had still not been recovered. It was hypothesized that a silencer had been used as well, since nobody could remember hearing a shot. All the articles summed up the same way—Howard, a celebrated novelist, was about to have a big book published, and had evidently been at work on his next, which no one would now have the chance to read.

I read page six over three times. There was no mention of a scented envelope, a strange love poem or a New York–style sex scandal. Had Didi been wrong? Would she just make something like that up? Did the police have any suspects? It just said they were investigating. Who would have wanted to murder Howard? These and other questions swirled through my head. I had the feeling that I ought to be doing something. What about the arrangements for the funeral? Do you even get to have a funeral if your body is currently being hacked up into a thousand little pieces in some police laboratory? And if there was to be no funeral, what about a memorial service? Was that my responsibility? Who was in charge of such things? Whom should I ask? Detective Fineburg? Didi?

But what I really thought about was Adam and that kiss. *That* I thought about all the time. I know this may sound trivial, especially with all this other stuff going on, but I will perhaps be excused on the grounds that it had been a very long time since someone had dealt with me romantically, and it stirred up all sorts of longings. Moreover, it wasn't like there was a herd of eligible (at least, I hoped he was eligible), attractive men hanging around the Berkshires just waiting to be rounded up. In the year or so I had been here, the only unattached men I had come in contact with were a contractor who chain-smoked Marlboros and was under court order to stay away from his former wife, a real estate developer who wore a gold pinky ring and a seventy-two-year-old retired advertising executive ("I'm young at heart," he assured me). What the Street would have called a real seller's market.

So, naturally, whenever anyone halfway decent appeared . . . When would he call? Was he going to call? Should I call him? Absolutely not, Elizabeth, I told myself sternly. He'll call.

But he didn't call.

Plenty of other people did, though, starting with my sister Susan in L.A.

"Elizabeth! I'm so worried about you!" she exclaimed as soon as I answered.

"It's all right, I'm fine," I told her.

"And Emily? I can't stand the thought of either of you being in danger!"

"In danger?" I repeated.

"I saw it all on the *Today* show," Susan announced. "You know I watch it every morning. Imagine my surprise at having to hear about the murder of my own brother-in-law from Gene Shalit," she added coolly.

"Of course," she went on, "I'm sure you were too busy to pick up the phone and call . . . Terrible, just terrible! How can I not be worried when my own sister and niece are exposed to a murderer?"

"Susan, we were not exposed to a murderer. At least," I corrected myself, "Emily was never exposed and, if I was, I didn't know it. There's absolutely nothing to worry about."

"Have they caught who did it yet?" my sister asked.

"No, I don't think so. At least, they haven't said so," I replied.

"Then how do you know whoever this maniac is isn't after the whole family?" she demanded reasonably.

"Uh—"

"Are you getting police protection?"

"Susan, I don't *need* police protection," I assured her, wondering for the first time whether or not I did.

"I wish there was something I could do for you," she said plaintively. She always says that. "Wouldn't you like to bring Emily out to L.A for a visit? This is a good time."

She always says that, too.

"No, Susan," I said. "Everything will be just fine."

In quick succession I heard from my parents (Howard's murder made the LA papers), my aunt and uncle on Long Island, Cousin Enid in Poughkeepsie and Great-Aunt Ann in Milwaukee. I was also called by my college roommate, two women I still keep up with from high school and an old boyfriend, now married. Each of these people touched on the same themes as Susan, expressing horror at what had happened and offering love, support and guidance. Such was the strength of their collective love, support and guidance that at the end of the last phone call I was so nervous that I went and locked all the doors and windows.

"Hello?"

"Elizabeth Hack, please."

"Halperin. I use my maiden name now."

"I have Caitlin Billings on the line. Will you hold please?"

I groaned inwardly. It was late afternoon and nearly everyone I'd known in the world (except Adam) had called. I wasn't sure I had the strength left to deal with Caitlin.

Caitlin Billings was Howard's attorney. He'd hired her after we'd separated to represent him in the divorce. I'd spoken to her on the phone many times and we had met once during a particularly unpleasant effort to resolve the child support issue. Caitlin was in her late thirties, with red hair that she wore long and loose, except for a single beaded braid on one side, giving her the look of a tourist who has just come back from a week on a beach in Jamaica. She wasn't pretty per se (her face was too round and her coloring too pale, in my opinion), but she was certainly attractive, with a knockout figure.

Caitlin was a great proponent of new wave health and healing. She believed that everyone was surrounded by an invisible energy field that connected with everyone else's energy field, and that the course of events could be influenced by brain waves. Whenever Howard and I came to a disagreement over a clause in the divorce contract, she would begin her negotiation with the statement that she was trying to surround me with love, so that I would see the reasonableness of Howard's position. She got away with all of this, I believe, chiefly because she was very good at her job and brought in a great deal of business, and because her father was a senior partner at the firm.

"Elizabeth?"

"Yes?"

"Hi, Elizabeth, it's Caitlin. Although I'm afraid I'm calling today in an official capacity, may I first say how sorry I am, how sorry all of us here at Lewton & Lord are at your loss? I was quite devastated when I heard the news. How are you holding up?"

"I'm fine, Caitlin."

"Good. I knew you would be. I've been trying to surround you with love ever since I heard about Howard."

Uh-oh, I thought.

"Elizabeth, it turns out that you and I have quite a bit to talk about. I was wondering if you could come into the city for a meeting."

"When?"

"As soon as possible. Tomorrow, if you can make it." She paused. "But, of course, you can't leave the baby."

I struggled against my irritation. Caitlin was herself the mother of two small children. But she had returned to work promptly. She had accomplished this by establishing her household with a full-time *au pair* and a husband whose hours as a Russian scholar were as flexible as hers were rigid. But she had done it. And she was constantly reminding me of this fact by being overly solicitous of my relationship with Emily, as though, having made my choice, I was unable to function in any capacity outside the role of mother. This was particularly galling since, after eleven months home with Emily, I wasn't so sure myself.

I stalled. "Can't we just talk about it over the phone?"

"I'm afraid not," she replied gently. "It concerns Howard's estate, you see."

"Howard's estate?" I began to twirl the phone cord around my hand and pace back and forth, something I do when excited or nervous.

"Yes, Howard left a substantial estate. I have a file full of documents on my desk that need signing. I—but first, Elizabeth, I have to be honest with you."

"Yes?"

"I sense hostility here. You may not realize it, but waves and waves of hostile electrical force are engulfing me. They are coming right through the telephone line. It is making it very difficult for me to carry out my professional duties."

"I'm sorry," I said automatically.

"I mention this for your benefit as well. It's not good for you. These are harmful waves. I am doing my best to counteract them with love, but, really, you must try."

I made an effort to control my hostile electronic waves.

"Now, where were we?" Caitlin continued. "Oh, yes, the will." She stopped. "Did you know Howard had scheduled an appointment with me about his will for this very morning? You know, I had a premonition about him. I felt the clouds surrounding him just last week when he spoke to me—"

"I'm sorry, Caitlin," I interrupted (to hell with the waves), "but I don't understand. Howard wrote me out of his will. He told me so."

"He intended to. He wanted to endow the Howard Hack Award for Achievement in Modern Minimalism. I had the papers all drawn up. That's what he was coming in for. As it stands, though, that will is invalid. Accordingly, I was forced to file his prior will this morning with the court."

"His prior will? You mean—" I checked myself. "But how can that be? We're divorced."

"Well, no," said Caitlin, "you weren't. I have your divorce papers here in my hand. They are also unsigned. Howard was to have signed them this morning, with his new will."

"Then—" I stopped. The one-million-dollar advance, I thought incoherently. The apartment in the city. The royalties from the sales of the book . . .

"That's right," said Caitlin. "You inherit everything."

Chapter

6

The next morning was a cold and blustery November day, but the house was warm and cozy. When I came into her room, Emily was standing up in her crib waiting for me. She'd slept on her hair funny again, so it stood straight up on the top of her head like a mohawk. As soon as she saw me her face broke into a big, wide, expectant four-toothed grin. She looked like a completely joyful extraterrestrial.

I lifted her out and gave her a big hug.

"I'm glad you're feeling better," I told her, "because I have some good news I want to share with you. We're rich."

Emily yawned and snuggled closer to me.

"You can act as nonchalant as you like," I told her, changing her diaper and then carrying her downstairs. "But you're not fooling anyone. I know how much you want one of those big plastic kitchens with the wall phone and the attached dinette. You're not putting anything over on *me*," I harrumphed, maneuvering her into her high chair and ladling oatmeal and raisins into her Big Bird bowl.

"Ppppppgagagaga," said Emily, picking out the raisins one by one.

"Who am I talking to here, a Buddhist? Did I say money was going to solve all of our problems? I'm just expressing a little natural enthusiasm. Unlike others," I retorted, refilling her apple juice.

Emily didn't say anything.

"Hey, you think you're the only one around here who knows money can be a trap?" I asked, feeding her a spoonful of oatmeal. The phone rang and I got up to answer it. "You're talking to someone who traded commodities, remember? You think I don't know it's important to keep money in perspective?" I demanded, reaching for the receiver. "Who's the mother around here anyway?"

"That's telling her."

It was Adam.

"How's Emily?" he asked.

"Much better, thanks. That was a wonderful prescription— I mean Emily's—" Oh, God, Elizabeth. You've got to do better than this. The man doesn't have to know you haven't had a date in almost a year. Play it cool for a change. "I mean, the pink stuff seems to be working," I added coolly.

"Good." He paused. "In that case, would you like to have dinner with me?" he asked.

"Dinner?"

"How about Friday?"

"Friday?"

"For dinner," he said.

"Oh. Right. Friday for dinner," I replied nonchalantly.

"Is that a yes or a no?"

"Uh, no," I said. "I mean, yes. It's a yes." There's such a

thing as being too cool. "Really, I'd love to." Okay, that's fine. End it. "I can't think of anything I'd rather do." That's *enough*, Elizabeth. "I mean it. Really."

Jeez.

"On second thought, I'm busy Friday night," he said.

"Oh."

"Just kidding," he said.

I hung up the phone, picked Emily up and waltzed around the kitchen with her until she screamed with delight.

Ordinarily, I don't rush out to get the out-of-town papers. But considering that my ex- or not-quite-ex-husband had been murdered three days ago, I decided to take a quick ride to Al's to see if Howard's death had made the big time.

Al's News & Variety was located right on the corner of Church and Housatonic, next to the Lenox Beauty Parlor. Since it is exactly four minutes by car from the door of my house to the front door at Al's (assuming that I got one of the parking spaces right in front, which I always did), I didn't think it would do Emily any particular harm to accompany me. Accordingly, I bundled her up warmly, pulled a pair of jeans on over my pajamas, threw a coat on over the whole ensemble, and got into the car.

But today there were no parking spaces in front of Al's. In fact, there were no parking spaces on the whole block. I deduced immediately that many of the cars belonged to out-of-town newspeople. I was helped in this deduction considerably by the presence of the logos of the Albany, Springfield and Boston news stations on the sides of their respective vans.

As I walked toward Al's holding Emily, I had to decline an interview with a woman in a red suit and black high heels who jumped into my path to ask if I knew Margaux Chase. I saw the plumber who had messed up the installation of my dishwasher gesturing enthusiastically at a short balding man in a plaid sport jacket who was taking notes on a pad.

I blinked a little as I entered the shop. Al's Variety is dark, small and L-shaped, stuffed with papers, magazines, baseball cards, baseball caps, sweatshirts, sweatpants, t-shirts, socks, toiletries and other sundries and staples. Al himself stood behind the counter as he did every day but Sunday. He was in his sixties, tall, white-haired, dressed in a clean checked shirt and neatly pressed pants. As was his habit, he stood with his reading glasses tipped at the end of his nose, an open Bible before him. There was nobody else in the store.

He looked up as I came in and nodded soberly to me.

"Very sorry to hear of your loss, Elizabeth," he said.

"Thank you, Al."

"Baby okay?"

"She had a little fever," I explained, "but she's better now."

"Good." He peered at Emily. "Hi, sweetheart," he cooed with a smile. "She's getting prettier every day." He winked. "Looks like her mother."

"Thank you, Al."

I went over to where Al kept the out-of-town papers, on a rack in the corner behind the football jerseys and the comic books. Emily, feeling the combined effects of the cold and the oatmeal, yawned and laid quietly against my shoulder as I riffled through the stock.

"Can I get a pack of Camels, please?"

I turned and saw a man standing at the counter. He wore a bombardier-style brown leather jacket, jeans and expensive-looking cowboy boots. I wondered how, with those boots on, he could have gotten in the store so quietly that I didn't hear him.

Al passed him the cigarettes.

"Thanks." The man took the package, tapped it thoughtfully on the counter and glanced at Al, who was still reading.

"And The Lord says, Let your way of life be upright, and let your behavior be rightly ordered: for my salvation is near, and my righteousness will quickly be seen," the stranger recited suddenly. "And let not the man from a strange country, who has been joined to the lord say, The Lord will certainly put a division between me and his people." He stopped, then grinned. "Isaiah, chapter fifty-six, verses one and three."

"Yup," Al agreed.

"Look. My name's Sherman Forrest and I'm with the *Christian Science Monitor*," said the reporter. "I don't want to bother you. I'm sure you've been bothered enough already. But I just have one question. Howard Hack had an ex-wife up here. Do you have any idea where I could find her?"

Al looked up from his Bible. I stood absolutely still.

"I'm sorry," he said politely. "I don't know her."

I snuck out of Al's without bothering to buy anything and drove straight home. As I pulled into my driveway I was greeted by the sight of Didi's station wagon blocking my garage. Didi herself was sitting in the driver's seat, waiting for me. As I pulled Emily out of her car seat, Didi got out, too.

"Elizabeth," she said, hurrying to embrace me. "How are you doing?"

"Uh—fine, thank you, Didi," I replied, endeavoring to save Emily from being suffocated between us and hoping my pajamas didn't show under my coat.

"I brought you something. You know, I thought you might not feel like cooking at a time like this . . ." She reached back into the car and pulled out a big white box.

"Didi. That's really sweet," I said.

"Oh, it's nothing. We always do that up here when somebody's had a—you know—"

While I did not particularly feel like having company this

morning, at least until I had taken a shower and brushed my teeth, Didi just stood there, clearly expecting to be invited in. And I could see that it was impossible to carry both Emily and the box into the house.

"Would you like to come in, Didi?" I asked graciously.

"Well, maybe just for a few minutes. I left Samantha and Sean with my mother. You never burden the bereaved with small children," she explained.

"Oh! That's very sweet," I said again.

I put Didi's box on the counter while I took off Emily's coat. I left my own on.

"Aren't you going to open it?" she asked.

"Oh! Of course," I said.

I opened the box. Inside was a double layer cake with white frosting. A little blue sugar angel was set in the center.

"I hope you like lemon," said Didi.

I gave up, made a pot of coffee, cut us each a small piece of cake and took off my coat. Didi looked right at my pajamas, but didn't say anything.

Didi took a small bite of cake. "Are you *sure* you're all right?" she asked with deep concern.

I assured her I was.

She took another bite and commented on the cheerfulness of my wallpaper.

I thanked her.

She took a third bite, looked me square in the eye and said: "So, who do you think did it?"

Without bothering to swallow her cake, Didi volunteered, "*I* think it was the Easter Bunny."

I paused. "But, Didi, weren't *you* the Easter Bunny?" I asked finally.

"No, the *other* Easter Bunny."

"*Was* there another Easter Bunny?"

"Oh, yes, and when I went up to compliment her on her

costume, she gave me a *very* funny look and walked away," confided Didi.

I nodded, although I didn't think the fact that someone had given a funny look to a woman in a pink sweatsuit with cotton balls stuck all over it should necessarily make her a suspect in a murder case.

"Of course, it *could* have been . . ." Didi continued.

I half-listened while she ran through a number of other gruesome scenarios. But I couldn't get the question out of my mind.

I had been so occupied, what with hearing that Howard was dead and sorting out the implications for myself and Emily and then fielding all the phone calls and then finding out that I had inherited over a million dollars, that I had almost forgotten that Howard had not, in fact, been hit by a truck or had an untimely heart attack, but had been *shot*.

More than that, the person who had pulled the trigger had almost assuredly attended the same party as I, made small talk with the same ghosts and goblins, eaten from the same canape tray.

Who *had* shot Howard?

It wasn't until after Didi left that I really had a chance to sit down and consider this question. Even then, I didn't get very far. I'm afraid my analytic skills were slightly rusty. I was reduced to pulling a yellow pad out of my desk drawer and writing at the top:

SUSPECT   MOTIVE   OPPORTUNITY

and then staring glumly down at it, tapping my pen against the little green lines.

"So, Em," I sighed. "Who did it?"

Emily pulled a little toy Easter bunny out of an old shoe box.

"Very funny," I said.

Well, there was the obvious, of course. I began writing H-O-L-

At that very moment, there came a short, efficient, demanding rap at the front door.

"Now, who could that be?" I said, putting down my pen.

Emily wrinkled her nose and began crawling across the floor in the direction of the door.

"Oh, that's okay," I said, sweeping her up just before she reached the landing, "I'll get it," and I opened the door.

There stood Holly Ivy.

She was dressed entirely in black. Black cashmere turtleneck, black stretch pants, shiny black shoe boots, a black onyx bracelet and earrings, a black shawl draped around her sleek dark head, sunglasses despite the overcast November sky. She looked like a society cat burglar.

"Elizabeth," she said as I stood gaping at her, reminded for the second time that morning that I was still in my pajamas, "such a terrible thing," and she stepped inside. "May I come in?" she asked over her shoulder, already moving toward the living room.

There didn't seem any point in responding, since, as far as I could see, she already *was* in, so I simply closed the door behind her. "Speak of the devil," I whispered to Emily.

"What?" Holly turned and removed the sunglasses. Those violet eyes popped out at me.

Maybe they're contact lenses, I thought. Aloud I said, "Nothing," and then, "Please come in." I shifted Emily in my arms. "May I get you something?" I asked. "Coffee? Tea? Angel cake?" I added hopefully.

"Hmm? Oh, no, nothing, thank you." Her gaze swept over

me and landed on Emily. "Oh," she said, "this must be—" there was a little silence.

"Emily," I volunteered.

"Yes, of course, Emily. I've heard so much about her," said Holly. "You know, from Howard."

"Really."

"Oh, yes, he was always talking about—"

"Emily."

"Emily. Yes. Right. He was *terribly* fond of her."

"I'm sure he was," I said. "Is there something I can do for you, Holly?"

Holly smiled. It was a warm, inviting smile, filled with perfect white teeth. "I knew I could come to you, Elizabeth. I felt a natural sympathy spring up between us when Howard introduced us at that dreadful party."

"Really," I said, for the second time.

"Yes. And I've been just broken up over this thing, really I have."

"Yes, I can see that."

"Of course, he told you that we were collaborating."

Yes, I thought. I had heard evidence of the collaboration. "No," I said, "as a matter of fact, he never mentioned that."

"Really." She stopped for a moment. "Well, it was no secret. Howard and I were writing a book together. Actually, that's not quite correct. It was my book. Howard was contributing in some small way, but it was, strictly speaking, *my* book."

"So what's the problem?" I asked.

"The problem," said Holly, "is the notes."

"What notes?"

"The notes to my book."

"What about them?"

"They've—disappeared."

"Disappeared?" I repeated. "Did you tell the police?"

"Well, no, perhaps disappeared is too strong a term. What I meant to say was that I had left them with Howard for safekeeping and now I can't find them and I thought just possibly he might have left them here."

"Here? If they're anywhere they're in the apartment," I said.

"Oh, no, I loo— I mean, I don't remember seeing them there," she said. "The last time we were there together, I mean."

"Well, they're not here," I told her.

"Are you sure? You might not recognize them. They might be handwritten or typewritten or even on a computer disk—"

"What do you mean, might be? Don't you know your own notes?" I asked.

"Well, you know, I kind of left all of that to Howard."

"Of course you did," I said.

"The point is, how can you be sure you don't have them? Have you looked?"

"I don't have to look."

"Well, how could it hurt? I'll help you."

"Holly, let me be as explicit as I can. Howard walked out of here six months ago. After he was gone, I went through the entire house. I discovered he did quite a thorough job of clearing out his possessions. He left two pairs of socks with holes in the heels, a container of used tennis balls and a pair of earmuffs. I believe they are still in the basement. You are welcome to them if you wish."

"No, thank you, Elizabeth," said Holly, who, once she caught the gist of my speech, had started turning away and was by this time already at the door. "Oh." She stopped and turned back for just an instant. "Oh, and good-bye—"

"Emily," I said, but she was already out the door.

*   *   *

After she left, I stood staring after her.

She did have a motive, all right, I thought grimly. And, Lord knows, she had opportunity. And, especially after this visit, I, personally, would have been thrilled to find out it had been Holly Ivy.

But seeing her again had reminded me, all too clearly, of those few minutes standing in Margaux's guest bedroom with my ear to the wall, listening to Howard have his orgasm. And something that I just couldn't get away from had occurred to me.

If I could hear Howard, silencer or no silencer, wouldn't I have heard a shot?

With a sigh I walked over to my list of suspects and reluctantly crossed out the H-O-L.

Chapter

7

Food and sympathy poured in all morning. I wouldn't have been surprised to see a United Nations relief truck pull up at my door. I received a zucchini-and-alfalfa-sprout pizza on seven-grain crust from Pat, a pork-and-rigatoni casserole from my neighbor Rebecca, who hadn't spoken three words to me since I moved in, and sixteen sour cream pumpkin muffins that I could hardly lift from Rose, Emily's baby-sitter. Even Faye Rudge, the chief's wife, sent over a chicken drenched in tomato sauce.

I stood in the kitchen surrounded by this bounty and realized that with all this food in the house, I had nothing to eat. So I wrapped Emily up and went shopping at Guido's.

Guido's is to the Berkshires what Rick's was to Casablanca. It speaks volumes about us, I am sure, that Rick's was a glamorous nightclub and Guido's is a food mart. Nonetheless, this past year, when *New York* magazine reviewed the Berkshires as it always does before the summer season, it listed Guido's ahead of Tanglewood as the area's number-one attraction.

And with good cause. Everything is available at Guido's: fresh meats, exotic cheeses, just-made pasta cut to specification in front of you, whole glazed turkeys and fruit-and-clove-studded hams cooked to order, every kind of fruit and vegetable grown within the two hemispheres. At Guido's it is possible to order a picnic of bok choy, haricots verts, venison sausage, fresh peaches, heavy cream, Perugina chocolates and lean pastrami on rye.

Since my separation from Howard and the acceptance of my reduced circumstances, I had heroically forgone the farm-raised salmon fillets at $10.99 a pound in favor of the $4.99 scrod. I had rigorously avoided turning my head in the direction of such dainties as the chestnuts in heavy syrup, the white asparagus, the herbed niçoise olives. Only very occasionally, as a special treat, did I indulge in fresh raspberries or sugar-snap peas, and then only because Emily seemed to like them.

But now—!

I don't believe that the full impact of Howard's death and my inheritance hit me until I walked through the door of Guido's that Tuesday afternoon. Oysters! Smoked salmon at $19.99 a pound! Caviar! Lobster! The crassest guest home-owner on *Lifestyles of the Rich and Famous* had nothing on me, and I hadn't even gotten out of the fish department yet.

"Elizabeth?"

I turned around, unseeing, still mentally debating the merits of homemade New England clam chowder ($3.50 a single portion) versus lump crabmeat as an appetizer.

"*Ja*, Elizabeth, are you okay?"

"Astrid," I managed, my sight clearing. There she was, dressed in jeans and a down vest, Maurits and his bottle plunked down in the shopping cart. "Look, Emily," I said in the idiotic high-pitched falsetto I use when I'm trying to get my daughter's attention. "It's Maurits and Maurits's mommy."

Emily and Maurits studiously avoided looking at each other.

"Elizabeth, I'm so glad I ran into you," said Astrid. "Didi told me . . . she said he was your husband . . ."

"My ex—" Out of habit I started to correct her, then remembered not to.

"Anyway, I am so sorry. Is there anything I can do?"

"No, nothing, thanks," I smiled.

"Take care of Emily for you? Maybe you don't want to be alone. *Ja*, I know. Why don't you and Emily come home with Maurits and myself tonight for dinner? We can make a little party—or, er, you know, just to take your mind off things. You can meet my husband, Jann. I told him all about you. He's dying—uh, he wants to meet you."

"Thanks, Astrid, that's sweet, it really is, but I don't think so."

"You sure? Maybe you want to come home with me for a little while, before dinner, just to talk? People shouldn't go through something like this alone. In Holland you'd have the whole neighborhood at your doorstep." She smiled. "Poof, what am I saying? You probably have plenty of people—"

Yes, it was true. I had had the whole neighborhood on my doorstep. Everyone was being terrific.

Still, Astrid was different. There was no morbid curiosity, no sense of rote obligation. Astrid just wanted to be friends. She liked me. She was making that first overture, the one that's the hardest to do, the one that nobody makes anymore.

I knew that if I went home with her she'd make me a cup of coffee and I could tell her everything. I could tell her about my relationship with Howard and how I'd hated him these past few months and she'd listen without judging. I could tell her how stunned I'd been at the news of his death, scared and saddened at the same time, and she'd sympathize. I could tell her the incredible story about the money and she'd be happy for me. I could tell her about Adam and she'd rejoice with me. And right then I wanted to go home with her. I wanted to tell her. I wanted to open up and let somebody in.

But I didn't.

"I'm sorry," I shook my head. "Some other time, maybe."

"Sure," said Astrid. "I understand. See you at the play group, then. It's at my house, *ja?*" She started to push her cart away.

"*Ja*—I mean, yes," I replied. "See you then."

I continued on my way, tossing items into the cart, but somehow I ended up doing only the most perfunctory shopping. If I hadn't known before that I should have accepted Astrid's invitation, I knew it as soon as I arrived home. There stood Sherman Forrest of the *Christian Science Monitor,* stamping his cowboy-booted feet on my front doorstep.

"Elizabeth?" he called, sidling down the steps and coming around to the driver's-side window before I'd even had a chance to turn off the ignition. It had begun to drizzle and he had turned up the collar of his jacket. I noticed it was trimmed with fur. "Elizabeth Halperin? Formerly Mrs. Howard Hack? I'm Sherman Forrest of the *Christian Science Monitor.* Mind if I ask you a few questions?"

I sat in the car with the windows closed and the doors locked, considering.

Ordinarily, I would have opened my door, grabbed Emily and invited him into the house for something warm to drink. I know this will sound naively trusting, especially to anyone who lives in a city, but really, that's the way it is up here. When someone turns up on your doorstep you don't treat him like he's just escaped from a prison van. You give him not only the benefit of the doubt, but whatever you happen to have to eat in the house as well, and, lord knows, this seemed a good way to get rid of those muffins.

This has a great deal to do, I believe, with the nature of crime in the country as opposed to that in the city. Howard's murder notwithstanding, wanton, random violence is still virtually unknown here. There is crime, even rapes and shootings, but they generally occur between people who know each other and who have had a little too much to drink at the local tavern or are in the midst of a messy divorce. To me, this did not constitute something to worry about. Since moving from New York I had not bothered to lock either my car or my house, except the latter at night, and then anyone with half a brain could scope out the spare key behind the flowerpot on the back porch without unduly exerting themselves. Up until recently, worrying about physical safety was something I'd left back in New York.

But now—I stopped with my hand on the car door handle. Now I was Emily's sole protector. I had to be extra cautious for her sake. What, I asked myself, did I really know about this man? So what if he *said* he was a reporter. He could be anyone. Why, for all I knew, he was the guy who killed Howard and was simply using the *Christian Science Monitor* ploy as a ruse to throw the police off the scent while he polished off the rest of the family. Had he been at Margaux's party? I tried to scrutinize his face through the glass, which was a bit difficult, as it had started to rain a little harder. All those costumes—would I even recognize him if he'd been dressed up as a dachshund or something? And just what was he carrying that made the pocket of his leather jacket bulge so . . .

He must have guessed my dilemma, because he took his wallet out of his pants very slowly and held his press card up to the window, like a cop flashing his ID. It had a picture of him on it and "*Christian Science Monitor*" printed in dark letters.

"So how do you like it?" he yelled through the glass and the rain, pointing his finger at the photograph. "Pretty good, huh? I had it done specially, by a professional, the guy who does Peter Jennings. Cost me a bundle, but it was worth it. Otherwise they turn out like your driver's license, like ya got malaria or something."

Still I just sat there, weighing the consequences, wondering if I shouldn't just hightail it out of there. As I did, it started to rain in earnest.

"Jesus Christ!" he exploded. "Would you look at this! And I just bought the fucking thing!" At first I didn't understand, but then I realized he was concerned about his jacket, which in truth was turning rapidly from a rich, warm tan color to streaky muddy brown. "Look," he begged, trying to shield himself against the car, "can't we talk about this inside? I've been waiting out here in the muck for almost an hour. I'm freezing. Have a little compassion. Look, I'll even carry your groceries."

I couldn't help smiling a little, he looked so pathetic.

"There," he said, reasonably, "you're starting to warm up to me. I know you are. And you're right to. My god, if I wanted to hurt you, or do something to you other than ask you a few lousy questions, d'ya really think I'd stand out here and freeze my butt off waiting for you? Lady, believe me, I've covered more wars than you got diapers. I been thrown in jail under both the Shah *and* the Ayatollah. I've covered gangs, drugs, the Mob, dictators, you name it, all *kinds* of bad guys. Believe me, if I want to get you, I don't stand in your driveway making a big public stink, get all your neighbors interested. I just jimmy one of your windows, let myself in, wait all nice and warm and dry until you walk in and then whack you out in the privacy of your own home. I tell you what I do not do. I do not stand out here in the fucking freezing cold and rain ruining a goddamn brand-new nine-hundred-dollar leather jacket for any other purpose than to impart trust, you got it?" He was really hollering now.

I opened the car door and swooped Emily into my arms. "Why jimmy the window," I asked, "when the front door was open?"

"You leave your front door unlocked?" he asked, blinking. "Ya gotta be more careful. You got the kid to watch out for now."

It took quite a while for the actual interview to get under way. As soon as we were in the house, the precious leather jacket and its owner were dispatched to the bathroom. There Sherman Forrest spent over a quarter of an hour engaged in the proper hanging of his garment from the shower curtain rod and in overall damage assessment. (I later discovered that several of my grandmother's hand-embroidered guest towels had been appropriated for the purpose of blotting the more severe watermarks.) Next came the boots, which were wet through. These were put beside the wood stove to dry, then moved back several feet on the grounds that the leather might crack from the heat, then inched forward again when it was discovered that they were too far away to benefit in all but the most indirect way from the fire. The boots having at last been placed satisfactorily, it was determined that the socks were wet as well (a circumstance of which I was already aware, their odor having preceded them), and these were hastily flung into the clothes dryer and an old pair of Howard's dug out as a substitute.

Thus restored, Sherman Forrest insisted upon helping me to unpack the groceries, during which time he told me how he had grown up in Valley Stream, Long Island, gave me the details of his *bar mitzvah* at the Oceanside Jewish Center with a buffet afterward at Arele's, told me how he talked his way into a job in the mailroom at the *Daily News* right out of college, how he worked his way up and how he had never been married, but listed by name the famous actresses and models he had slept with ("Those were the days when everybody wanted to sleep with a journalist," he noted). About this time Sherman Forrest felt a pang of hunger and insisted upon whipping us up some omelettes, so that in addition to attending to Emily I had to keep yelling instructions down the stairs on where to find the very groceries that we had just finished putting away.

At last, however, Emily was in bed and the omelettes were consumed along with a very nice bottle of wine that he had uncorked without asking and that I had been saving for a special occasion. I would have been more upset except for the fact that my omelette was terrific.

We removed ourselves to the living room, where I threw several more logs on the fire. As I watched Sherman Forrest settle himself comfortably into my sofa I finally got to ask something that had been bothering me for the last few hours.

"Excuse me for asking," I said, "but what is a Jewish guy like you doing writing for the *Christian Science Monitor*?"

"Nothing wrong with the *CSM*," he yawned, jamming two pillows under his head. " 'Course, it's not the big time. They can nickel and dime a guy to death. Not like the old days at ABC."

"*You* were at ABC?" I asked, not without a certain measure of incredulity.

"Foreign correspondent," he nodded, pulling himself to a sitting position. "Traveled everywhere. 'This is Sherman Forrest reporting from Honduras,' " he said in round tones. " 'This is Sherman Forrest reporting from Saudi Arabia.' Won an Emmy for disguising myself as a priest and interviewing political prisoners in the Philippines under Marcos," he confided.

"So what happened?" I asked.

He shrugged and slipped back down. "Oh, you know the

old story. New guy comes in at ABC, tries to make a name for himself by cutting back. Let go a whole bunch of pros from the news department. That's why their coverage eats shit now," he observed.

"Oh."

"Point is, I had to work somewhere, might as well be *CSM*. Mind if I smoke?" he asked, taking out his Marlboros.

"As a matter of fact I do," I said. "I don't like smoke in the house. It's not good for the baby."

"Oh," he said unhappily, laying the cigarettes down on the table. "Sure. I understand. Where was I? Oh, yes, ABC. The thing is, all I need is a hot story and they'll beg me to come back. No doubt about it. That's where you come in," he said, taking a cigarette out of the pack.

"Me?"

"Absolutely. This Howard Hack case is it."

At last, I thought. "Why?" I asked. "Why is everybody so interested in Howard?"

"Honey," said Sherman Forrest simply, "this case's got sex written all over it. And sex sells. It sells better than violence, it sells better than heroism, it sells better'n anything. It's that simple.

"Of course," he continued absently, rolling the unlit cigarette between his fingers, "it helps that there's violence here, too. And a decent corpse. Not as good as a movie star or the head of a Mob family or a high-priced gigolo or someone like that, but a chi-chi author'll do in a pinch."

"Uh-huh," I said, trying to absorb this reasoning. "So, you think Howard was killed by—"

"A female," said Sherman Forrest flatly. "No question about it."

"How do you know?" I asked.

"Elizabeth," said Sherman Forrest solemnly, "I want you to look at my nose."

I inspected his nose. It was on the large side, but otherwise unremarkable.

"This nose," he said, laying a finger against one side of the appendage in question, "has been sticking itself where it didn't belong for years. It stuck itself into Cambodia during the secret raids and almost got itself shot off. It stuck itself into Colombia and got itself put on the death list of a major drug lord. More to the point, it's stuck itself into Beverly Hills prostitution rings, Long Island princess fatal attraction slayings and I don't even remember how many he-cheated-on-me-and-he-had-it-coming-to-him-the-bastard murder trials. When this nose says your ex was killed by an unhappy gun-wielding female, you can take it to the bank."

"Uh-huh," I said again.

"Look," he sighed, sitting up with the air of a much-tried sixth grade teacher, "it's like this. We already know the bullet came from a twenty-five-caliber handgun. A twenty-five's a small gun—one of the smallest you can buy. A little, itsy-bitsy gun. Now, I don't know what the statistics are on this, but it's generally been my experience that it's the women who favor the cute little itsy-bitsy guns. Call it sexist of me, but they do. Little itsy-bitsy guns fit better into expensive pocketbooks. Guys as a rule favor the larger guns. Makes more of a statement."

"Really," I said.

"Yup. Then there's the angle of delivery. Right there at the left earlobe. Assassin gets in that close, victim knows 'em. Knows 'em and isn't afraid of 'em."

"But Howard had earphones on," I objected. "He might not have heard whoever it was come in."

"He might not have heard her, but he'd have felt her," said Sherman Forrest. "Guy was naked. You got no clothes on, somebody opens a door behind you, you gonna feel a draft from the hallway. Oh, no, he knew whoever it was popped him. *More* than knew her. Sitting there naked, didn't jump up and try to put on a robe. Didn't even turn around. Just kept on writing. I'd say he was intimately acquainted with whoever did it. Shit, from the way he was found he was probably *expecting* her. Unless the guy was an exhibitionist. *Was* he an exhibitionist?" It was the first question he'd asked all evening.

"Not to my knowledge," I said.

"That's what I thought. Few people really are. I don't care what kinda shape you're in, you tend to see only your pimples and love-handles, know what I mean? Puts a big damper on taking your clothes off in front of people you don't know."

"I see what you mean," I said slowly. "Tell me, have you informed the police of your theory?"

"The police?" He laughed. "I don't have to tell the police. I'm not telling them anything they don't already know. You think the police haven't figured this out? It ain't exactly nuclear physics."

"So you think the police will catch whoever did it?"

"Sweetheart, you can bet on it. And that's where the fun comes in." He put the cigarette to his lips but made no move to light it.

"What do you mean?"

"Look, soon as the perp's in handcuffs it's basically all over for the press. Oh, sure, you got your 'brave boys and girls in blue' story, your back-patting DA press conference, your trial, but really, what you've got is whatever it is the authorities want you to have, which is usually jack shit. No interviews with the suspect, no interviews with the victim's family or friends beyond the simpy 'Thank God that's over' statement, no interviews with all the other people who had the motive but not the guts to pull the trigger. In other words, you got no mystery. And if there's one thing that is a surefire, one hundred percent, complete-satisfaction-or-your-money-back guaranteed sell, it's a mystery with sex in it." He leaned back and took out his lighter.

"You know," I said slowly, "I get the feeling you're proposing something here, but I'm not quite sure what it is."

"I'll tell you what I'm proposing. I'm proposing a partnership." He flicked the lighter on and held it there in his hand.

"What kind of partnership?"

"A partnership where everybody gets what they want. What the hell other kind of partnership is there? And here's what I want. I want *perspective*."

"You mean you want information," I cut in.

"No, that is not what I mean. If I had meant information I would have said information. Information I can get. By the time I'm done with him I'm gonna know this guy Howard Hack like we were Siamese twins since grade school. I'm gonna talk to everybody from his choir leader to his latest squeeze. Information's easy. It's perspective I need, and only one person can give it to me." He eyed me, raised the lighter a little.

"Me? Give you perspective on Howard? You must be kidding."

He shook his head. "With all due respect, there's no one like an ex-wife for perspective. An ex-wife's got all the inside dope on the guy and no stars in her eyes blocking the vision. And I wouldn't be saying this if the guy was still alive. *Then* you'd be right, an ex-wife'd be useless. Still too busy hating the meatball. But with the guy dead everything changes, see? Then an ex-wife is invaluable. Nope. You're it."

"So let me get this straight," I said. "You want me to help you blow Howard's murder up into a big, sleazy sex scandal so that you can sell the story to the networks and get your old job back?"

Sherman Forrest looked hurt. "That is not at all what I

mean. For your information, it already *is* being blown up into a big sleazy sex scandal. That's inevitable. I'm just asking you for your help in putting the puzzle together before the authorities take away all the pieces."

"Uh-huh," I said for the third time that evening. "And just what exactly do *I* get from this partnership?"

Sherman Forrest finally lit his cigarette. He took a deep drag and leaned back against the cushions.

"You get to find out who did it," he said.

Chapter

8

Sherman Forrest's visit was still fresh in my mind the next morning. It had taken an age to get rid of him, his idea being, first, to sleep in my bed with me and, second (finding the first notion rejected out of hand), to sleep in the guest room. (It did not escape my notice that he seemed every bit as cheerful about the second alternative as the first.) It was only by adopting the firm, no-nonsense sort of voice that I use to discourage Emily from crawling too near the wood stove that I was able to bundle him out, cowboy boots and all, into the night.

The next morning, Emily was so much better that I decided to go ahead with my plan for the day, which was to leave her with Rose while I took the train into New York.

"Now, Rose," I said, as I hovered guiltily around Emily like the last fly of the season, "that should be about it. Do you think you have everything or should I go over it again?"

"We-ell," Rose drawled, squinting at the sheet of typewritten instructions I'd provided, "this all seems pretty clear. You're going into—"

"New York," I supplied quickly.

"—New York," Rose continued, "on the eight-thirty-five—"

"Leaving from Hudson," I encouraged. "There's the number for Amtrak," I said, pointing to the sheet.

"Oh, yes," said Rose. "Now, you'll get to New York at about—"

"Ten-forty-two," I cut in.

"—which gets you to that lawyer's office—"

"Caitlin Billings," I said, enunciating clearly and pointing out the name on the page. "Here's the number—"

"Oh, yes," said Rose. Then she looked up. "I hate lawyers, don't you?" she asked.

"Yes," I said. "See, here's the number—"

"I once knew a lawyer, tried to sue everybody in sight. Sued 'em at the drop of a hat. Damn silly things, too," said Rose.

"Yes," I said. "Now, I don't know when I'll be back but *probably* I'll take the two-fifty-five—"

"'Course some of them were real," Rose mused. "Like the time old man McCoy—he really thought he was somethin' because they let him volunteer at the fire department—anyway, he tried to stop up the creek, claiming it was a beaver dam—"

"Yes, Rose, that's very interesting, please remember that Emily's already had her medicine, but try to get her to eat something green, all right? Like peas or beans—"

"—then there was the time Jesse Hillcock—she's that stuck-up old biddy runs the Sweet Pea Moss Inn over on Route 102—backed her Lincoln into his—"

"Yes, well, Rose, I really have to run if I'm going to make that train. Bye-bye, sweetheart, Mommy has to go to New York now. I'll be home in time for dinner," I said, grabbing my briefcase and sweeping Emily up in my arms. "I'll miss you," I whispered, cuddling my face into hers. "Wish me luck."

Emily pulled back so that she could see into my face. For a long moment, we just stood there, looking at each other.

Then, just before I put her down, I could have sworn I saw her wink.

"Elizabeth. I'm so pleased you could make it. I hope this wasn't too inconvenient for you."

Caitlin strode out from behind an impressively large, polished antique desk that dominated her equally impressively large, polished office. She was dressed in heels and a long, obviously expensive pearl-white cashmere dress that clung to her softly.

"No problem, Caitlin," I returned, shaking her hand. An understated, truly exquisite little diamond bracelet dangled from her wrist.

"Is there something I can get for you? Coffee? Tea?" As I shook my head, she continued solicitously. "Well, then, would you like to call home before we begin, to make sure everything is all right with the baby?"

As a matter of fact, I had been intending to call Rose since Poughkeepsie.

"Oh, that won't be necessary," I said lightly, and immediately hated myself.

"Good. Well, then, why don't you sit here"—she indicated a chair in front of her desk—"and we'll get started."

I sat down and began to take a pen, paper and calculator out of my briefcase. Caitlin, who had returned to her swivel chair behind the desk, stopped me.

"If you don't mind, Elizabeth," she said, in a tone of gentle reproof, "I'd like to take sixty seconds to cleanse our souls before actually getting to the business of Howard's estate."

"Excuse me?" I said.

"It's something I learned over the weekend at a seminar at

the Living Alternatives Institute. Do you know Living Alternatives? It's in Sheffield."

"I've heard of it," I replied. Sheffield is about twenty miles from Lenox.

"Oh, it's a fabulous place, really. Superb. I would go so far as to call it the premier facility for health and healing on the East Coast."

"Really," I said.

"Anyway, the guest lecturer, Dr. Bombay . . . he wrote *Heal Your Way to a Better Business Life* . . . suggested taking a few moments every so often during the day—like before a discussion of the sort we're going to have—to close our eyes, hold hands with our neighbors, and look deep into ourselves as a way of focusing our personal energy fields for maximum effectiveness. I've implemented Dr. Bombay's thinking into my own schedule over the last few days and it really works. My productivity levels are up over sixty percent."

"Really," I said again. "How exactly did you measure that?"

"So what I'd like to do," said Caitlin, ignoring me, "is to employ Dr. Bombay's technique before we begin." She reached across the desk and grasped my hands firmly in hers. She has long, thin fingers and flawlessly manicured nails, which had been painted the color of pomegranate seeds. "Now, close your eyes," she counseled, "and breathe deeply."

I made a show of lowering my eyelids, keeping Caitlin in sight through my lashes.

"All the way."

I closed my eyes all the way.

"Good," she said. "Are you breathing?"

"I believe so," I answered.

"Concentrate, please. Now, when you inhale, I want you to think good, positive thoughts. Are you ready?"

"Yes."

"Good. Inhale."

I took a breath and thought about what a pleasure it would be when I finally got to let go of Caitlin's hands.

"Hold it," said Caitlin in a strained voice.

I held it.

"Now, at the count of three, exhale. And when you do, I want you to think about exhaling all of your negative energy. I want all those unhappy, negative thoughts to tumble out with your breath, leaving only the good, positive thoughts inside. Ready? One, two, THREE!"

I opened my eyes and exhaled loudly. Caitlin did the same.

"Aaahhh," she sighed suggestively, rolling her neck as though she'd just had the massage of her life. "Now, isn't that wonderful?" she asked, finally letting go of my hands. "Don't you just feel like a new person?"

"Absolutely," I assured her.

"Good. I'm so pleased." She stretched sensually one last time. Then she reached into her desk, removed a manila folder stuffed with documents and slapped it in my direction. "The net asset value of the estate is in the nine-hundred-thousand-dollar range," she began crisply, "of which six hundred thousand is exempt from inheritance tax . . ."

She went through it all. It took over an hour. The manila folder contained an up-to-date typed list of Howard's assets, some of which, like the equity in the apartment, had originally been mine. (I had committed the cardinal sin of divorce settlement negotiation, the one that every single article, book and seminar on the subject warns you never, ever, ever to do. I had agreed to a lousy deal just to be done with it. There was some real satisfaction in getting back my own money.)

Basically, the estate consisted of the Park Avenue two-bedroom, currently valued at $350,000 ("Let's knock that number down to $295,000 for tax purposes," said Caitlin, forehead contracting over her spreadsheet. "We'll use the firm's real estate assessor. That way we can limit the amount you'll have to pay in inheritance tax. If you decide to sell it we'll deal with capital gains later. *Will* you be selling it?" she asked. "I don't know," I replied. "Of course you don't," she said, and went on), one brand new black convertible Mercedes roadster valued at $70,000 ("Fifty-thousand, for tax purposes," said Caitlin, writing. "We'll use the firm's auto specialist.") and $500,000 in some securities and a money market account. ("Not much we can do about that, I'm afraid," she sighed.)

As executor, Caitlin would convert as much of the estate as possible into cash and put it in a special account labeled "Estate of Howard Hack." Out of this account she would pay all taxes and fees, including her own. After that, the money would be mine. "It will take about a month, I would say," she reported. "Of course, you have up to six months to get everything in order, but really, I don't think that will be necessary with such a straightforward case."

"Nine hundred thousand dollars," I said softly, little goose bumps breaking out all over my arms.

Caitlin laughed, a little tinkling laugh. "Hardly. That's it for the purpose of determining the magnitude of the estate at the time of death. But that doesn't count receivables, of course."

"Receivables?" I asked. "What receivables?"

"Receivables from the sale of additional rights to Howard's book. The sale of foreign rights, for example, or film rights. Maybe even television rights for a movie of the week about the murder."

"Do you think they could be significant?" I asked with a straight face.

Caitlin looked at me as though I'd just questioned the potency of her energy field. "They could run into the millions," she said.

Millions. Millions. Millions.

". . . a service the firm provides to all new clients," I heard Caitlin finish smoothly.

"Uh, I'm sorry, I didn't catch that last part—"

"I was just saying," Caitlin repeated, "that I would be happy to draw up a list of potential investment strategies to meet your needs. You know, when a person inherits a substantial amount of money all at once the way you have, they don't always have the time or energy to research opportunities properly. Even someone with your financial background can be unprepared for the enormity of the enterprise. Management of sums like these can be a full-time job," she noted.

She had a point. If I wasn't going to go back to work to trade other people's money full-time, I wasn't going to go back to work to trade my own money, either. "Um, that's very nice, Caitlin . . ." I began.

"It's a service the firm provides free of charge to all new clients," Caitlin rushed along. "You know, sometimes, because of our size and expertise, we have access to deals that others— overlook. I'm just saying I'll keep my eyes open and if anything comes along that looks interesting I'll go ahead and jot down the particulars for you. How does that sound?"

"That's certainly very considerate of you," I said.

"No problem," said Caitlin with a wave of her bejeweled wrist. I saw her steal a glance at the clock on her desk. "Well, that's about all I have to say," she concluded, putting her hands on her desk as a prelude to rising. "Do you have any questions?"

"Uh—no—"

"Good." She rose and shook my hand firmly. "Remember, Elizabeth," she said, as she swept me out of the office toward the reception area, "we at Lewton & Lord are here to help you. If there's anything we can do—anything at all—just let me know."

It wasn't until I was already down the hall on my way to the elevators that I realized that one thing she could have done would have been to let me have a key to the ladies' room before hustling me out so abruptly. I had to double back to the receptionist.

"To your right, around the corner, fourth door down," the receptionist replied crisply.

I took the key and followed her instructions. On the way back, I turned the corner and stopped short, then quickly backed away. A woman had emerged from the elevators and was making her way to reception.

"I have an appointment with Caitlin Billings," I heard her announce.

"Oh, yes, Ms. Billings is expecting you," the receptionist replied. "Go right in."

The woman opened the door that led to the inner offices and disappeared. Although I only saw her face for a moment, I knew her instantly.

It was Holly Ivy.

I walked out of Caitlin's office building more disturbed by this chance encounter than I cared to admit. Of course, Holly had every right to visit Caitlin. Her and those precious notes, I sniffed. She'd probably heard Howard mention Caitlin in passing and knew she was his lawyer, so she'd come to see if he'd left her his writings in escrow or something. Well, she'd be disappointed, I thought. Caitlin hadn't said a thing about any notes.

Although this should have been a source of some satisfaction, it wasn't. I still felt irritated. It took me a while to figure out why, but in the end, I had to be honest with myself.

It was that between the two of them—Caitlin and Holly—I had begun to experience feelings of misgiving. Seeing them reminded me that while they were both out there being so, well, professional, I was at home making Elmo talk.

Where was *I* going? I wondered as I walked down a crowded Park Avenue. What was *I* doing? Should I use Howard's legacy for a fresh start? What *was* a fresh start, exactly? Should I drag Emily to New York, get my old job back and wear clothes that require dry-cleaning, like Caitlin? Had I been doing the right thing all this time, by putting my own life on hold to be a mother? When you do that, do you get it back at the end?

And then, suddenly, I thought not of Howard, or Holly Ivy, or ambition, but of Emily. And suddenly, I wanted nothing more than to be home.

I glanced at my watch. If I hurried, I could still make the 2:55.

I did make it. I rode home in the November twilight and stared out the window until all I could see was my own reflection. When I got to the house I wrapped my daughter up in her blanket and sat on the rocking chair in the nursery looking at all the familiar baby things until the two of us were nearly asleep. I laid Emily in her crib and looked down at her.

I'm home, I thought. I'm safe.

Chapter

9

The next day I was upstairs reading to Emily when a police car turned into the driveway.

"Goodnightstarsgoodnightairgoodnightnoiseseverywhere," I jumbled all in one breath as I watched Chief Rudge and Detective Fineburg emerge from inside and head up the steps to my front door.

I put my daughter in her crib and hurried downstairs. Although the door was unlocked as usual, the two men stood outside stiffly, waiting for me to invite them in. They might have been holding up a sign flashing "OFFICIAL POLICE BUSINESS."

"Ma'am," acknowledged the chief politely when I swung the door open.

"Good morning, Elizabeth," the detective smiled. He was wearing an old felt hat pulled down low over his brow and a green tie with a hot pink bunny rabbit embroidered in the center.

"Good morning," I returned. "Won't you come in?"

"Sure," Detective Fineburg began.

The chief coughed.

"Oh, I forgot," laughed the detective. "Before we come in, the chief here wants to read you your rights."

"My rights?" I repeated.

"It's routine, ma'am," Chief Rudge announced impassively. Detective Fineburg shrugged and smiled at me from behind the chief's back.

"Uh—okay," I said.

The chief recited my rights in a low monotone. They sounded exactly the way they do on TV.

"Do you understand everything I've said?" he finished.

"Yes."

"May we come in now?" asked Detective Fineburg.

"Sure," I said and held the door open.

They trotted in after me. "I hope this isn't too early," said the detective.

"Not at all. It's a good time, actually. I just put Emily down for her nap."

"She goes to sleep just like that?" he asked, astonished. "No crying, no carrying on?"

"You have a problem getting one of your daughters to sleep, Detective?" I guessed as the chief trailed us into the living room.

"My youngest, Cara. She won't go to sleep without a tussle . . ."

I went over to one of the bookcases. "Here," I said, getting down a well-worn paperback and handing it to him.

"*Change Your Child's Sleep Habits*," he read. "Hey, I think I've heard of this book. Isn't this that sleep doctor from Boston?"

"Uh-huh," I said.

"It really works?" he asked doubtfully, turning the book over in his hands.

"Absolutely," I assured him. "But you have to read it from the beginning. You can't skip around," I cautioned.

"Well, that'll be a tall order for me," he conceded. "But I'll give it a try. Do you mind if I keep this? It might take me a while. I was never very good at reading." Detective Fineburg squinted at my bookshelves. "Unlike you," he noted. "This is quite a collection."

I laughed. "I love to read," I admitted.

"You got a favorite author? Favorite subject? Favorite period? I'm partial to mysteries, myself," he said, still gazing at my books. "What about poetry? You like poetry?"

"I like good poetry," I said.

He sighed and plucked a volume entitled *English Romantic Writers* from my shelf. "I never could understand poetry," he complained. "Take these guys, for example." He opened to the table of contents. "Keats." He uttered the name with the sort of enthusiasm that most children exhibit for cauliflower. "Never could understand Keats. Had him in school. Nearly killed me, Keats did. And Wordsworth. He was a little easier, but still. Ah, but here's a name that rings a bell. Blake. William Blake. Always liked William Blake." He took a step back and recited:

"Tyger! Tyger! burning bright
"In the forests of the night,
"What immortal hand or eye
"Could frame thy—could frame thy—" he faltered.

"Could frame thy fearful symmetry," I finished for him.

"Serves me right for trying to show off," he said shame-facedly. He shut the book abruptly. "Mind if I keep this, too?" he asked.

"Uh—sure," I said, a bit startled.

"Thanks," he said, tucking it under his arm. "I'm afraid we've got to ask you a few more questions," he apologized.

"Is something wrong?" I asked, looking from one to the other.

This time the chief answered. "No, ma'am. Just routine."

"I see," I said, and sat down.

"You see, Elizabeth," said Detective Fineburg, taking a chair and moving it so he was directly across from me, "we've got a problem."

We've? I thought.

"What kind of problem?" I asked.

"Well, it's a *discrepancy* kind of problem," the detective confessed, pulling at his ear.

I waited.

The chief reached into his back pocket and flipped out his notebook with one hand, as though it were a switchblade. "During our previous interview you stated that you were divorced from the deceased at the time of his death. Is that correct?"

"What the chief means," Detective Fineburg cut in hurriedly, "is that we've had some conflicting information on this subject, and we thought just possibly that we had misunderstood you the last time—"

I explained that Howard had not signed the papers after all, even though he had told me he had done so.

"But he *was* going to divorce you?" asked the chief, pen poised above the note pad.

"He said so." I paused. "His lawyer said so, too. She said he was to have signed the papers on Monday."

"His lawyer, ma'am?" The chief wrote. "Would you happen to have the lawyer's name and address handy?"

"Caitlin Billings," I replied. "Three-fifty Park Avenue. In New York," I finished lamely.

"You know her address just like that?" asked Detective Fineburg softly.

"I just saw her yesterday," I pointed out a little defensively.

"Why?" asked the detective.

"Why?" asked the chief.

I swallowed. "Howard—left me some money," I said.

"Really." The detective's eyebrows shot up. "Without being too indelicate, might I inquire—was it, would you categorize it as a *substantial* sum of money?"

"Yes." I swallowed again. What the hell, I thought, they're going to find out sooner or later. Might as well hear it from me. "About nine hundred thousand dollars," I said.

I thought I saw the chief's hand shake a little as he wrote, although otherwise there was no indication that he had even heard what I said. But Detective Fineburg whistled.

"Whew! All from writing a book? Beats the hell out of the detective business." He stopped. "That was pretty generous of him," he noted. "I mean, leaving so much money to the person he was divorcing."

"He didn't mean to," I told him. "He had another will all drawn up. But he never got a chance to sign it, so—" I left the sentence unfinished.

"Who told you about the other will?" asked Detective Fineburg. "His lawyer?"

"Yes and no," I said. "She did mention it. But Howard had told me about it first over the phone."

"He threatened to cut you out of his will?"

"Yes—I mean no—I mean, I didn't care. It didn't matter to me," I said.

"You're pretty casual about nine hundred thousand dollars," Detective Fineburg observed.

"I didn't know it was nine hundred thousand, I mean, I wouldn't have cared, I mean, I think I wouldn't have cared, I just wanted him out of my life . . ."

"But you did argue with him about money. I mean, it was an issue between you," said the detective.

"Of course it was an issue. I wanted Emily to have some security . . ."

"Emily was an issue with you too, wasn't she?" Detective Fineburg asked, glancing away.

I stopped. "To whom have you been speaking?" I asked stiffly.

He held up his hands. "Just doing my job."

I shifted in my chair. "Of course Emily was an issue. Howard and I had different ideas about raising her."

"Such as?"

"Oh, the usual." I waved my hand in the air. "You know, he wanted me to go back to work and leave her with a nanny, or put her in day care . . ."

"Did he ever say he was going to try and take her away from you?" asked the detective.

I blinked. "Of course not," I sputtered. "Whoever gave you that idea?"

"Just trying to fill in all the holes." Detective Fineburg looked over at the chief. "Well, I think we've cleared that up. I don't have any more questions, do you, Chief?"

"No," Chief Rudge answered, closing his pad with deliberation. I led the way to the front door and they followed without speaking.

But on the front steps Detective Fineburg turned around once more. "Uh—" he began, "we might have a few more questions on this inheritance thing. Are you going to be around over the weekend?"

"I suppose so," I replied.

"Not going anywhere? New York again, for example?"

"I wasn't planning on it," I said.

"Good." The detective smiled. "Then it shouldn't be too tough to get in touch with you."

They turned to go. "Oh, Chief Rudge," I called after him.

The chief spun around. "Yes?"

"Please thank Faye for the chicken."

"Astrid, these are positively sinful," sighed Didi, helping herself to another cookie.

It was our second play group and Didi, Astrid, Pat and I (Margaux had yet to arrive) were all standing around Astrid's dining room table, which had been heaped with enough food to support the occupants of a lifeboat for two months. In addition to the cookies there were brownies, pink-and-white petit fours, miniature cheesecakes glistening with peaches, caramel-and-pecan-filled Danish, custard tarts, three different kinds of cheeses, a bowl of strawberries accompanied by a crock of sweetened whipped cream and a silver chafing dish that opened to reveal an array of meatballs stuck with those fancy colored cocktail toothpicks. They looked like mudballs waving little flags.

Astrid beamed. "I'm so glad you like them," she said, plopping a spoonful of whipped cream into her coffee. "They come from an old family recipe. It's very simple. You take three sticks of butter and two cups of sugar . . ."

I saw Pat's lips work but nothing came out.

Although these meetings had been my idea, I almost hadn't come this time. The last thing I wanted to talk about was Howard, his death or his murder investigation. I just wanted to be alone. This would be the last time, I told Emily as we drove up to the house, and then we'd just quietly drop out.

But since we'd gotten to Astrid's, nobody had mentioned Howard at all. Everyone had been enormously friendly, but the talk had been of cookies, ear infections and potty training. As Emily was wholly absorbed by the discovery of a fire engine among Maurits's toys, I let myself relax a little and think.

". . . Elizabeth?"

"I'm sorry?" Didi's voice had jolted me out of my reverie and I realized that all three faces were staring at me with concern.

"Elizabeth's in—how do you say it—outer galaxy?" said Astrid.

"Outer space," I corrected automatically.

"*Ja*, that too." Astrid smiled impishly and everybody laughed.

"I'm sorry," I said. "It's just that this last week—" I stopped. The concern in the faces around me deepened.

"If there's anything we can do—" Didi began.

"It might feel good to talk about it—" Pat seconded.

"We only want to help," Astrid finished.

I looked from face to face. "No, no, I'm fine, really it's—" I began. And then, all of a sudden, I started to cry.

I hadn't cried when I'd heard about the murder, I hadn't cried during that dreadful second interview with the police when it was clear they suspected me, in fact, I hadn't cried the whole week. But I guess I had a lot of crying in me, because when I finally let go it was a lulu.

I sobbed. I wailed. I hiccuped. My mascara ran down my cheeks. My skin got all blotchy. My nose ran. Oddly enough, the children showed no interest in me whatsoever, all except Maurits, who immediately crawled over and, sucking contentedly on his bottle, never took his eyes off me, as though I were a television set tuned to *Barney*.

But the mothers sprang into action. Didi put her arms around me and rocked me gently. Astrid stroked my hand and murmured soothing nothings in Dutch. Pat patted my back. Then Didi smoothed my hair and dried my tears, Astrid made me blow my nose and Pat handed me two cookies.

When I had stopped heaving and sighing sufficiently so as to be articulate, everyone pulled up a chair and Didi said, in a voice of soft command, "So. Tell us."

And I did.

I told them everything. Fact, hypothesis, pure conjecture—
I left nothing out. I told them how I'd heard Howard upstairs
at the party that night with Holly Ivy and her subsequent visit
to my house, I told them about Howard's book and the inheritance and Caitlin, I told them about Sherman Forrest and the
Christian Science Monitor and his theory of who did it and our
deal. I even told them about Adam and how my first date in
years was scheduled for that very evening. And I ended with
Chief Rudge and Detective Fineburg and how I was sure they
thought I'd done it.

"Of course," I hiccuped, "I'm probably just being paranoid
about that—"

"No, you're not," Didi cut in firmly. "I've been wondering
for days how to tell you this, so I'm just going to come out and
say it. They do suspect you. In fact, Cousin John says you're
one of the prime suspects."

"But how can that be?" I stammered. "I've never handled a
gun in my life."

"They don't know that," she pointed out reasonably. "And
you inherited. It's a lot of money. That gives you motive," she
said simply.

We were all quiet.

"Well, somebody else had motive, too," Astrid piped up
suddenly. "Because Elizabeth didn't do it."

I could have kissed her.

"What you need is a good lawyer." It was Pat, speaking for
the first time. "A lawyer will help organize the investigation,
maybe hire a private detective . . ." Her voice trailed off as she
saw us all looking at her.

"Pat, that's a good idea. Why don't you do it?" suggested
Astrid.

"I should have said a good *criminal* lawyer," Pat corrected
herself. "I'm not qualified. I just do real estate . . ."

"My goodness, I never knew anyone better at organization than you, Pat," Didi protested mildly. "Why, just look how you organized that pancake breakfast at the church bazaar last year."

"This is entirely different. I don't have the experience . . ."

"That's just what she said last year about the church bazaar," Didi observed placidly, "and she just about knocked everyone's socks off. They're still talking about it," she confided.

"If you *were* going to do it, Pat, what would you advise?" I asked.

She stopped and thought a moment.

"I guess the first thing to do would be to find out exactly what the police have on you and try to refute it. If you didn't do it, it must be circumstantial. But it would be even better to come up with someone else who had motive and try to place them at the scene. That means combing through a list of possible suspects and investigating their activities around the time of the murder," she said.

"*Ja*, we can do that, no?" Astrid demanded.

"I don't see why not," said Didi.

"Don't be ridiculous, Didi," Pat snapped. "What do we know about a murder investigation? There are all kinds of technicalities we know nothing about. Forensics and the like."

Didi looked hurt.

"*Ja, ja,*" Astrid stepped in soothingly. "Nobody's saying we'll be perfect. But it won't hurt to try, would it?"

"No, of course not," said Pat, sounding unconvinced.

Didi turned to me. "Can you think of anyone else who might have done it?" she asked.

As a matter of fact, I could. I had been thinking about it seriously ever since I realized that the police suspected me. Someone with motive. Someone with access. Someone who felt protected enough to get away with anything. I opened my mouth to answer, but at that moment the doorbell rang. We all turned around as the front door swung open and a familiar figure appeared in the entranceway.

"Sorry I'm late," said Margaux. "Did I miss anything?"

Margaux. Of course it had been Margaux.

This is how I pictured it: Margaux and Howard are lovers, have been since before he left me. As publication of his book nears, Howard begins to spend more time in New York. Margaux, hampered by the children, remains in the Berkshires, but believes Howard to be, if not exactly faithful, at least still interested. She naturally invites him to her Halloween party. Then he shows up with Holly Ivy.

Betrayed, Margaux works herself into a fury. She watches Howard and Holly all evening. She sees them slip upstairs. She has been Howard's lover long enough to know, just as I did, his propensity for public sex. She knows he is with Holly in *her* house, at *her* party, right under *her* nose. She goes crazy with rage. She fetches the small gun she keeps in her bedroom drawer in case of an intruder. She waits, hidden, until after Holly and then I go back down the stairs. Then she slips out of her room and opens the door.

Howard feels the draft. He turns.

She smiles at him.

Howard smiles his smile at her. He says: "Just a minute, I've really got something here" (Howard always wrote after sex), and turns back to his laptop.

Margaux says, sweetly, "So have I, darling." She comes up behind him and . . . BAM!

Or . . .

Margaux and Howard *were* lovers. Then Howard cheated on her. Margaux found out. There was a big scene and Howard walked out on her. Margaux, who had never had anyone leave *her* before, is stung. She wants to get even. She wants to get more than even.

She plans it all out in advance. Coolly, calmly, rationally. She lets Howard know that bygones are bygones and invites him to her party. Perhaps she even tells herself that she will first wait to see if he throws himself at her feet again. Just to be sure, though, she makes a point of inviting me. If she goes through with it, she knows she will need a credible suspect. Perhaps she even knows about Howard's Monday appointment with Caitlin and the divorce papers and the new will. After all, Howard might have mentioned all this in an offhand sort of way when he responded to her invitation. He might have said, "Great, but just for the weekend. I have to be back in New York Monday morning to get Elizabeth out of my life forever." Then she sees me at that first play group and it comes to her. I will be the perfect suspect. That's why she made that insincere gesture of friendship and invited me to her party.

Now she knows she is safe and plans carefully. She takes the small gun she keeps in the drawer of her nightstand in case of intruders and slips it into a concealed pocket made specially for her hoopskirt. The party begins; Howard arrives with Holly and she knows there will be no reconciliation. She will do it. She acts her part as hostess, biding her time. At last she sees Howard and Holly sneak upstairs, followed moments later by me. With complete calm she waits, hidden, until after Holly and then I go back down the stairs. Then she slips up the stairs and opens the door.

Howard feels the draft and turns.

She smiles at him.

He smiles his smile at her and says: "Just a minute, I've really got something here," and turns back to his laptop.

Margaux comes up behind him and . . . BAM!

There it is. It's all there for anyone to see.

So how do I prove it?

Chapter

10

John Andrews is one of my favorite restaurants in the Berkshires. The food is excellent and the wine is fairly priced. Although it is almost impossible to get a reservation while Tanglewood is in session, once the summer is over and the leaves are down it is not that crowded, even on the weekends. We were seated at a quiet table near the big fireplace. It was my first date in nearly three years and I knew it was important to come up with a clever topic of conversation.

I picked up my wine glass. "I used to be married, you know," I volunteered. "My husband left me."

Adam nodded slowly. "Any chance of reconciliation?" he asked.

"It doesn't seem likely," I told him. "By the way," I added brightly, "who do you think killed Howard Hack?"

"I figure it was the ex-wife."

"Really," I said.

"She lives up here, you know."

"Yes, I heard that." I took a large sip of wine. "What do you think her motive might have been?" I asked.

"The money," he said.

"*What* money?" I demanded, starting to squirm in my seat.

"Oh, there's always money."

The appetizers arrived.

"There isn't always money," I said, stabbing one of my pan-fried oysters.

"Okay."

"I mean, there are lots of other people who could have done it," I told him.

"Okay."

"I mean, why does everybody always pick on the wife?"

"Especially when she's got such a cute little kid," he agreed.

"Yeah, espe—" I stopped.

"It's a funny thing," said Adam, calmly scooping up some smoked salmon mousse. "You know those medical charts we keep? Occasionally we read them. And right at the top of Emily's it says: FATHER: Howard Hack."

"Oh, right," I said.

"So how are you getting along?" he asked. "I'm assuming this is the first time you've had an ex-husband murdered."

"Yes, of course—" I blinked at him. "You're not a cop or something, are you?"

"Nope."

"I guess I don't know how I'm getting along," I said. "I thought I was doing pretty well until the police decided the ex-wife did it."

"And what do the police think the motive is?"

"The money," I replied.

Adam nodded slowly once more. "See?" he said.

I thought this would be a good time for a shift in the discussion. "So," I said, with an airy lift of my arm. "How well—uh, long—have you known Margaux?"

"Oh, a long time."

"Really."

"Oh, yes, let's see. Umm—let's see. Uh—must be—three weeks now."

"Oh." I paused. "How did you meet her?"

"Impetigo," he replied.

"Hers?" I asked hopefully.

"No. Tolin's."

Too bad, I thought. "Office visit?" I asked.

"Uh-huh."

"On a Sunday?" I inquired sweetly.

"Oh, it's hard to remember that far back."

"Did anything unusual happen during her visit?"

"No. Just routine."

"DID YOU KISS HER?" I demanded finally. The people at the table across the room glanced briefly in our direction.

"No."

"Why not?"

"She's not my type," he replied.

"Really?"

"Really."

"Oh." I thought I'd let that one rest where it was. "Why did you pick Rasputin?" I asked.

"I always wanted to be a mystical, satanic seducer of women. Besides, black doesn't show as badly when somebody spills on you."

"You don't seem very satanic," I said.

"Don't be so sure," he said, pouring more wine into my glass. "Why did you pick Sally Bowles?"

"Desperation. Besides, Emily liked it."

"You have nothing to be desperate about," he said.

We sat drinking wine and talking in that darkened room until everyone else had left and they basically shooed us out the door. I don't remember what we talked about on the ride back to my house. He pulled into the driveway, shut off the lights and turned off the car. I felt him looking steadily at me in the darkness and suddenly I got goose bumps.

If I turn and look at him now, he'll kiss me, I thought. I turned and looked at him.

He began to stroke my hair. I leaned closer to him.

He's going to do it, I thought. He's going to kiss me, the kind of kiss I've been waiting and waiting for. I turned more fully toward him, slid my chin up so that my lashes brushed his cheek.

He held me tighter, bent lower and—

And at precisely that moment, as his lips were about to touch mine, I felt something . . . a presence . . . and I glanced over his shoulder out the window on the driver's side. There, squinting at me through the glass, was the interested face of Sherman Forrest.

"WHAT IS THE MATTER WITH YOU?" I yelled.

Sherman Forrest and I were alone in my house. Adam was gone. Rose was gone. I was so angry I didn't even care if I woke Emily up.

"WHAT IS THE MATTER WITH YOU?" I yelled again. "Who goes sneaking around on other people while they are out on a date?" I paused. "Do you need more ice?"

He pulled the ice bag away from his jaw and fingered the spot where Adam's knuckle marks were still firmly embedded. "No, that's fine. I've been hit harder than that plenty of times. And I was *not* sneaking around," he added with dignity. "I was concerned about your safety. I thought you might need help."

"I DID NOT NEED ANY HELP!"

"I saw that," Sherman Forrest agreed.

"Aghh!" I think I actually stamped my foot.

"Look," he pleaded, spreading his hands palms-up. "I don't know what you're so upset about. It was a little misunderstanding, that's all."

I did not condescend to respond to this. As Sherman Forrest well knew, the only reason he was here in my living room instead of Adam was that he'd been the one lying flat on his back in the grass. And as tempting as it was, I had decided not to leave him there.

"Hey," said Sherman Forrest, standing and placing the ice bag ceremoniously on the coffee table, "I can take a hint. I know when I'm not wanted . . ."

"Good," I said, marching over to the front door and holding it open.

". . . I just thought you might want to hear who did it."

I stopped. "You know who killed Howard?"

"In so many words . . . yes," he said, plopping down on the sofa and taking out a pack of cigarettes.

I closed the front door very carefully, walked over to the armchair directly across from the sofa, sank down precariously on the edge of the cushions, leaned forward and said: "Who?"

"You mind if I smoke? It's been a hell of a day," he said.

I nodded mutely and shoved an empty candy dish in his direction so he wouldn't just flick his ashes on top of the wood stove.

"In retrospect, it was the obvious choice," he said, lighting his cigarette.

I nodded.

"Of course, not everybody catches on at the same time," he shrugged, snapping his lighter shut.

"Of course not," I murmured, never taking my eyes off him.

"You have to be practiced . . ." He took a deep drag. "You know what really gave it away?"

"No, what?" I asked.

He leaned forward. "The costume," he whispered.

"The costume?"

"Yes." He nodded gravely.

I stopped and thought. "*Whose* costume?" I asked. "Howard's?"

"No. The killer's."

"Oh!" I wet my lips. Here was the moment of truth. I felt it.

Sherman Forrest nodded to himself. "As soon as I heard the description, I knew. The difficulty was in concealing the weapon. Where, you might ask, would a woman wearing a skin-tight bodice, little black shorts and fishnet stockings hide a twenty-five-caliber pistol? But I knew right away. The hat. The bowler hat. Probably taped to the inside."

I stared at him.

"The killer was wearing fishnet stockings?" I asked slowly.

"Uh-huh," he nodded smugly.

"And black shorts?"

"Yup," he said, taking another deep drag.

"And a bowler hat?"

"You got it. That's what tipped me," he said.

"You're describing a Sally Bowles costume," I said.

"Huh?"

"Sally Bowles. From *Cabaret*," I said.

"Oh. Yup, I guess I am," said Sherman Forrest. "My source didn't know that, but now that you mention it . . ."

"*I* WAS SALLY BOWLES!" I yelled.

Sherman Forrest blinked at me. Then he took a final puff of his cigarette and crushed it out in the candy dish.

"Hey, I knew that," he said.

Chapter

11

The next morning, the phone rang at 7:00 A.M.

"Elizabeth?" whispered a voice on the line.

"Adam?" I answered groggily.

"I didn't wake you up, did I?" the voice asked in the same hushed tone.

"Who is this?" I demanded, sitting up in bed and aware of my surroundings for the first time.

"It's Didi," whispered the voice.

"Didi!" I squinted at the clock on the nightstand. "What is it? Is something the matter?" I asked, getting out of bed and pulling on my bathrobe, hoping that she wasn't on her way over and calling from a car phone or something.

"No. I have something—"

"Didi, I'm sorry, I can't hear you. Can you speak up, please?" Wait a minute, I thought. There was all sorts of background noise. *Was* she calling from a car phone? I grabbed the cordless phone from the hall, replaced the receiver on the one by the bed and shuffled downstairs to put on a pot of coffee.

"No, I can't—I don't want anyone to hear me—"

"Didi, where are you?" I demanded, checking out the refrigerator to see if I had anything acceptable to go with the coffee.

"At the gym," Didi whispered.

"The gym?" I repeated blankly, closing the refrigerator door. "What are you doing at the gym?"

"Working out," she mumbled.

"What?"

"*Working out*," she said, slightly louder.

"Oh," I said, walking over to the front door to get the morning paper.

"I have a *clue*," Didi reported.

"A clue?" I stopped with my hand on the doorknob.

"You know, to the *murder*," she whispered.

"Oh!"

"That's why I'm here. Cousin John always works out at Cousin Joe's fitness center on Saturday mornings."

"Cousin John the policeman?" I asked, light finally dawning.

"Yes. So that's why I came, you see, to pretend to work out but really to see what I could find out about the case. That's why I have to whisper. Joe is letting me use his phone but it's not exactly private."

"How's it going?" I asked, excited.

"Terrible. My back is killing me—"

"No, I meant with Cousin John. You said you got something?"

"Yes. Elizabeth, there *was* a poem! The police are holding back the evidence."

"Didi! You're wonderful! Can you get a copy?" I asked eagerly.

"No, but I don't have to. I know who wrote it."

"Who?" I whispered.

"What? I can't hear you," said Didi.

"Who wrote it?" I nearly shouted.

"Black. William Black," she said.

"William Black? Who's that?" I asked.

"I thought you'd know him. He's very famous."

I searched my mind for a William Black. "A contemporary poet?" I asked.

"No, no, a dead one," said Didi.

I thought harder. Someone had just asked me if I liked poetry. Who was it . . . ? Detective Fineburg. *English Romantic Writers . . .*

"Blake!" I said. "William Blake!"

"That's it," said Didi.

"The poem," I said. "Do you know the name of the poem?"

There was a pause. "I've got it written down somewhere here . . ."

While I was waiting, I opened the front door. There, lying on top of the newspaper, was a florist box. Who gets flowers delivered in the Berkshires at seven in the morning? I removed the lid. There, nestled in the green tissue paper, were twelve long-stemmed apricot-colored Osiana roses. I looked for a note, but there wasn't one.

"Ohhhh," I breathed.

"What?" the phone cackled in my ear.

"Oh, I'm sorry, Didi, I couldn't hear you," I said dreamily. They had to be from Adam. Didn't they? I thought about Sherman Forrest. *Please, God, no,* I thought. Then: "I'm sorry, Didi. What did you say?"

"I said, 'Oh yes, here it is,'" said Didi. "*The Garden of Love.*"

THE GARDEN OF LOVE

I went to the Garden of Love,
And saw what I never had seen:
A Chapel was built in the midst,
Where I used to play on the green.

And the gates of this Chapel were shut,
And "Thou Shalt not" writ over the door;
So I turn'd to the Garden of Love
That so many sweet flowers bore;

And I saw it was filled with graves,
And tomb-stones where flowers should be;
And Priests in black gowns were walking their rounds,
And binding with briars my joys & desires.

I read these words at the Lenox library. I had to. Detective Fineburg had taken my copy with him.

Actually, I was in the children's room, which was set off from the rest of the library. There was a toy kitchen, a toy fire engine and a multitude of worn, filthy stuffed animals. There were also two tables, eight straight chairs, a rocking chair and a sofa, none of which were over three feet high.

While Emily went off to pull all the little pink and white cups and saucers out of the kitchen cupboard, I settled myself on one of the tiny chairs, which put my knees in the vicinity of my chin, and read Blake.

I read the poem over three times. I studied individual words, looking for clues. There were none. Except—

Except that it was Blake.

William Blake had been Howard's favorite poet. When he was courting me, he had often recited bits of Blake's poems—usually after sex—although never this one, I was sure. He'd said Blake was the most powerful master of imagery the world had ever produced. It was Howard who'd given me the volume of *English Romantic Writers* that Detective Fineburg had seized, the one they were undoubtedly fingerprinting or chemically analyzing or whatever they do when they're trying to prove you shot your ex, or almost-ex, husband.

But I knew something the police didn't know. I knew—it had been made manifest to me over the past week—that just because he'd married me, that didn't mean Howard had treated me specially. In fact, Howard, for all his talent, didn't seem to have much imagination. That meant that whatever Howard had done for me—like quoting Blake, or giving me a book—he had most certainly done with other lovers. *That* meant that if I searched Margaux's house I was almost sure to find—

"Elizabeth."

I looked up. "Pat."

Pat had called about a half an hour after Didi. "Elizabeth," she'd said, before I'd even had a chance to say good morning, "I wonder if you have time to see me this morning. There are several aspects of your case I think it is important we discuss."

I had hesitated. I had not, in fact, wanted to talk to Pat that morning. Of all the members of the play group (excepting Margaux, of course), she was my least favorite. Didi was nice and Astrid was smart but Pat was just—officious, in my opinion.

"I'm sorry, Pat," I began, "but I'm afraid I'm busy this morning."

"Oh," said Pat. "Are you sure it isn't something that can be put off? This is important."

"I'm afraid not. You see, I have to go to the library. Didi called and I want to check . . ."

"Yes, I know, she called me, too," said Pat.

"Besides, I have Emily and she likes the little kitchen in the children's room," I said, feeling the need for further explanation. "She plays by herself and it gives me a chance to get some work done."

"Oh," said Pat. Her disappointment was palpable.

Don't give in here, Elizabeth, I told myself sternly. If you do, all you are going to do is end up wasting an hour or so filling out forms or something.

"Unless you think you could meet me at the library . . ." I heard myself say.

"Well, all right," said Pat. She hadn't sounded very happy about it, but now here she stood, wearing a powder-pink cable-knit sweater that could only have come from Talbots and juggling Oliver on one arm and her briefcase on the other.

"Oh, look," said Pat to her son. "There's Emily playing with the refrigerator. Don't you want to go play with her?"

"No," said Oliver firmly, clinging to her leg.

"I was afraid of this," she sighed to me. "He's scheduled for reflective downtime. I'm not sure he'll interact. Oliver, darling, Mommy has to work right now—"

But Oliver had spotted a giant stuffed tarantula.

"Aahhh!" he croaked excitedly, tottering over to the toy and beginning to throw it around the room.

"Maybe you just have to find the things he likes to interact with," I said, as we watched Oliver stage a spirited one-on-one wrestling match between the tarantula and a two-headed dragon.

"Maybe," said Pat, staring after him.

"Pat," I said, reaching up and touching her on the arm. "What did you want me for? I'm kind of busy right now . . ."

"Huh? Oh," she said, turning around. "Well, it is just that I did a little work on your case last night and I thought it might help to sit down with you and go over a few points again."

She looked around to see if there was any adult-sized furniture. Finding none, she pulled up a chair at the little table beside me. She perched herself precariously on the edge and started laying out piles of papers from inside her briefcase on the table in front of her. Since the table was completely covered by two piles, she was forced to put one of the piles on the little chair beside her, one on the floor and one on the rocking horse. "I've been boning up on my criminal," she explained.

"I hope you haven't gone to too much trouble," I replied, looking at all the piles.

"Oh, no. It's just that I like to be prepared," she said, removing two Number Two pencils and one ballpoint from the briefcase and anchoring them carefully with a block on the pile closest to her. Then, without further preliminaries, she turned to me. "Elizabeth, I believe that the best way to proceed in matters such as these is to have a thorough grasp of the opponent's case. In this way we can anticipate what they are likely to do and be prepared to act accordingly." She looked at me over the top of her glasses. "Don't you agree?"

"Well, I guess so . . ."

"Good." She leafed through a pile and picked out a paper that was filled with bullet points. "All right," she began, studying it, "you should understand that there are two main elements to any criminal case. Motive and opportunity. Unfortunately, at this point, you have both against you." She stopped and looked up from her paper. "I don't mean this to be upsetting, but we have to think like the enemy," she said.

"Uh, sure," I said uncertainly.

"Now, as regards motive—naturally, the motive against you is the inheritance. I should warn you that monetary advantage is generally considered to be a compelling motive. But, worse than that, we have here what is called immediacy of motive. Immediacy means that you not only had a motive to kill him, but a motive to kill him at that very party since if you didn't, your chance to inherit those funds would disappear. Immediacy of motive is *very* compelling," she added with relish, ticking off a bullet point on her sheet with one of the pencils.

"Uh-huh," I said, trying to think like the enemy and not get depressed and failing miserably.

"Now, as to opportunity," said Pat, obviously warming to her task, "there, too, they have you. In fact, not only can they place you generally at the scene of the crime, but they can place you almost at the exact spot at the exact time the crime was committed."

I felt compelled to defend myself. "But Holly Ivy was there, too," I pointed out.

"And that's how they'll know," said Pat reasonably, smiling pleasantly at me.

"Oh," I said, deflated.

She shuffled through the pile at her feet and came up with what looked like an organizational chart. "And yet," she mused, examining it, "the case against you remains incomplete." She looked up at me again. "We know that because you haven't been arrested yet," she explained.

As I found myself unable to answer this, I simply nodded.

"There were apparently no eyewitnesses and the murder weapon does not appear to have been recovered," she continued thoughtfully. "Without either of these, there is nothing to link you specifically with the crime, despite all the other indications that you did it." She stopped and marked the paper. "So that's it. That's what they are looking for."

"What?"

"Something specific to link you to the crime. To make the case complete they must show that the preponderance of evidence points to you and you alone. That no alternative explanation exists that fits all the facts."

I began to feel a little hope. "You mean, like someone else did it in a jealous rage," I volunteered.

Pat took off her glasses to look at me. "Elizabeth, in dime-store novels the jilted lover works, but in real life a judge and jury are much more likely to believe nine hundred thousand dollars," she said dryly.

"Oh," I said, deflated again.

"So now we know their game plan. They are going to try to link you to the note, to the room . . . Is there anything you can think of that they might try and use against you?"

"They already have my book," I said and explained about the volume of Blake.

"That, in and of itself, is not enough," said Pat.

"That's a relief," I said.

"Although it is not good," she continued.

"Oh," I said.

"Elizabeth, can you think of anyone else who might have profited from Howard's death?" asked Pat.

"No," I said.

"This is important. Think hard. It might not be obvious."

I thought hard. "No," I said.

Pat frowned. "It's here somewhere. We just don't see it. I wonder . . . Elizabeth, may I have a copy of the will?"

"Do you mean the will where I inherited or the will that Howard meant to sign but never got the chance?" I asked.

"Both," said Pat. "There might be something there . . . if we look hard enough . . ."

"Sure," I said. "I'll call Caitlin and . . ."

"Why don't I do that?" Pat suggested, removing the stack on the rocking horse and making a note to herself on the front page. A child of perhaps four ran over immediately and, throwing her a reproachful glance, dragged the horse away.

"Well, if you want to," I said and gave her the name and address. "Caitlin is rather odd," I felt compelled to add.

"Odd or not, you never know what you may pick up from another lawyer," said Pat.

"Oh, right," I said.

"Well," said Pat, "I think that's all for now. I'll let you know what I come up with." She began repacking the files into her briefcase.

I handed her the file closest to me. "Thanks, Pat," I said.

"My pleasure," she said, taking the papers. "It beats real estate law all to hell." She glanced at the top sheet. "Oh, and Elizabeth, there is one more thing."

"What?"

"The police will probably come to your house with a search warrant."

"Oh," I said. Then: "I guess I have to let them in."

"Of course you have to let them in. That's what a search warrant means. They don't need your consent."

"Oh," I said.

"But, Elizabeth, this time, when they do . . ."

"Yes?"

"Don't volunteer anything," said Pat.

Although I was grateful to Pat for outlining the case against me—sort of—and certainly for preparing me for possible future actions on the part of the police, and while she had impressed me with her diligence and approach, what she had not done was to convince me that Howard's murder was a crime of greed rather than passion. I knew him better, knew Margaux better. The existence of the poem cinched it for me. It was a grand, dramatic gesture, the sort of grand, dramatic gesture that was Margaux's trademark. She *always* did everything larger than life. Just look at her clothes. The way she entertained. Her numerous love affairs. Her height. Not to mention her literary pretensions. It was *like* Margaux to leave a Blake poem, just to show that her taste was better than everybody else's.

I had been making it too easy for her, I decided abruptly as

I backed out of the library parking lot. I had been letting her set me up from a distance. The thing to do was to go to her house and see her face to face. Make her look me in the eye. Gauge her reaction to my presence. See how she conducts herself under direct scrutiny. Perhaps even goad her into making a mistake. Also, once in the house, I could look around for *English Romantic Writers*.

All that was needed was a reason for my just dropping by her house. Any obvious, transparent excuse should do. But which obvious, transparent excuse should I use?

"I'm sorry to bother you, but I really need someone to talk to," I said a few minutes later when Margaux opened her door.

"Elizabeth! Of course. Come in," said Margaux.

I followed her into the foyer, trying to hang onto Emily, who, perhaps sensing that she was in the presence of her father's killer, and certainly overtired from the mammoth labor of having turned the library's toy kitchen inside out, had started fussing.

"I was just about to put Alden down for a nap," said Margaux, taking our coats and then heading up the stairs. "Tolin is out playing at a friend's house," she added.

We walked down the second-floor hallway. We must have passed the room where Howard had been killed but it was hard to tell because all the doors were closed. Alden's bedroom was at the very end, near a second, back staircase. We found him sitting on the lap of a teenager who was reading *Green Eggs and Ham* to him.

"Time for a nap," Margaux sang out, lifting Alden up in her arms. She laid him in bed, kissed him and covered him with a blanket. "Perhaps Emily would like a nap as well," she said over her shoulder.

Of course Emily would like a nap. She had just done the

toddler equivalent of cooking Thanksgiving dinner for twenty. I tightened my grip on my exhausted child. "Oh, she's fine," I said cheerily, clutching Emily closer as she, spying Alden's blanket, let out a particularly piteous wail.

"Are you sure? She looks a little tired. It's no trouble, you know. That's what the extra bed is for. And Whitney can watch them both while they're sleeping, can't you, Whitney?"

"Uh, sure," said the teenager unconvincingly.

"And it will give us more time to talk," said Margaux, looking at me.

"Well—all right, I guess. Only I'm not sure she'll go down in a strange place . . ."

"Here, sweetie," said Margaux, handing Emily a blanket similar to Alden's.

Emily stopped crying and, kicking on a dime, took the proffered blanket and jammed as much of the lining as she could into her mouth in order to suck it.

I shot her a look that said, "Thanks a lot, you don't have to look *that* comfortable," but she ignored me.

"Why don't you just lay her on the bed?" Margaux suggested.

I laid her on the bed. Emily readjusted the blanket once and fell immediately asleep.

"Well, that's decided," said Margaux brightly and led me out of the room.

I trailed her back down the hallway. I had forgotten how huge the house was. How was I ever to find *English Romantic Writers*?

"I'll just pop into the kitchen and see if the cook can scrounge up some coffee for us," said Margaux as we headed down the stairs. "Why don't you wait for me in the library?"

Some days, you just live right.

"That sounds good," I agreed and, following a wave of her

hand to the right, found myself alone in the very room I'd most wanted to see.

One glance confirmed that I had a big job in front of me. Bookshelves lined the walls around the fireplace. Glassed-in cabinets filled with rows and rows of books peeked out from behind lamps and vases and plants. I'd seen bookstores smaller than Margaux's library.

I started on the north wall. Aristotle, Flaubert, Erica Jong . . .

"Got it," said Margaux, coming in behind me with a tray.

I turned abruptly and tried not to look guilty.

"Why don't we sit down over here?" she suggested, settling the tray on the coffee table in front of the sofa.

I went over to her and took a seat adjacent to her on the couch. From this position I could still see plenty of books.

She poured out some coffee.

Women Who Run With the Wolves, You Just Don't Understand, Eat More, Weigh Less . . .

"Milk or sugar?" she queried.

"Both." Margaret Atwood, Joyce Carol Oates, Jackie Collins . . .

"There you go," she said, handing me my cup. She settled back against the sofa cushions. "Now," she said solicitously, "what do you want to talk about?"

I sipped my coffee and tried to adjust my demeanor to reflect my role as distracted widow. "Well—it's Howard," I began. "All this—"

"Yes, it is most upsetting," Margaux agreed, cutting me off. "Do you know, the police have been here all week?"

"Really," I said. *Zen and the Art of Motorcycle Maintenance, The Complete Guide to Children's Diseases* . . .

"Oh, yes. Fingerprinting the house, taking pictures of the room, asking questions. It's been terrible," she complained. "I only just got them out yesterday."

"Really," I said. Jane Austen, Charles Dickens, Helen Gurley Brown . . .

"It would have been much worse, though, except—Elizabeth, may I tell you a secret?"

"Umm." Edgar Allan Poe, Somerset Maugham, Dave Barry . . .

"I'm in love."

"Umm . . . what?" I said. "I'm sorry, what did you say?"

"I'm in love," she repeated. "Oh, Elizabeth, he's wonderful. Tall, handsome, cultured, civilized . . ."

I put down my cup.

"Did you say in love?" I asked.

"This time it's really it," she said, leaning back dreamily among the pillows. "L-U-V love," she said.

"Uh . . ."

"And I'll tell you, now that I've experienced the real thing I can't believe I even thought I was in love ever before. All those other times . . . Well, I'm not going to think about them *now*." She picked up her cup and took a sip of coffee. "Of course, he feels the same way about me," she added.

"Of course," I said mechanically.

"He says he doesn't know how he could have stood being with other women, it's so different with me. Isn't that wonderful?"

"Wonderful," I echoed.

"And the sex . . . well, I've just never had sex like this. He's insatiable. I'm insatiable. It so rarely happens that way, don't you think?"

"Uh . . ."

"Of course, it was a little difficult with the police constantly underfoot, but I really think that added to the spice of the thing."

"Uh-huh," I said.

"But you know what I can't decide?" she asked.

"No, what?" I said.

"Whether to get married in June or September. You know, I've always found the words 'June bride' to be irresistible. They conjure up such marvelous images. It could be in the little church on the hill, small, just two hundred or so guests. I could wear something off-the-shoulder and carry irises—no, better yet, lily of the valley with just a hint of violets. But then again," she reflected, playing with her hair, "autumn is so glorious here. Almost magical, don't you think? All those brilliant colors—the leaves, the sky, the grass. If we did it in autumn we could have the ceremony outside. You can't do that in June because of the bugs. And it could be formal. I could wear something striking and carry roses . . ."

I sat there listening numbly as she chattered on and on and eventually it came to me: She's crazy. Margaux is crazy. Who begins an affair a week after her lover is killed right under the noses of the police? (Well, I reflected, I had—with Adam, sort of—but that was different.)

". . . of course, he hasn't asked me yet, but that's only a formality between two people as wildly in love as we are . . ."

I found myself staring intently at her as she spoke, trying to gauge her sense of reality. Someone in Margaux's condition, I decided, might have killed Howard and not even remembered she'd done it. Blocked it out. That happens sometimes with people who are insanely jealous, doesn't it? I asked myself.

". . . I can't wait to bear his child. I hope we have a boy . . ."

By that time, I didn't care whether she had done it or not. I just didn't want to have to listen to any more. I happened to glance toward the fire and there it was, on the shelf to the right, lying on its side as though someone had pulled it out to refer to it and then, in her haste, forgotten to put it back exactly.

English Romantic Writers.

Chapter

12

The next day was Sunday. I woke up full of plans. I would leave an anonymous tip with the police telling them to search Margaux's house. No, I would call and use my own name. I would say: "Chief Rudge? Elizabeth Halperin here. I think you would be very interested to know that I just happened to see a copy of *English Romantic Writers* at Margaux Chase's house. This proves she did it. I'm sure if you searched carefully you'd find the gun as well . . ."

I sniffed the flowers that I had set in a vase on the chest of drawers in the bedroom. I had debated for the past twenty-four hours or so whether to call Adam and thank him, but I simply couldn't shake the horrible fear that I would do so and he would say *"What* flowers?" Then I'd be back to Sherman Forrest. I preferred to live in ignorance.

Get a grip, Elizabeth, I told myself sternly. Give it a rest. I think you're starting to lose perspective. So I fed Emily her breakfast, got the papers from the porch, gathered up Emily,

Mr. Bear and Floppy Dog (two of Emily's special stuffed animals) and flopped back into bed to read.

I get the *Times* and the *Berkshire Eagle* on Sunday and the very first thing I look at, even before the front page, is the *Times Book Review*. So I settled myself against the pillows, smiled at Emily, who was practicing rolling on Mr. Bear, unearthed the *Book Review* and—

"Look! Emily! It's your father!"

There it was. The front-page review.

"Look, Emily!" I repeated. "Daddy's book is reviewed on the front page of the *Times*. This is a very big deal," I told her solemnly.

Emily stopped rolling on Mr. Bear and looked at the paper I had thrust in her direction.

"See? Here's the name of the book—*Passion Palace*, it's called—and here's Daddy's name—Howard Hack. And here's the name of the person who reviewed it—K. McKinsey. K. McKinsey is a very important writer," I continued, staring at the paper.

(Actually, K. McKinsey [no one knew what the initial stood for] was one of a group of new, upcoming writers who had all gone to college with one another, and had produced, one by one, a series of extremely commercial books on the difficulties of being young and rich. While he was alive, Howard had hated K. McKinsey, but I didn't think Emily needed to know that.)

"Want me to read it to you?" I asked. Emily picked up Mr. Bear and Floppy Dog and snuggled into my lap.

"At first," I began, "when one picks up *Passion Palace*, one is beset with doubts: how to separate fact from fiction, art from artifice, quest from query . . . and then, suddenly, precipitously, *stupendously*, one becomes aware that it is this very distinction which lays bare the creativity, the complexion, the very essence of the genius that was Howard Hack . . ."

Emily climbed off my lap and went back to rolling on Mr. Bear.

I read the remainder of the review to myself. It was a glowing tribute to Howard. He would have loved it. I remember thinking, Howard's going to sell a lot of books with this review before I realized that there was no Howard anymore. Then I remember thinking that when it came to the royalties, *I* was Howard.

Ha, I thought. Justice.

I remained pleased with myself all the way through the *Times* and up to the front page of the *Berkshire Eagle*.

"ADMINISTRATION OFFICIALS SAY USE OF FUNDS WAS JUSTIFIED . . . ," "OUTBREAK OF HOSTILITIES IN . . . ," "MYSTERY SURROUNDING AUTHOR'S DEATH DEEPENS."

I'll read that, I thought.

Suspicion that a disgruntled lover was behind the murder of author Howard Hack eight days ago deepened today when authorities connected with the case confirmed that a note containing a love poem was found with the body. Chief Ned Rudge of the Lenox Police Department disclosed that a poem which has since been identified as "The Garden of Love," written by the eighteenth-century poet William Blake, was found typewritten on scented blue notepaper and left atop the victim's laptop computer.

Howard Hack, author of the critically acclaimed *Passion Palace*, was found shot to death in the nude a week ago Saturday while attending a costume party in Lenox. Sources close to the deceased confirm that Hack had been romantically involved with several women over the past few months and had even boasted of a liaison with an undisclosed member of the British royal family. Police confirm that at least two women with whom Hack had had a recent affair attended the same party at which he was murdered, although neither has been charged with the crime.

At the time of his death, Hack was separated from his wife, who, coincidentally, also attended the same costume party. "It was a little like old home week," said Francine Weezle, Hack's literary agent, who was also present that evening. "Everywhere you looked, there was a woman glowering at Howard." Ms. Weezle, head of Weezle Associates, declined to speculate further on the question of whether the motive behind the murder was romantic revenge. "I do books," she said, "not investigations."

Ms. Weezle did, however, deny the rumor that the clue to Howard Hack's murder is contained in his just-published novel. "People should read *Passion Palace* because it is a work of great fiction," she said. "Whether the identity of the real-life murderer is to be found within the covers of the book is immaterial."

I lowered the newspaper.

"Emily," I said. "We've got to get a copy of that book."

"What do you mean, you don't have it?" I demanded that afternoon to Sheya, the owner of the Lenox Book Store. Good God, I thought, I sound like Howard.

Sheya shrugged nervously. Sheya was always nervous. She was a tall, thin woman in her early sixties with fluffy white hair who fluttered among her books like a sparrow.

"I *had* it," she murmured, "but it just flew out of the store. Perhaps I underestimated demand. I'm expecting another shipment any day now, though. I can put your name on the waiting list, if you like."

"Uh, well, I guess so," I said unhappily.

Sheya picked up a pen, hunted around on her desk and came up with a clipboard. I saw quite a few names ahead of mine.

She cleared her voice. "Now, shall I put you just on the list for *Passion Palace* or do you want the other books as well?"

"*What* other books?" I asked.

She readjusted her glasses. "Well, he had two previous books, *The St. Paul Du*—"

"I know he had two other books! But they are out of print," I said.

"Well, no, actually—" Sheya consulted a chart, "they're being reissued."

"They are?"

"There's such a demand," Sheya murmured again.

"Well, what do you know," I said under my breath.

"Shall I put you down?" she asked, pen poised.

"Uh—no," I said, thinking of the twenty-five copies of each of Howard's previous works that were packed in boxes somewhere down in the basement, a piece of information that, for some reason, I had decided to withhold from Holly Ivy. "Just for *Passion Palace*," I said.

"All right," said Sheya and turned to the woman who had been waiting patiently behind me.

"I *had* it," I heard her murmur as I headed to the door, "but it just flew out of the store. I'm expecting a new shipment any day now. May I put your name on the waiting list?"

Then, Monday morning at nine o'clock, the phone rang. There he is, I exulted. So it was Adam who sent the flowers. I knew it all the time. Shall I let it ring a couple of times, I wondered, just so he doesn't get too confident?

"Hello?" I answered in a throaty voice, grabbing the receiver before it could ring a second time.

"Elizabeth? It's Caitlin," reported the voice on the other end of the phone.

"Oh."

"Elizabeth, I've just had a Pat LaFountain on the phone. Do you know this person?" Caitlin barked.

"Pat? Sure—"

"I thought as much. Well, I think you should know she asked a number of questions about your finances and even requested a copy of Howard's will. Naturally, I told her nothing," Caitlin continued. "This happens sometimes with celebrity accounts. It's nothing to worry about. Usually such interlopers are discouraged with a single phone call. If it happens again, I can certainly take the appropriate action . . ."

"*What* appropriate action?" I asked.

"Well," said Caitlin with a little laugh, "obviously we can't have just anyone privy to your and Howard's confidential information . . ."

"What are you talking about? I told Pat to call. She's a friend of mine who also happens to be a lawyer—*my* lawyer," I retorted.

There was a pause.

"Elizabeth, this is highly irregular," Caitlin began.

"Why?"

"I cannot urge you vigorously enough to reconsider. I'm your lawyer, too, and, as your lawyer, I must advise you, in the strongest possible terms, against this kind of dissemination of information. You never know where it may lead," Caitlin warned in her deepest tones.

"But why shouldn't she have a copy of the will?" I persisted. Come to think of it, I thought, I hadn't seen a copy of the will either.

Caitlin paused again. I could almost feel her shifting gears.

"Elizabeth," she began again, warmly. "Elizabeth, I realize

that we've had our differences in the past, but you must believe that I want only the best for you. It's my duty to protect and serve you. That's what I'm here for. Can't you feel it?" she asked.

She's surrounding me with love, I thought with alarm. I held the receiver as far away from my ear as I could while still being able to hear her.

"Elizabeth, if you felt the need for additional legal representation, why didn't you come to me?" Caitlin's voice floated toward me over the distance. "Don't you know that we have one of the most highly trained, prestigious criminal departments in the country? They are at your service—"

"Thank you, Caitlin," I interrupted, "but I'll stick with Pat." Did I just say that? I wondered. Tell me I didn't just say that.

Silence. Then: "Just who is this person Pat?" asked Caitlin. "Why don't you let *me* check her out for you? It's nothing for me to run a background check. I'll just call up some of my friends at the Bar Association and we'll have her vital statistics in a jiffy . . ."

"That won't be necessary, Caitlin," I said.

"Don't be silly, it's no trouble. I'll just—"

"Caitlin, I already know her background."

"I'll tell you what I'm going to do right now," said Caitlin, "I'm going to get Clayton Nemeroff on the phone with us. He's the senior partner in charge of criminal here at Lewton & Lord. Elizabeth, he's the best in the business. He has twenty years' experience behind him and thirty lawyers and I don't know how many associates and assistants underneath him. Just hold on—"

"No, please don't do that, Caitlin."

"Elizabeth, enough fooling around. You don't know what you're dealing with here. Amateurs can get you into some very serious trouble," Caitlin snapped.

"Caitlin, just answer Pat's questions and send her the will," I said. "And while you're at it, I'd like a copy, too," I added.

There was a moment of silence.

"I'm not sure I can do something that goes against my ethical principles," said Caitlin finally.

"Of course, you have to follow your conscience, Caitlin," I said. "If you want me to find someone else to handle the account . . ."

There was another moment of silence.

"That won't be necessary," she grunted and hung up.

No sooner had I hung up than the phone rang again. There he is, I thought, this time with relief. I knew he'd call, I thought smugly.

"Hello—" I almost said "Adam."

"Hello. Elizabeth. This is Phillip Laramee."

"Phillip?" I repeated blankly.

"Yes. Phillip Laramee. You remember, we met at Margaux's party."

Phillip Laramee? What did he want? "Hello, Phillip," I replied cautiously.

"I was just wondering how you were."

"I'm fine."

"I also called to say that I enjoyed our conversation at Margaux's party, although I'm afraid it got swallowed up in all the unpleasantness that came later."

Unpleasantness? "Yes."

"I recall that at the end of that conversation, I mentioned that it would be fun to continue it sometime. I also recall that you agreed."

Well, yes, that was true. But at Margaux's party, Howard was still alive, I had yet to become either an heiress or a suspect in a murder investigation and, most important, Adam

Rothstein had been nothing more to me than someone whom I had spilled beer on.

"Do you still feel the same way?" he continued.

On the other hand, Phillip Laramee was Howard's publisher. Phillip Laramee was Margaux's publisher. He might know something. Besides, he obviously had some business matter he wanted to talk to me about. He was trying to soften me up. Maybe they were selling the Japanese rights to *Passion Palace* or something . . .

"Of course," I said.

"How about Wednesday?"

"The day after tomorrow?"

"Yes. Wednesday. The day after Tuesday. For lunch."

"You're coming to Lenox?" I asked, trying to remember if the Church Street Cafe, the best place in town for lunch, was open or closed on Wednesdays.

"No. Actually, I was hoping you'd come to me," said Phillip. "I always eat at Café des Artistes on Wednesdays . . ."

"Oh," I said.

"Yes," he continued. "They always hold the same table for me. Quite a good table, actually."

"How thoughtful of them."

"Yes. I think so, too. Shall we say one o'clock?"

One o'clock, the day after tomorrow, in Manhattan? No way. Even if I called Rose right now and she was home and she said yes, she was free to baby-sit Wednesday, I'd still have to drive to Hudson, take the train for two hours (if I were lucky), take a cab to Café des Artistes, then, after lunch, reverse the whole procedure. Seven hours of travel for a two-hour lunch. No way. He had a lot of nerve.

I paused for a moment in the entranceway to the restaurant, having just given my coat to be checked, and glanced surreptitiously at my reflection in the mirror on the left to see if I had lipstick on my teeth. Then I squared my shoulders a little under my suit jacket and approached the maître d'.

"Yes?" he said politely.

"I'm meeting Phillip Laramee," I announced.

"Of course. Ms. Halperin. Mr. Laramee hasn't arrived yet. Would you care to be seated or would you rather wait at the bar?"

I made a show of looking at my watch, which was completely unnecessary as I knew quite well it was one-fifteen, having just walked around the block twice so as not to arrive first.

"I'll be seated, thank you."

"Very good. Would you follow me, please?"

He led me through to the middle room to a table placed directly beneath a large mural depicting two naked anatomically perfect wood nymphs frolicking in a stream. It was like an oversize *Sports Illustrated* swimsuit issue, only without the swimsuits.

"Enjoy your lunch, Ms. Halperin."

"Thank you."

The maître d' disappeared and was immediately replaced by a waiter.

"Good afternoon," he said as another waiter filled my water glass. "May I get you something from the bar or would you prefer to wait for Mr. Laramee?"

"I'll wait, thank you."

I was left alone. There was nothing to do but sit up very straight and pretend to be looking at something off in the distance, what little distance there was.

A couple of minutes later I saw Phillip bustle in. He waved at the maître d' and came straight to the table.

"Elizabeth. Sorry I'm late," he said, grasping my hand and shrugging out of his raincoat and scarf at the same time. He held these articles of clothing out generally behind him and one of the waiters trotted up and took them away.

He slid into his seat and perused my side of the table. "Have you ordered a cocktail?" he asked.

"No," I replied.

"Good," he said, lifting his right hand slightly. Seemingly from nowhere, a wine list appeared in it. "Is chablis all right? I realized after I called that I should have asked you for dinner. That would have justified champagne."

"I don't want anything, thank you."

"No?" he said, raising an eyebrow. He paused for a moment. "Okay. Well, I'll just order a bottle anyway, in case you change your mind." He turned about ten degrees. "Forty-two, please," he said to the waiter who had appeared in much the same fashion as the wine list.

"It's not that I never drink at lunch . . ." I began.

"Of course not," nodded Phillip.

"I mean I like to drink . . ."

"I'm sure you do."

I took a breath. "I don't drink when I'm discussing business," I said purposefully.

"Are we discussing business?" asked Phillip.

"Well, not yet. But I assume we're going to."

"What did you have in mind?"

"You called me," I reminded him.

At that moment, the wine steward arrived. He showed the bottle, then, upon Phillip's approval, uncorked it with that mixture of flourish and underplay that is particular to good sommeliers everywhere. He poured, Phillip tasted.

"Very good," said Phillip.

The wine steward angled the bottle in the direction of my glass. "None for me, thank you," I said firmly.

The wine steward filled Phillip's glass, then reached to take mine away. Phillip stopped him.

"No, Henri. Leave the glass. And while you're at it, pour

some wine in it." He looked at me with a smile. "Just in case we finish with business early."

I ignored the wine. Phillip lifted his glass. "Cheers," he said, taking a sip. "I know I should drink California wines . . . they're really every bit as good and it helps the trade deficit . . . but I just can't think of wine as coming from anywhere but France. I suppose that means I can never run for Congress."

"A great loss to the nation," I agreed.

Suddenly Phillip got very serious. He leaned even closer. "Now, Elizabeth," he whispered. "Don't turn around until I finish speaking . . ."

"Yes?"

"There's a woman sitting at a table, diagonally behind you to your left . . ."

"Yes?"

"Wearing the most hideous red floral suit . . ."

"Yes?"

"That's Sigrid Buffin. She was just made fiction editor at *The New Yorker* . . ."

"Yes?"

"I understand that she used to sleep with the editor-in-chief at . . ."

"Why are you telling me all this?" I interrupted.

Phillip leaned back and spread his hands palms-up. "I thought you said you wanted to discuss business."

Enough of this, I thought. "I thought you said you wanted to discuss literature. Like at Margaux's party. By the way, how long have you known Margaux?"

Phillip raised an eyebrow. "A rather awkward segue, wouldn't you say?"

"No, I'd probably say inept."

"Don't be so hard on yourself. What do you want to know?" asked Phillip.

I stopped and considered a number of subtle ploys to obtain the information I sought. Then I leaned forward. "Do you think she could have killed Howard?"

"Margaux as a murderess? Well, I don't think I can comment on that specifically, but suffice to say that if I ever had bad news to impart to Margaux I would make sure there was a third party present," said Phillip.

"*Have* you had bad news to impart to Margaux?" I inquired. "I mean, of a personal nature?"

"I can't say that I ever have," Phillip replied mildly. He raised his menu. "Shall we order?"

Two hours and two bottles of chablis later, Phillip once again leaned toward me conspiratorially. "Elizabeth, I have a problem."

"Hmm," I sort of hummed, finishing off the last few drops in my glass.

"It's what to do with the rest of the afternoon. It's a question of priorities, don't you think?"

"Absolutely."

"There's always work. I could go back to the office. It's what I usually do."

"How depressing for you."

"We could both go back to my office. But I'm afraid it's not very congenial. It's cluttered. Cutbacks, you know. The nineties. And then there are all those other people around."

"That is a problem," I agreed.

"On the other hand, my apartment is quite roomy. And, by coincidence, just upstairs."

"You live in this building?" I asked.

Phillip nodded. "That's how my apartment came to be upstairs."

"How convenient."

"Yes. I've always found it to be."

"But not for me, I'm afraid," I said.

"A pity. Another time, perhaps?"

"Perhaps."

The ride back to the Berkshires from Penn Station seemed interminable. My mouth was dry and my head ached. There was something wrong with the heat on the train and after a while I couldn't feel my fingers or feet. The farther we got from the city the more deserted the cabin became until at last only I and an overweight woman with sausage curls and a polyester suit reading *Reader's Digest* were left.

People who say that virtue is its own reward are full of shit, I decided as the train finally chugged into Hudson and I stepped off wearily for the hour's drive to Lenox.

"Stop said the mama fish or you'll get lost/But the three little fishes don' wanna be bossed."

I arrived home to find Rose entertaining Emily, singing in a hideous falsetto, the *Evening News with Peter Jennings* on in the background. ". . . And, later in the broadcast, the life and loves of a celebrated murder victim, an ABC exclusive report," I heard Peter Jennings announce.

I stopped. I knew instantly, in the way you know from the tilt of the mechanic's head as he surveys your car that it is going to be bad news, that they were going to talk about Howard.

"Bye, Rose," I said, shoving a wad of bills into her hand.

"But isn't that gonna be . . ." she protested, turning back to the set.

"Drive carefully," I said cheerfully, pushing her out the door.

I left Emily on the kitchen floor, where she was happily pounding Lego blocks with a plastic hammer, and sat down on the arm of a chair directly across from the television. I sat there fixedly if unseeingly until, at last, Peter Jennings folded his hands in a deliberate manner and looked directly into the camera.

"And now," he began, "a story about an unsolved mystery. You will remember that last week we reported on the murder of Howard Hack, the famous novelist, at a country home in western Massachusetts. At present, the identity of the killer is still unknown and many questions remain unanswered. But the killing has had an enormous effect on a small New England town, known up until now more for Tanglewood than tangled webs. Here, with our report, is our special correspondent on the scene in Lenox, Massachusetts."

The screen shifted to a picture of Main Street. The big white church on the hill was plainly visible.

"This is the picturesque town of Lenox, Massachusetts," announced the unseen commentator. Wait a minute. I knew that voice. "A quiet New England community set in the heart of beautiful Berkshire County."

Switch to a scene of Monument Mountain.

"An area as proud of its contribution to American literature as of its natural beauty. Herman Melville and Nathaniel Hawthorne climbed this mountain together. Edith Wharton fêted Henry James at her country home not five minutes from here. It is all the more ironic, then, that such a place should be the scene of the violent death of one of the country's greatest writers."

The screen changed abruptly to a picture of a house, a large house . . . Margaux's house. Then the camera zoomed in on a man standing in front of Margaux's house. He was dressed in an expensive-looking gray suit, with a muted silk tie. He was holding a microphone and looking into the camera. He was . . . he was . . .

"Good evening. This is Sherman Forrest reporting from the Berkshires," said Sherman Forrest in round tones.

"Behind me is the house where Howard Hack was shot at close range while attending a costume party eleven days ago. The murder came just days before the publication of Hack's most important work, *Passion Palace*." Sherman Forrest held up a copy of Howard's book.

"The novel addresses the very subjects that probably killed the writer—sexual infidelity and romantic intrigue. In fact, the coincidence is so strong that there are rumors within the publishing industry that the book is a thinly veiled parable of Hack's life story and that consequently the solution to the mystery surrounding his death lies within its covers.

"Adding to these rumors was the presence of a sheet of scented notepaper found beside the body. On the paper was printed the poem 'The Garden of Love' by the eighteenth-century English poet William Blake."

Switch to a picture of a middle-aged man with wispy red hair and wire-rimmed glasses, sitting in a book-lined study.

"Dr. Harley Grimmfich, head of the English Literature department at Williams College and an authority on William Blake, identifies 'The Garden of Love' as a poem about passion and betrayal."

"Like much of Blake's work, 'The Garden of Love' contains echoes of sexual tension overlaid by images of violence," said Professor Grimmfich. "It would be an appropriate choice for someone who felt seduced by erotic infidelity."

"All I can tell you is we've never had something like this happen here before!" The picture had changed again, this time to a wholesome-looking baby-faced blonde woman of about forty. The caption beneath her read "Marion Thornewood,

Lenox Town Selectwoman." "This is a family sort of place. You know, skiing in the winter and school fairs and Tanglewood in the summer." Marion Thornewood laughed nervously. "I mean, we don't *have* sex in Lenox."

Cut back to Sherman Forrest.

"But they do now. Howard Hack was apparently carrying on a number of love affairs simultaneously. But ABC has learned that suspicion is falling most heavily on Hack's estranged wife, who lives here. If she turns out to have killed him, this quiet town in the Berkshires may well be known not for the quality of its ski runs or the beauty of its open-air concert hall, but as the site of one of the most infamous sexual triangles in literary history. This is Sherman Forrest, reporting from Lenox, Massachusetts . . ."

I stood there in front of the television, dumbfounded. Then, three things happened at once. The phone rang, Emily banged her hand with her plastic hammer and someone knocked loudly on the front door.

I swooped a wailing Emily up in my arms and grabbed the phone. "Oh, sweetheart, I'm sorry, did it hurt? I'll bet that hurt. Oh, honey— What? Oh, hi, Susan," I shouted over Emily's screams. "No, I—just a minute, Emily hurt her hand, shh, honey, shh, it's all right, baby, let Mommy see it," I crooned, trying to cradle Emily and examine her right hand while hanging onto the phone.

The knock sounded again, this time louder. "Just a minute!" I bellowed.

"Waaaahhh!" screamed my daughter, tears streaming down a purple face.

"Oh, sweetheart, please let me see—no, Susan, I—yes, I saw it, yes, I—shh, shh, who is it?" I shouted in the direction of the door. "Wait a minute, Susan, there's someone—just a second, sweetheart, I'll be right with you—no, not you, Susan, Emily—all right, all right—" This in response to a third knock as, hoisting Emily up over one shoulder and the phone over the other, I swung the door open and hollered "All right, all right, I'm coming!" right in Adam's face.

"Hi," he said pleasantly, walking past me into the house.

"I'll call you back, Susan," I said and immediately hung up.

"Kitchen in there?" asked Adam, inclining his head to the right and not bothering to take off his coat. He was carrying a couple of large shopping bags.

"Uh, yeah—"

"Great," he said and walked into the kitchen.

I stood in the hallway for a minute, then closed the front door and followed him, still holding Emily, who had stopped crying and was sucking her hand and peering interestedly after Adam over her shoulder.

We found him in front of the refrigerator, stuffing mysterious bags and cartons onto the top shelf. "What are you doing?" I asked.

"Be with you in a minute." He continued his unpacking, then looked up. "You haven't had dinner yet, have you?"

"Uh, no—"

"Good," he said and closed the refrigerator door. Then he moved to the oven. "Let's see, we'll turn this on to three-fifty"—he turned the dial, opened the oven door and slid in something wrapped in foil—"and let me just open the red so it can breathe for a while—"

Oh, God. More wine? The phone rang shrilly. I'd forgotten I still had it under my arm. I jumped and Emily started to cry again.

"Hello?" I said into the mouthpiece, trying to hold the receiver in the crook between my head and my left shoulder blade. "What? I'm sorry, I can't hear you. Can you just—"

Adam took the phone away from me. "I'm sorry," he said

into the receiver, "but she can't come to the phone right now.
She'll have to get back to you," and he hung up. Immediately
the phone rang again. "I don't think we need this right now,"
he said. He picked up the receiver, hung it up immediately,
then picked it up again and tossed the receiver into the closet.

I stared at him, but he was busy looking at Emily. "What
happened here?" he asked, taking her away from me and patting her soothingly.

"Uh—she hurt her hand—"

"Let's see. Oh, that's not too bad," he said. "You know what
you need?" he asked Emily. She had stopped crying and was
looking intently at his face. "You need a raisin." He produced a
box from the pocket of his shirt and handed a raisin to Emily.
"I always keep raisins available, in case of an emergency," he
told her.

Emily shoved it in and held out her hand for another.

"You're absolutely right. That was a two-raisin boo-boo,"
he said seriously and handed her another. He looked at me
over her shoulder. "She's tired. Has she had her bath yet?"

"Uh, no—"

"Shampoo and stuff upstairs?"

"Uh, yes—"

"Okay, we won't be long," he said and carried my daughter,
who was leaning quietly against his shoulder and gazing at him
with the sort of adoration she generally reserves for Mickey
Mouse, up the stairs to the bathroom. "Have I told you the
story of Tubby Turtle yet?" I heard him ask her on the way.

I stared after him and then at the shopping bags still
unpacked on the counter. As I sank into a kitchen chair I
became aware that whatever that was he'd slipped into the
oven was beginning to give off the wonderfully satisfying
aroma of baking and that the house itself was suddenly, bliss-
fully, quiet.

*   *   *

Two hours later we were in the living room, leaning against pillows in front of the fire. The remains of a candlelight supper lay on a table behind us. Music was playing softly in the background. Emily was asleep upstairs.

"That was wonderful," I sighed. "How did you know?"

"How did I know what?"

"About the ABC story."

"What ABC story?"

I looked at him. "The ABC story that ran tonight. The one where Sherman Forrest—"

"Sherman Forrest? How did he look?" asked Adam.

"Like always," I said.

"Too bad."

"Anyway, he basically said I murdered Howard as part of a sex triangle."

"Really?" Adam perked up. "Who was the third person?"

"He didn't say."

"Too bad."

"Well, if you didn't know about the story, why did you come over tonight?" I asked.

"I thought it would be a good idea," said Adam.

"It was," I said.

"See?"

"Except that I've eaten more in the last twenty-four hours than I've eaten in the previous month," I said.

"Don't worry about it. They have great weight rooms in prison."

I looked at him. "You're making fun of me," I said.

"On the contrary," he said, pulling me down. "I am smiling at you."

And after that it was all wonderful. Absolutely wonderful. For that brief time I even forgot that I had just been targeted, on perhaps the most watched news program in America, by that sneaky, scummy (if I ever got my hands on him I *would* be guilty of murder) Sherman Forrest . . .

Early the next morning, this mood had carried over. Adam and Emily were still asleep. I slipped out of bed, stretched luxuriously and peeked out from behind the bedroom curtains to see what kind of day it would be.

Not good. There were eight news vans parked on the street in front of my house.

13

"Adam?" I said, poking him gently.

"Hmm?" he murmured sleepily.

"I have a favor to ask."

"Anything for a pal," he mumbled.

"Adam? How do you feel about wearing women's clothes?" I asked.

"How do I look?"

"You sure you want the high heels?" I asked.

"If you're going to go in drag, I figure you might as well do it right." He looked at himself in the mirror. "Perfect," he said. "I missed my calling."

"No, you didn't," I replied. "And don't forget to strap the doll into the car seat," I said, shoving Raggedy Ann into his arms.

He looked down at the doll. "Come on, Emily," he chirped. "Time for Mommy to take you to work."

He grabbed the plastic bag with his own clothes in it, gave me one last kiss, said: "Watch out for my lipstick," and started to totter down the basement stairs to the garage.

"Hey!" I said and he turned back. "I never thanked you for the flowers."

"What flowers?" he replied and disappeared into the garage.

I went back upstairs and peeked out the window. As soon as the garage door began to go up, loitering newsmen tossed aside cigarette butts and styrofoam coffee cups. Some made for the garage while others waited expectantly at the bottom of the driveway.

Adam backed out around his own car, did a quick U-turn and was out of the driveway so fast that even I didn't know it was him under the broad-brimmed hat.

"It's going to work, Em," I sang out as one, then two, then three, then four vans turned to follow.

I waited a little longer, then turned back to my daughter. "All we need is another plan to shake the last four."

Ten minutes later I stood at the door leading to the open garage, Emily in one arm, the spare car seat in the other, my purse and a well-stocked diaper bag slung across my shoulder.

"Here's the thing, Em," I whispered. "Adam left me the keys to his Wrangler. All we have to do is run outside, get in the car, strap you into your car seat, throw the diaper bag on the floor and plow out of here before the rest of those reporters surround the car. I figure we have about twenty seconds. What do you think? Think we'll make it?"

Emily blew a spit bubble.

"You're right," I told her. "Piece of cake. One, two, three . . . GO!"

We sprang into action. We were at Adam's car almost before they noticed us. One, the car seat. Two, strap Emily in. Three, dump the diaper bag on the floor.

And then, there they were.

"Mrs. Hack, we have a report . . ."

"Mrs. Hack, is it true . . ."

"Mrs. Hack, can you give an interview . . ."

"Time to get out of here," I told Emily and took off down the street.

"I wonder how many will follow us," I mused as we sped down Housatonic Street toward town. "Let's see, there's one, two, three—oh, look, that's ABC in the Ford—four. That last one's a Boston station, honey. Okay, we've got them all. What's that, Emily? Why, yes, sweetheart, I'm sure they'd love a tour of the Berkshires. What a nice idea. What do you say we start with Mountain Road?

"What's that, hon?" I asked as I pulled out of town and turned down a narrow street to the right. "You don't remember Mountain Road? Sure you do. It's this one right here," I said, taking a sharp turn to the right and beginning to climb up a steep incline. "The one that goes straight up the mountain. The one with all the hairpin twists and turns. The one that's not paved. The one you need—" I scanned the console, "this for," I finished triumphantly, pulling a lever and throwing the Wrangler into four-wheel drive. "Let's see how they like it."

BUMPBUMPBUMPBUMP. "That's what we call potholes, sweetheart," I said to Emily.

THUMPTHUMPTHUMPTHUMP. "Those are heaves. Oh, look, we lost the Springfield van," I reported.

BRRRBRRBRRRBRRR. "People call that a washboard, Emily. It's kind of like riding a bucking bronco.

"Oh, look, Em. Here are some swales they put in the road for runoff." WHAM! WHAM! WHAM! "Oh, too bad, we lost the Ford . . . Ooh, Em, look how narrow the road gets here.

And you know what? On the other side of this little turn right here it's almost straight down."

By the time we reached East Street in Richmond we were alone on the road.

"Where are we going now?" I asked. "That's a very good question, Em. We can't very well go back home. And anyway, we weren't doing much good at home. What we need is to do some investigating. You know, look for clues. And I thought of the perfect place," I announced, turning south toward the Taconic Parkway. "A place where no one will bother us. Where they won't think to look. And, conveniently, a place where I still have the keys.

"We're going to Daddy's apartment in New York."

We made it in just after the morning rush hour. It was a quiet time of day and the lobby was empty except for Joe, the doorman, who was taking advantage of the lull to sneak some Fritos and read the racing forms.

I lugged Emily and the diaper bag up to the desk. "Hello, Joe," I said.

He looked up and recognized me immediately. "Hey!" he said, jumping up in mid-crunch and reaching out to shake my hand. Then he remembered that his was all greasy so he wiped it on his pants before pumping mine energetically. "Haven't seen you in a while! Where you been keeping yourself? How've you been?" Then he looked at Emily and broke into a big smile. "Aw, don't tell me—it ain't possible—look how big she's gotten!"

I held Emily up proudly. "Emily, this is Joe," I announced. "He's the doorman here in our building. You haven't seen him since you were a tiny baby."

Emily favored Joe with her big four-toothed grin.

"Aw, gee, Mrs. Hack. She's beautiful." Joe put down the racing forms and held out his arms. "Think she'll come to me?"

I hesitated. "I don't know, Joe . . . this is all kind of new to her . . ."

"C'mon. Sure she'll come to her ol' Uncle Joe." Joe reached for Emily. She gave me a half-startled look, unsure, and then tentatively put her arms around him. Joe beamed with pleasure. "That's right, that's right," he crooned, patting her softly on the back. "You know your ol' Uncle Joe's a good egg. What a darling. Gee, I wish I had somethin' for her. Hey, I know." He dug into his pocket and came up with a package wrapped in cellophane. "Beef jerky," he said with satisfaction. "Want some, honey? Think she'll like beef jerky?" he asked me over his shoulder.

"Umm, maybe not just now, Joe," I said.

"Yeah, you're probably right. She's a little young yet. But just you wait 'til you're five or six, Em," he said, wagging his finger at her. "You're gonna be all over me for this stuff."

Then, on the spot, his face fell. " 'Course you're here 'cause of—'cause of—" he seemed unable to bring himself to mention Howard's death aloud. "Jeez, I was real sorry—we were all real sorry—to hear—it's a terrible thing—I mean, did they find who did it yet?"

I shook my head and gently pried Emily loose from his grasp. "We're just on our way up to take a little inventory, Joe," I said and coughed nervously. What had sounded offhand and perfectly reasonable practiced in the car sounded utterly suspicious here in the lobby. "You know, sort things into boxes, make sure Emily has something special to remember her father by . . ." I made a movement toward the elevators.

Joe snorted. "If there's anything left."

I stopped. "What do you mean?"

"Well, between the police and that Holly broad Emily'll be lucky if there's a pair of her dad's socks left."

"The Holly broad?"

He made a face. "I don' know why I have so much trouble remembering her last name . . . it's some kind of vegetable, I think, or a tree, maybe . . . no, let's see . . . Rose? . . . Oak? . . . "

"Ivy."

He snapped his fingers. "That's it. Holly Ivy."

"Holly Ivy has visited the apartment since Howard died?"

"Couple of times."

"How'd she get in?"

Joe looked away. "She's gotta key." He cleared his throat. "Fact is, she was kinda living here the week or so before the . . . before the . . . you know."

"I see."

"I'm not saying I watched her walk off with the microwave or anythin'. It's just a feeling I got. You know, a hunch."

I nodded.

Emily and I took the elevator up to the sixteenth floor. It was a big, old-fashioned lift, more like a miniature room than an elevator, really, and on the walls were hung an antique mirror and an oil painting. Then the door opened and we found ourselves in the hall.

Ten steps to the right. Put the key in the door. Turn the lock. Walk in.

It was just the same. He'd done nothing to it, really, since the separation, except to throw a leopard skin on the bed. Oh, there were signs that the police had been there, of course, someone had clearly been through the desk and the bookshelves and in the drawers of the nightstand, but the rooms certainly hadn't been torn apart the way I'd come to expect from the way such searches were depicted in the movies. It just looked slightly disheveled, as though it hadn't been picked up after for a few days, which, of course, it hadn't.

I looked around with a critical eye. What was missing?

"Okay, Em," I sighed, after I'd changed her diaper and handed her a sippy cup of apple juice. "I need your help here. We're looking for something, but we don't know what it is, see? It could be anything. But whatever it is, it might help us figure out what happened to your father. So don't hesitate to call my attention to whatever you find, no matter how small or insignificant, okay? Now, where do you suppose we should begin?"

Emily scarfed down her apple juice and crawled over to Howard's desk.

"Daddy's desk," I agreed, coming up behind her and lifting her up so she could see. "What a good idea. You're sure you haven't done this before?" I asked her as we both stared down at the dusty mahogany surface.

Howard's desk was a three-drawer affair. On the top stood a computer, a printer, a pile of MasterCard receipts, a Garfield cup containing a number of pens and pencils, a little plastic container of colored paper clips, a stapler and a pocket calculator.

"Here," I said, handing Emily the pencil holder. "You search this. I'll go through the desk."

Emily accepted the Garfield cup with gravity. She sat down on the rug and started removing the pens and pencils and examining them one by one.

I began with the MasterCard receipts. The latest was dated October 29, just two days before the murder. Bloomingdale's was printed across the top. Underneath were the following charges:

Armani shaving cr	$ 90
1 pr. Bloomies mens shorts	$ 28
1 Natori night ensemble	$225
Subtotal	$343

The one before that was stamped SAKS FIFTH AVENUE. It read:

Fogal pantyhose	$ 95
Fogal pantyhose	$105
Ch. Dior nightwear	$150
Subtotal	$350

The one before that came from La Lingerie on Madison and East Sixty-first Street. It said simply:

Bra and panties set $395

"I hope it all runs in the wash," I said to Emily and tossed the receipt pile aside.

Next I pulled out the top drawer. It contained a dog-eared copy of James Joyce's *Ulysses* and another of Norman Mailer's *The Naked and the Dead*, three blank legal pads, a pair of Carrera sunglasses and a half-used package of breath mints. There was also a manila folder marked "Pending." I opened this eagerly. Inside was a circular from the 92nd Street Y announcing a lecture series in which Howard had been asked to participate, entitled "Dating in the Age of Minimalism: A Novelist's Perspective," a circular from PaineWebber, where Howard had an account, inviting him at a cost of $250 to attend a seminar entitled "Putting on Your Game Face: Global Investment Strategies for the New Investor," the business card of Sharon Lewis, an associate producer at *Prime Time Live*, the business card of Marissa Petersen, an assistant director at New Line Cinema, and two dry cleaning tickets.

The drawers on either side were similarly disappointing. The one to the right contained supplies of computer paper, blank envelopes, mailing labels and stationery. The one to the left was entirely filled with publicity photos of Howard, dressed in a black turtleneck, leaning on his fist and staring intently into the camera.

That left the computer. I switched it on.

"I hope he didn't change his password," I worried aloud.

Most writers don't even bother with a password, but Howard had been completely paranoid about his work, convinced someone would steal it.

Psswd:, flashed on the screen.

H-O-W-A-R-D, I typed in.

The WordPerfect logo appeared.

"We're in," I reported to Emily.

(Fortunately, Howard had also been completely paranoid about forgetting his password and not being able to get into the computer himself, so he'd picked something he wouldn't forget.)

I called up the directory of his files.

> *DIR: TAX*
> *CAR*
> *STORY*
> *LTR*

TAX turned out to be an accounting of his estimated tax payments, which I printed out, just to make sure Caitlin knew about them so the estate didn't pay twice. *CAR* contained the name, address and phone number of the dealer who had sold Howard the Mercedes, the garage where it was parked and the name of the mechanic who serviced it. In my opinion, this was the first really useful information I'd found and I printed it out, too. I'd forgotten all about the car.

Then I turned to *STORY*. If Howard had really written something new just before he died and hadn't showed it to anyone, I could probably sell it for a substantial sum of money. Maybe *The New Yorker* would take it, or the *Atlantic*. Who would I ask about that? I wondered as I waited for the file to come up. Maybe I could use Francine Weezle. After all, she was still Howard's agent, wasn't she? Could you be someone's agent after they were dead . . . ?

"I think I've got something here," I said aloud as the screen flickered. Then the following words appeared:

THE PHENOMENOLOGIST
A Short Story
By
HOWARD HACK

. . . and nothing else.

I looked at Emily. "Oh, well. There goes college," I said and went back to the directory.

That left *LTR*.

It was a long file—over seventy pages. There were letters dating back over a year. Some of them were written during the time we were still living together, before Howard got his big contract. This one, for example:

Writer's Press Magazine
New York, NY
Attn: Alexander Fontaine, Editor
RE: Three unanswered query letters

Dear Mr. Fontaine,

I am writing to congratulate you. You have just won the Howard Hack Literary Award for Rudeness and Unsavory Behavior as Regards an Author of Some Standing. Do not underestimate the honor being bestowed upon you. There were several candidates of no mean ability running against you. They were unmannered, rustic boobs to a man (actually, there were several women involved as well) with little or no appreciation for art beyond that which appealed to their sexual organs. But you persevered and in the end I had to hand it to you.

How dare you leave my letters unanswered?

Then there was this one:

Complete Health Network
P.O. Box 1785
Newark, NJ
Attn: Mr. Todd Crossgate

Dear Mr. Crossgate,

I am writing to complain about your proposal to increase my premiums by ten percent, effective at the end of this month.

What do you mean by sending me a letter telling me that if I do not pay the increase as planned my policy will be canceled? I think I should warn you that, as a writer of some standing, I am considering making you and your company the subject of my next piece for the *Times*.

Perhaps you would care to reconsider.

I leafed through the rest of them. This was clearly Howard's business letter file, since I did not find a single page where the heading did not contain a company address of some type. Where had he put his personal file? I wondered.

The last letter had been sent the day before he died. It was addressed to Caitlin.

Dear Caitlin,

In reference to our telephone conversation, I regret to inform you that, on the advice of my new financial planner (you know Jillian at PaineWebber, don't you?), I have decided against authorizing you to purchase shares in my name in the Locomoro Land Trust.

P.S. How about dinner?

The Locomoro Land Trust? Was this one of those "interesting" deals that Caitlin had mentioned were part of her firm's service to new clients? I made a note to look it up.

"Well, that's it," I sighed as I turned off the computer. I looked around for my daughter.

She was sitting on the floor absorbed in playing with something she'd dug out of the pencil holder. It wasn't a pencil or pen, though, because all of those were scattered around the Oriental rug. The Garfield cup wasn't in sight, either, but a little investigation confirmed that it had rolled under the sofa. I got on my hands and knees, retrieved the cup and was in the process of scooping up the carnage when I got a quick look at whatever it was Emily was playing with.

I crawled a little closer. It flashed silver in the sunlight.

I crawled a little closer and intercepted it just as she was about to put it in her mouth.

It was a key.

I lay flat on the floor and looked up at Emily. "Bingo," I said.

The safe deposit box. Of course. How could I have been so stupid as to forget it?

We'd gotten the safe deposit box when Howard and I were first married. It was at my insistence. Not that we had anything particularly valuable to save. It was just that Howard was driving me crazy.

Like other writers, Howard often worried about losing his

work, but unlike other writers he carried this anxiety to extremes. Howard worried that his computer would break down and melt his files. He worried that an electrical storm would hit Manhattan while he was typing and his computer would blow up and melt his files. He worried a fire would break out in his study and melt his files.

But, worse than natural disaster, Howard obsessed that his work would be stolen. Someone would break into the apartment and take the computer. Someone would break into the apartment and break the computer. Another writer would break into the apartment and steal his files.

At first I tried soothing words, a surge protector and an extra lock on the door. But when he got up three times in one night just to turn the stupid machine on and check, I suggested a safe deposit box. If he kept copies of all his files in a safe deposit box, I'd argued, he wouldn't have to worry like this. And if he *really* wanted to make sure they were safe, he could make copies of certain files and then delete those files entirely from the machine. That way if another writer went to the trouble of stealing his machine, all he or she would get for their pains was a dated copy of WordPerfect.

Howard had thought this was a great idea. But it demanded a trip to the bank and a certain amount of administrative paperwork. Howard didn't like administrative paperwork and Howard didn't do things he didn't like. So I had ended up going with him and filling out the forms for him. I'd put the box down in both our names. That way, I'd figured, if he got sick or something I'd be able to retrieve his stuff for him.

Murder was a rather severe form of illness, but it justified a peek into that box. If Howard *had* left a clue or suspected someone of wanting to kill him, he might just have tucked the information away in a file. The question was, after we'd split up, had Howard had my name stricken from the bank's records? Or, even if he hadn't, would the guard let me open a box that belonged at least partially to a murder victim?

There was only one way to find out.

It wasn't until Emily and I were actually walking down the stairs of the bank to the safe deposit box section that I realized how awkward this might look if Howard had had my name taken off the box. Trying to get into somebody else's safe deposit box was a crime, I realized. What you were *supposed* to do was to inform the lawyer in charge of the estate of the existence of a box, so that she, in turn, could inform the courts, so that the courts, following procedure, could appoint somebody official to go with you to open the box. Since this was a murder case, the police would probably demand to have somebody there as well, which meant that all those official people would have to coordinate all their official schedules, which meant the box wouldn't have gotten opened until after Christmas. It went without saying that if there was anything good in there, I'd be the last to see it.

Back in the apartment, this line of reasoning had appeared to more than justify the risk of shortcutting official procedure in favor of trying to get into the box myself. But now I froze in front of the front desk. If I were discovered, there'd be an inquiry, at the very least. I'd have to talk to someone in security at the bank and quite possibly the police. It would come out that Howard had been murdered and that I was a suspect . . .

"May I help you?" asked the young man behind the desk.

I just sort of stared at him, debating. He looked to be about nineteen years old, although I guessed that he was somewhere between twenty-one and twenty-three, putting in his two-year stint at a New York bank before applying to Harvard Business School. A lot of people do that. He was wearing a somber gray pin-striped wool suit, no doubt off the rack at Brooks Brothers, a blue Oxford shirt with a white collar and a maroon tie. His hair had been carefully parted and slicked down and his horn-rimmed glasses shone dully in the fluorescent lighting. He looked like a prep student playing Gordon Gekko in the school play.

"I'd like to get into my safety deposit box, please," I announced abruptly. It simply wasn't possible, I thought, that I would be caught by someone with pimples.

"Number?" he asked smoothly, looking at Emily and me over his glasses.

"Six-oh-nine," I reported. Howard had taped the number to the key. He never could remember anything, unless it had been written by a dissident émigré.

"Name?"

"Elizabeth Halper—er, umm, uh, Elizabeth Hack," I said.

He stopped for a moment and scribbled something down on a piece of paper. Then he took off his glasses deliberately and cleaned them. "Have you been away, Ms.—"

"—Mrs.," I cut in.

"Mrs., umm, Hack?" he asked.

"Away?" I repeated.

"I haven't seen you in here before," he said, putting his glasses back on.

I blinked. "We've been in the country," I said and shifted Emily on my hip. Emily put both arms around my neck and turned to regard our interrogator.

"I see. Would that be Long Island?"

"No, Massachusetts."

"Oh, Massachusetts." He smiled. "I love Massachusetts. I went to Williams College," he volunteered.

"Umm, we're in Lenox," I reported reluctantly.

"Practically neighbors, then," he noted, still smiling.

"Yes." I shifted Emily back the other way. "I'm sorry," I

said, "but we're in something of a hurry . . ."

"Of course," he said, making no move to hurry. "Well, why don't you sign the book while I look up your card?"

I signed the book and he fished through his files and came up with a slim folder. He opened it and stared at it for a long time. Then he looked up at me.

"You are Mrs. Howard Hack," he said.

I wet my lips. "Yes," I said.

"Howard Hack, the novelist," he said.

Shit. "Yes," I said. "Is there some problem?" I asked coldly, deciding to tough it out.

"Yes, I'm afraid there is." He paused and pressed a button. A buzzer sounded. Almost immediately, a guard appeared behind him.

Oh, God, I thought and clung to Emily.

"Mrs. Hack—"

"Yes?" I whispered.

"Your annual fee is thirty days overdue."

My lips worked. "My annual fee . . . uh, can I still look in the box?"

"I'm afraid not."

"I can't?"

"Not until the account is current."

"How much?" I asked.

"One hundred and fifty dollars." Howard gets me again, even in death.

There was obviously no question of using a check or credit card with the name "Halperin" prominently displayed. That left cash, which would leave me with about ten dollars to get home on.

I glumly counted out the money.

"Thank you," he said, then handed me a receipt and turned authoritatively to the guard. "Six-oh-nine," he said.

The guard nodded.

He turned back to me. "Mr. Lewis will take you to your box." He pressed another button and the gate in front of me swung open. "Have a nice day, Mrs. Hack. And thank you for banking with us."

Mr. Lewis led us down a hallway and into the vault. He stopped in front of number 609, took my key, inserted it and his own into the lock and lifted out the box. It was a midsized box, long and shallow.

"Would you like a room?" he asked.

"Yes, please."

He carried the box to a windowless cubbyhole fitted with a small table and chair. He put the box on the table and closed the door behind him.

I waited until I could hear his footsteps receding down the hall and then I took a deep breath. "Here we go, Em," I whispered, and threw open the box.

We both blinked and stared down. The box was empty but for a single computer disk.

It was marked "Diary."

Chapter

14

August 3—I think I'll begin this diary with a disclaimer. I don't intend this to be the ordinary, quotidian recitation of events that commonplace people use to wax prosaic over a stifling two-week bus tour of Europe. This diary will be an extension of myself and, by default, my work. I will use it to record those ephemeral life experiences, those rabid sensations, those feverish impressions and only those experiences, sensations and impressions which I, in my capacity as a novelist, wish to recall for the purposes of deepening my future work and coalescing the artistic flames . . .

So began Howard's diary, which I began reading late Thursday night, after an exhausting drive back to Lenox. Of course, the smart thing to do would have been to spend the night in the apartment, get a good night's sleep and rest up for my next confrontation with the fourth estate. I'd have to see them eventually. I wasn't going to keep driving on Mountain Road forever. But, as tired as I was, the second Emily and I got back from the bank, I realized that this was no longer the apartment, or my apartment—this was Howard's apartment. Besides, I had Adam's car and I wanted to get my high heels back. Not to mention Adam.

. . . to this end, I've determined not even to use the established sequential format common to other diaries, but to record my impressions in order of their potency, their lasting effect upon my art . . .

For the last half-hour of the trip I had rehearsed what I would say to the microphones and cameras that would no doubt be thrust in my face. I had just decided on "No comment" when I turned off Route 7 onto Housatonic Street. A completely quiet and deserted Housatonic Street. Just like Housatonic Street on every other night, when one of its residents is not the chief suspect in a murder case.

I turned into my empty driveway. Where had they all gone? *This must be good news*, I thought. *Maybe they caught her.*

As soon as I got in the house I slid Emily, still dressed and sound asleep, into her crib. It was too late to call anyone, so I hurried into my office and switched on my computer. I couldn't wait to see what was in Howard's diary.

. . . Although, for ease and consistency's sake I'll try to use alphabetical order wherever possible, so as to be able to refer to specific instances in the future . . .

Wait a minute, I thought. Alphabetical order? In a diary? What the hell did that mean? I skipped ahead a few pages until I came to:

ALICE
Met Alice (dog psychologist and part-time hairdresser) while

waiting for the M1. Quoted Proust to her, brought her back to the apartment and banged her twice, once on the kitchen counter. Afterward, had a cappuccino and wrote three pages. Never saw her again, but remember she didn't shave under her arms.

ALICIA

An assistant editor at Brides magazine, I met Alicia when she responded to a query letter I'd sent asking if her publication would be interested in a 3000-word essay entitled "A Deconstructionist's View of Marriage as Portrayed in Moby Dick." We held several conferences on the subject. On the second occasion of our meeting she went down on me behind a mannequin at Bergdorf's. She has very nice tits. I still speak to her occasionally although, due to artistic differences, the piece was never published.

AMANDA . . .

This isn't possible, I thought, staring at the entries. This isn't . . . Margaux. Is Margaux here? I wondered. I paged down quickly until I came to the Ms. Mabel, Maddie, Marcy . . .

MARGAUX . . .

Yes! I exulted and then I stopped. Wasn't this like eavesdropping or spying, only much worse? Did I have the right to pry into another woman's most intimate secrets—particularly one whom I couldn't stand? Was I really going to do this thing—to read about Margaux?

What nonsense. Of course I was.

MARGAUX

My relationship with Margaux began the day I met her, at a reading. It was a meeting of two spirits, a coupling of art and passion. Afterward, we did it twice at a party at her house—once in the upstairs bathroom and once in the pantry.

Bastard, I thought, and kept reading.

During the first months, Margaux was my guardian angel, my mystic muse, my lyric temptress. She succored my soul. She nurtured my talent.

But then—and it gives me great pain to write this—she became unreasonable, so unreasonable, I would venture to say, as to be unstable. She was insatiably jealous. She wanted me all for herself and if she couldn't have me, she threatened to do violence both to herself and to me.

I knew it!

She demanded that I leave my wife. When I pointed out, in the clearest possible way, that leaving Elizabeth was entirely unnecessary, since Elizabeth was still overweight and rather saggy and dumpy from childbirth—

Arrgh!

—and was therefore no threat to her, and, furthermore, that I had found Elizabeth to be an excellent source of income for some time with hidden resources in that field and as such should not be discarded too hastily, Margaux became vindictive. One night, after I'd put myself out for her (I had had a headache but had gone ahead and done it with her anyway, just to be generous) I woke up and found her poised over me with a pillow, as though deciding whether or not to suffocate me—

Homicidal!

—naturally, I split up with her after that, although for a long time she refused to accept it. I had moved out by this time and I thought that my living in New York would prove our relationship unworkable, but Margaux simply hounded me and in the end it was only when I threatened to reveal what I knew about her to her father that she became reconciled to our altered circumstances and even invited me to her annual Halloween bash.

So it *was* Margaux. It had to have been Margaux. Howard had something on her and she decided to get rid of him. What could it be? The entry ended there.

No wonder she was so upset when Howard showed up at her party with somebody else. Not only was he rubbing her nose in it, she must have had a terrible time getting him away from Holly long enough to—

Holly. Holly Ivy. Was *she* in here, too? I wondered. She was so new. And yet . . . I hit a key.

SEARCH FOR? asked the computer.

H-O-L-L-Y, I typed in carefully.

The screen went blank and then:

HOLLY

I met Holly at the New York Public Library. I was there ostensibly to do some last-minute research on my novel but, really, I go there for the sex. The women who go there are generally the mousy, studious type who aren't expecting anything anyway and who are usually so thrilled to have an author take any notice of them whatsoever that you can bang 'em in the stacks and still have time left over to look up the year Richard the Lion-hearted embarked on his second crusade.

Not that this was what happened with Holly. Far from it. As a matter of fact, I met Holly while *she* was banging a research librarian in the Greek Antiquities section. She was trying to get him to write her prologue for her. Holly always bangs people to do her work for her. The guy did promise to do it for her, but then I stepped in (rather gallantly, I thought) and when she found out who I was she thought it would be much better to have her prologue written by Howard Hack than by some unknown schmuck NYPL research librarian and . . . that is how we became acquainted.

I have great admiration for Holly. To be so young, so beautiful, with such a talent—I really don't know anyone as limber as she.

I will just mention, however, that Holly does have a rather deplorable propensity for stealing other people's work. In fact, I did catch her once trying to steal mine. (Luckily, I always use a password when working on the computer.) Naturally, I told her that if I caught her doing it again, I would be forced to publicize the fact that she did not, in the strictest terms, compose her own prose. We had a big scene over this but eventually I calmed her down by offering to bring her to Margaux's Halloween party.

Margaux, Holly—who else was there? I paged rapidly through the file. For a long time there was nobody else I recognized, although I did come across this entry:

SARAH
I will write only a few brief words about the woman I have chosen to call Sarah. Suffice to say that, as Sarah is a Royal, it behooves me to be as discreet as possible in relating the circumstances and nature of our relationship. However, I feel I owe it to my work— to my commitment to my art—to my very essence as a novelist to describe with as deep an honesty as that which I am capable of the feelings and sensations which Sarah evoked in me during our brief rendezvous. And so, it is with this determination in mind that I strip our affair of all frivolity to reveal its fundamental core.

When I think of Sarah, I think of only one thing. Tits. BIG tits. What a set.

And then, on a whim—I couldn't even say what made me

think of it—I hit *SEARCH FOR* again and typed in:
C-A-I-T-L-I-N

CAITLIN
I met Caitlin in February at a "Deepen Your Love" seminar at the Living Alternatives Institute.

Wait a minute, I thought, *I remember that seminar—*

Elizabeth and I were bickering at the time. The problem, of course, was Elizabeth's inability to handle the demands of motherhood—the child was, after all, six weeks old by this time and did not require the level of attention which Elizabeth mawkishly bestowed upon it. Nonetheless, I consented to examine my own behavior through an intermediary and enrolled for a weeklong seminar.

The class was not what I expected. For one thing, it was predicated upon both partners' participation. Having assumed that the most effective way to deepen my love for Elizabeth was to leave her at home, I was adrift—until I met Caitlin. She, too, had left her spouse at home. As we were the only uncoupled persons present, we decided to pair off in order to benefit from the exercises. We ended up spending the entire week together, deepening our love approximately three times a day.

By then, I understood that what was really wrong with my relationship with Elizabeth was that she was selfish and incapable of loving. I resolved to divorce her. I was initially apprehensive of such a step, but Caitlin convinced me that such a move did not necessarily mean financial discomfort and promised to help me through the whole unpleasant scene.

Yup, I thought. That's just what I remember.
Well, is that it? I wondered. I didn't have much desire to leaf through the rest of Howard's musings—all the Julies and

Janices, the Ingrids and Inezes. Was there anyone else I could think of? Wait a minute.

SEARCH FOR:

E-L-I-Z-A-B-E-T-H, I typed. A blank screen and then:

NOT FOUND, OK?

I blinked. *Not found?* I tried again.

SEARCH FOR:
E-L-I-Z-A-B-E-T-H
NOT FOUND, OK?

Okay, I thought. *Then how about—*

SEARCH FOR:
L-I-Z-Z-I-E
NOT FOUND, OK?
L-I-Z
NOT FOUND, OK?
L-I-Z-A, E-L, E-L-I, B-E-T-H, W-I-F-E, S-P-O-U-S-E
NOT FOUND, NOT FOUND, NOT FOUND, NOT FOUND, NOT FOUND, NOT FOUND, OK?

It took about fifteen minutes, but eventually I understood that the man who had devoted whole paragraphs to the size of a chance encounter's breasts hadn't bothered to write a single word about his own wife.

It's a good thing for you you're dead, Howard, I thought grimly as I turned off the computer and climbed wearily into bed.

*   *   *

The first thing I did the next morning was to peek out the window to see if the news vans were back. They weren't. That was good, because I was tired and my head ached. I was just about to turn on the radio to try to catch the end of the local newscast to see if there had been a break in the case when I heard Emily chirping in the next room. "Don't give me that smile," I told her as I lifted her out of her crib. "When are you going to learn to wake up miserable like everybody else?"

Having missed the news, I carried Emily downstairs to get breakfast started. There, I forgot to put water in the coffee machine, then put it in too late so the coil sizzled and water leaked all over the counter. I stepped in the piece of mashed banana that Emily had conveniently left by the side of her high chair. I went into the little bathroom off the kitchen—no toilet paper.

Things could be worse, I thought as I reached into the darkness of the cabinet under the sink. I could be out of toilet paper altogether. The stores could be out of toilet paper. Toilet paper could not have been invented yet—"What's this?" I said as my hand touched something cold, metallic and unfamiliar. I pulled it out. It was a gun.

A small gun. A little, itty-bitty gun. The kind of little, itty-bitty gun that fits well into expensive pocketbooks.

I have never claimed to be a gun expert. I'd never even held a gun in my hand before this. I didn't even know how to check to see if it was loaded. But all the same, I knew that the gun I was holding was the gun that had killed Howard. Just like I knew that it wasn't me who had put it there.

What to do? Call the police? Oh, right. "Hi, Chief Rudge, this is Elizabeth Halperin. You know, your prime suspect for the Howard Hack murder case? Well, I just happened to find the murder weapon in my downstairs bathroom this morning and I was wondering if you'd like to come over and search the rest of the house to see if the person who planted it here left any other incriminating evidence around?"

No, I don't think so, I thought. But should I tell someone else? Who? Who would believe me? *I* didn't believe me.

No, I thought. There's only one thing to do.

"Emily," I called out. "We have to go for a little ride now."

"Now, listen, Em," I said as I wheeled out of the driveway and sped off down the street, the gun wrapped up in one of Emily's cloth diapers and tucked away deep in the diaper bag in the back seat. "There's something I want to talk to you about. It's about—it's about—" I struggled for the appropriate way to approach my topic. "It's about right and wrong, Em," I said finally.

She turned her head my way and looked at me expectantly.

"Right and wrong," I repeated as I pulled up into the parking lot behind the cemetery a couple of miles down the road. "You see, Emily, it's very important to learn to do what's right in life. Not because of some misguided sense of morality, but because when we do wrong we're likely to end up hurting either ourselves or other people. Doing right, which is often much more difficult in the short run, always ends up making a person feel better about themselves."

Emily blinked and touched her nose. I took that as a sign that she was with me on this.

"Which brings me to what I wanted to talk to you about," I continued as I pulled her and the diaper bag out of the car and carried them both down the path alongside the cemetery and into the woods beyond. "You probably wonder what we're doing out here in the woods first thing in the morning in the freezing cold. Well, the fact is that this morning Mommy was faced with one of those right-and-wrong decisions."

We had come to the edge of a rise. Off in the distance were

more trees and woods. Directly below us was the remains of an old dump, no longer in use. Everywhere below us was trash. Old cars, broken refrigerators, smashed appliances, tires, metal, glass, plastic and every conceivable form of garbage lay spread out like a particularly nasty obstacle course.

"You see, Em," I said as I shrugged out of the diaper bag, "this morning Mommy found a piece of material evidence in a criminal case. Now, if *you* ever find material evidence lying around, I don't want you to touch it. You just go straight to the police and tell them everything you know about it." I unearthed the gun and started rubbing it all over with the diaper. "I'm just rubbing this to clean off Mommy's fingerprints," I explained in response to her questioning look. "Mommy shouldn't have picked this up in the first place, and just in case somebody else finds it, I want to make sure it's clean." I finished rubbing. "You know, I always want to be honest with you, Emily. So what I have to tell you is that, technically, what I'm about to do now is wrong. There's a name for what I'm about to do, Em, and I want you to understand. It's called—"

I heaved the gun over the rise. We both watched it fall and disappear into the muck.

"Extenuating circumstances."

I didn't say much on the ride back home. To tell the truth, I felt a little lightheaded. It was such a brazen act. What if someone had seen me? In retrospect, wouldn't it have been better to wait for cover of darkness?

As if in response, the second I pulled into the driveway, a car pulled in behind me. I clutched until I realized it was Astrid's Subaru.

Astrid? I wondered. What's she doing here? Unless—wait a minute. What day of the week was it?

Didi's car pulled in behind Astrid's.

It was Friday. What happens on Fridays?

Pat's car pulled in behind Didi's.

Friday is play group. Whose turn was it to host play group this week anyway?

Margaux's car pulled in behind Pat's.

Mine.

Okay, I thought. Don't panic. For all they know, you just took a quick hop to the store. Just act natural and everything will be fine.

"HI!" I bellowed, waving jauntily at nobody in particular. "GREAT TO SEE YOU!" I yanked Emily out of the car seat. "COME ON IN!"

They all trooped into the house behind me. The main room was littered with last night's clothes. The remains of Emily's breakfast, including the mashed banana, were visible in the kitchen beyond. The door to the little bathroom off the side was open, as was the cabinet under the sink. There was still no toilet paper.

"COME ON IN!" I repeated, sliding my dirty socks and underwear behind a sofa pillow as nonchalantly as possible. "COFFEE, ANYONE?" The coffeemaker was still leaking and a puddle had formed beneath it. "IT WON'T TAKE ME A MINUTE TO CLEAN THIS UP," I reported.

Rat-tat-tat. Someone was knocking very loudly at the front door.

"I'll get it," Didi offered, rather tentatively, I thought.

"NO, NO, I CAN—" I rushed back to the door. "I'M SURE IT'S JUST—" I stopped. "Chief Rudge," I said. "Detective Fineburg." I took a step backward.

Both men stood on the front step regarding me somberly. Two uniformed officers stood behind them.

"Ma'am." The chief nodded curtly. "We have a few more questions to ask you. Would you please accompany us to the station?"

"Uh—" I took another step back and became aware of the play group gawking behind me. "Now is not the best time," I mediated, looking at Detective Fineburg.

"I'm afraid this is not negotiable, Elizabeth," Detective Fineburg responded, gently but firmly. "Please get your coat and come with us."

"What seems to be the problem, Chief Rudge?" Pat had appeared magically at my side.

The chief's face took on a strained expression. "I'm sorry, ma'am, but this is between us and Mrs. Hack—"

"Mrs. Hack—uh—Ms. Halperin just happens to be my client, Chief."

Detective Fineburg looked at her. "Your client was just observed tossing this into a dump not two miles from here." He held up the gun in a small plastic bag.

"Didi?" said Pat without bothering to turn her head. "Could you watch the children for a while? Elizabeth and I have to go out now."

"Tell us again about the way you discovered the gun," said Detective Fineburg.

We were sitting in a small gray cinderblock room around a cheap rectangular table, just me, Pat, the chief and Detective Fineburg. In the center of the table a tape recorder was rolling, as it had been from the time we'd sat down and begun the interrogation—nearly two hours ago. It turned out that the reason there had been no reporters at my house was that the police had ordered them out so as to be better able to monitor my actions just in case I decided to do something incriminating—which, of course, I had.

"But I just told you about that," I protested.

"Tell us again. I'm not clear on all the details," said the detective.

I looked at Pat. She nodded imperceptibly.

I sighed and began again. "I came downstairs and made

Emily her breakfast. Then I went into the bathroom off the kitchen—"

"Was this before or after your trip into New York?" interrupted the chief.

"After, of course. Anyway, I went into the bathroom and there wasn't any toilet paper, so I—"

"Did you notice anything suspicious?" asked the chief.

"Suspicious?"

"You hypothesized a break-in," cut in Detective Fineburg. "To account for the gun. Was anything else out of place?"

"No-o, but there might have been. I wasn't noticing too much this morning—"

"Why not?" asked the detective briskly.

"Well, you know, it was a late night last night—" I fumbled. I didn't want to slip up and mention that I'd spent most of the previous night reading Howard's confidential diary. This just didn't seem the time to point out that I'd bluffed my way into a murder victim's safety deposit box and filched new evidence out from under the noses of the police. Besides, how was I to account for the fact that Howard hadn't mentioned me? They'd have thought I'd deleted that part for sure. I swallowed. "All that driving back and forth . . ." my voice faded out weakly.

"Hmm. Go on," said the detective.

"Uh—"

"There wasn't any toilet paper, so you—" the chief prompted me, reading impassively from his notes.

"Uh, right. I went to look for some in the cabinet under the sink. That's when I discovered the gun."

"Yes," said Detective Fineburg. "Let's talk about that."

"Talk about what?" I asked.

"Finding the gun. What did you do when you found the gun?"

"What do you mean, what did I do? I told you. I decided to

just get rid of it. I was afraid you wouldn't believe that it wasn't mine, that I had nothing to do with Howard's being shot, so I—"

"But what made you think that that was the gun used to murder your husband?" asked the detective.

Because it was planted in my house, I thought. "Well, I didn't—I mean, I couldn't know for sure," I said. "But—I—it was a small gun," I finished lamely.

"So?"

"Well, Howard was killed with a small gun," I said.

"Really? How do you know?" asked Detective Fineburg.

"Uh—" I hesitated. Should I bring Sherman Forrest into this? I didn't think so. Bringing Sherman Forrest in had never been particularly advantageous in the past. "It was—it was in the paper," I said, remembering suddenly.

"Which paper?'

"The *Eagle*."

"Hmm," said the detective again. He played with his pen. "How long had the gun been there?" he asked.

"I have no idea."

"Who do you think could have put it there?"

"I don't know."

"You didn't put it there yourself, did you?" he asked. "I mean, and forgot about it?"

"You don't have to answer that," said Pat quickly.

"Of course I'll answer it," I said. "No, I didn't put it there myself. I never saw it before today. I never even touched a gun before today."

"And yet you knew to wipe it down," interjected the chief.

"I said I'd never touched a gun before," I returned. "I didn't say I never watch television."

There was a momentary silence, which Pat broke.

"Chief Rudge, Elizabeth has been here quite a long time. She has answered all of your and Detective Fineburg's questions to the best of her ability. She is cooperating fully with the investigation. Unless you are intending to charge her, I think she should be able to go home now. She has a small child to look after."

The chief glanced quickly at Detective Fineburg, who stared down at his pen for a long moment before answering.

"Ms. LaFountain, I'm going to be straight with you. I am sorely tempted to charge her. At the very least, I've got obstruction of justice and withholding evidence." He stopped. "But in answer to your question, no, I'm not going to charge her—just now. Just now I am going to ask her questions, and she is going to stay and answer those questions until I am satisfied that I have the truth. I don't care if her kid comes down with whooping cough, she's going to stay here until I am good and ready to let her go. Is that understood?" Without waiting for a reply, he turned to me.

"Now," he said, just as if nothing had happened. "Tell us again about the way you discovered the gun."

It was dark when they finally let us out.

"What time is it?" I asked Pat as we made our way out of the station.

"Nearly seven."

I realized then that Pat had spent her entire day with me. I cleared my throat. "Pat, I—I just want to thank you," I began. "You were really—" I felt my throat constrict.

Pat patted my arm reassuringly. "Forget it," she said. "Besides, I'm representing you, remember? This is my job. Come on. I'll drive you to Didi's. She's got Emily."

We got into Pat's car and I stared out the window until we turned a corner and the police station passed from view. I wish I could have gotten a message to Adam, I thought. I wish I could see him tonight. It's only been two days, but I miss him . . .

I became aware that Pat was clearing her throat. "Umm, Elizabeth, there's something we need to talk about," said Pat. She looked very serious.

"Yes?"

"I want you to know, before we begin, that although what I have to say now may sound callous, perhaps even disloyal, it is absolutely necessary that you should hear it and understand it. I wouldn't be living up to my responsibilities as your attorney if I did not present you with all of your alternatives and portray those alternatives as realistically as I possibly can."

"Go on," I said.

Pat sighed. "Elizabeth, I believe they intend to charge you with the death of your husband. They *want* to charge you. They are waiting for ballistics to come back, certainly . . . but after that . . ." her voice trailed off, then came back firmer. "And, Elizabeth, when they *do* charge you, in all probability it will be with murder one." She turned to look at me.

I looked back. "I know," I said steadily.

"No," said Pat. "I don't think you do. First-degree murder is what they will go for if they have to go to trial. They don't necessarily want to do that."

"They don't?"

"No. The DA rarely wants to go to trial, particularly in a capital crime. It's a no-win situation for him. If he does win, well, people assume that if you're going to accuse one person of killing another you should have a pretty good case and he doesn't get any credit. He's *supposed* to win. If he loses, he looks like a big jerk. Obviously, he would like to avoid that at all costs. And no matter how strong a case he has, you can't predict what a jury will do. So the answer is, no, they don't want to go to trial. They will if they're forced to, of course, but they don't want to." She stopped. "What I'm trying to say is that we might have an opportunity to plea-bargain."

"Plea-bargain?" I was shocked. "But Pat, I didn't do it!"

"Hear me out," she insisted. "You can't make this kind of a decision unless you are in possession of all the facts. You must consider all of your alternatives. I am not advocating that you accept a plea bargain. But I want you to understand it.

"Elizabeth, in the Commonwealth of Massachusetts, if you plead innocent to first-degree murder and then go to trial and lose, the penalty is life imprisonment without parole. And I have to point out that even if the DA's case isn't airtight, what we have isn't terrific. We have the appearance of a crime for profit. Even if there were extenuating circumstances . . . he beat you, mental cruelty, things that could come out during the trial . . . a jury is likely to discount them because you would have the *appearance* of profit against you, just like you have the *appearance* of trying to get rid of the murder weapon."

"But what good would a plea bargain do?" I protested. "Then I'd be admitting guilt."

"But you'd be admitting it to first-degree, possibly second-degree *manslaughter*," Pat rejoined gently. "Those charges carry harsh sentences, it's true, but they're not life. With good behavior you'd be out in fifteen, perhaps ten years. You'd still be able to have some sort of relationship with Emily. You might be with her through high school . . ."

Not have Emily! Not have Emily! What was this woman saying to me? She might just as well have told me to live without my heart or my lungs. Not have Emily! Not know her as a child! Not nurse her through the chicken pox! Not watch her in the school play, or at her first ballet recital!

All those times when I hadn't given her my best came crashing down on me. When I thought I'd go out of my mind if I had to read *Pat the Bunny* one more time. When I cursed the food on the floor, or the diapers or the piles of laundry she produced . . . all now precious, precious. Emily in her bath, Emily standing in her crib, Emily crying out in the night and my coming in to soothe her . . . not to be there to soothe her!

And then, the hollowness of all those months of agonizing whether being Emily's mother was enough. Whether I wasn't my own person unless I was out there building a career for myself instead of on my hands and knees on the floor building bridges and houses out of brightly colored blocks. Not have Emily! Not have Emily!

We spent the remainder of the drive to Didi's house in silence.

"Thanks, Didi," I managed once I was in the house with Emily secure in my arms. "I don't know what I would have done . . ."

"Don't be silly, Elizabeth. That's what friends are for," said Didi. "Can I get you something to eat? There's plenty."

I had interrupted their dinner. Sean was in a high chair, but Samantha was seated at the table with her mother and father. I realized I had never met Didi's husband before, didn't even know his name. What a great time to be introduced, I thought. I'll bet he's just thrilled to have a murder suspect in his dining room. It's probably right up there with finding termites in your mashed potatoes.

Didi read my mind. "Elizabeth, this is Tom," she said quickly. "Tom, this is Elizabeth."

Tom put down his fork and stood up. We shook hands awkwardly. "Nice to meet you," he said. "Just give me a moment and I'll get my coat and drive you home."

I was touched. "No, no, I've put you out enough already. I'll call a cab," I said.

"Don't be silly, Elizabeth," said Didi. "Tom will drive you."

"No, please, finish your dinner," I pleaded.

"Well," said Tom. "If you don't mind waiting just a little—"

"Please," I said again. I took a deep breath and realized my legs were shaky. I looked around and spotted a rocking chair in the next room. "Didi, Tom, you've been so kind—would you mind—would it be all right if Emily and I just sat and rocked for a few moments?"

"Of course," they said together.

I moved into the next room and sank into the chair with Emily. We rocked and kissed and cuddled as though Detective Fineburg was standing just outside the front door, which, for all I knew, he was. What to do? I wondered. What to do?

I'll call Adam when I get home, I thought. He'll help us. I miss him, I thought again. I wish he were here.

And then, slowly, the feeling of being watched—by someone or something—began to steal over me. I shuddered and looked around. What could it be? There was no one in the room. I looked down, and there it was on Didi's coffee table.

Howard. Or, rather, Howard's picture. There he was, in his black turtleneck, his chin on his fist, eyelids lowered, staring at me from the back cover of his book jacket.

I reached down and turned the book over. The now-familiar words—*Passion Palace*—leapt up at me in red from the cover, a reminder of everything that had occurred and a foreshadowing of what was to come.

I stared at the book on the coffee table. There was something incongruous about it that at first I couldn't place. Then it came to me. It was the only book in the room. Indeed, now that I thought about it, except for one dog-eared paperback and a Weight Watchers cookbook in the kitchen, it was the only book I'd seen in Didi's house.

"All set?" asked Tom, coming in behind me.

I jumped.

"Elizabeth, are you sure you're all right?" asked Didi, deep concern in her voice. "Wouldn't you rather stay here tonight? We have room."

"No, thank you, Didi," I said, still mesmerized by the book. Didi followed my glance. "Oh," she said, picking up the book and holding it with her fingertips, as though it were a piece of rare china. "Does this bother you? Let me put it away."

"No, no," I said. "On the contrary—Didi, may I borrow it?" I asked suddenly.

Didi looked startled. "Of course," she said. "Here." She handed me the book.

I turned it over and looked at it. "Oh, but you haven't finished," I said, noting the bookmark about a quarter of the way through.

"Oh, that's all right."

"Are you sure?"

"Oh, yes. To tell you the truth"—Didi looked embarrassed—"it's not exactly my thing. You know, I never buy this kind of book, but with all the publicity and the murder and everything I thought, well, just this once."

"Uh-huh," I said.

"And I know it's a good book," Didi hastened to assure me. "It's just that I'm not used to it—I mean, I probably can't appreciate it."

"Uh-huh," I said again.

"So, really, if you want it, go ahead. And there's no hurry about getting it back to me. I mean, I might finish it sometime . . . later . . ."

"I'll return it as soon as I can," I promised, getting my coat. "And thanks again, Didi," I whispered, as I gave her a little hug. "Thanks for everything."

"Nonsense," said Didi, but she looked pleased.

Tom tried to be nice on the way home. He really did. He told me how pleased he was to have finally met Emily and what a beautiful child she was. He talked about how much Didi enjoyed the play group and what a good idea it had been to organize it. I smiled and murmured my "Thank you's" and "Really?'s" and waited for the ride to be over. Be home, Adam, I thought.

When we got to my house, my car was parked out front and in the darkness we could just make out a man's figure leaning against the front door. Tom frowned. "I'll go see what he wants," he volunteered. "If there's any problem, we'll just turn right around."

"No, it's all right," I assured him. "It's—it's a friend of mine."

I got out of the car and lifted Emily out of the child seat in the back. I came around to the driver's side. "Thank you, Tom," I said.

He nodded. "Take care."

I walked up the front steps to where Adam was waiting. He didn't say a word. He just put his arms around both of us and helped us into the house.

I gave Emily a long bath that night. I did everything I could to please her. I made the yellow duck quack and the man in the boat sing. I poured half a bottle of bath soap in the tub so there would be enough bubbles. I splashed her and tickled her and played fishie.

Afterward I toweled her off and rubbed her skin with baby lotion. Then I slipped her into the feetie pajamas with the pink dolly stitched on the front, wrapped her in her white blanket and rocked her until she was almost asleep. I laid her in her crib and stood by, watching her sleep and breathing her scent.

Adam came up behind me. He slipped his arm around me and I rested my head on his shoulder. "Come to bed," he said.

I shook my head. "You go ahead," I said. "There's something I have to do first."

*   *   *

And so it was that I settled myself cross-legged on the floor in Emily's room, close by her little pink teddy bear night-light, and opened *Passion Palace*.

I read that book cover to cover, from the inside front jacket cover to the inside back jacket cover. I read the title page, the copyright page and Library of Congress numbers, the acknowledgments, the dedication and every word of the text. When I would start to slow down and feel myself nod off or read the same sentence over and over I had only to remind myself of my conversation with Pat to pick it up again with renewed vigor. It must be here, I thought. It is here somewhere. Keep looking. Keep looking.

It was about six-thirty the next morning when I read Howard's final sentence. I closed the book quietly, got to my feet and peeked out from behind Emily's rosebud curtains. The sky outside the window was lightening from blue-black to a dull gray.

I padded quietly into the bedroom. Adam was asleep, stretched out on the far side of the bed. His back was turned to me and I could see his hair tousled against the pillow. I slipped into bed next to him and cuddled up close. Adam was very warm.

Well, what do you know, I thought, as I fit my body next to his. For once, the publicity people were right.

The answer *was* in the book.

And this time, I even knew how to prove it.

Chapter 16

"Company?" queried the guard at the front desk.

"Laramee, Buford & Young," I said firmly.

"Whom do you wish to see?" He picked up a phone receiver.

"We have an appointment with Phillip Laramee."

"Names?"

I cleared my throat. "Jacqueline Olsen and—" I glanced at Astrid, who stood silent beside me, "Dr. Gerte Theilen, from Begelmann AG."

"Just a moment."

Well, I thought, as I stood there in one of my old blue business suits, a briefcase in one hand, here's the first cut. It was 1:10 on Wednesday afternoon. Phillip should be en route to his regular table at Café des Artistes. If he'd decided, just this once, to have a tuna salad sandwich at his desk instead, it was over. If he was out, but the *real* Dr. Gerte Theilen from Begelmann AG had been here before, it was over. If—

"What were those names again?" interrupted the guard.

"Olsen and Theilen, from Begelmann AG."

I stole another glance at Astrid. She looked a little pale, I thought, but otherwise she was perfect. If anything, her blue business suit was snappier and more expensive-looking than mine. And she'd worn sunglasses, which gave her a more European look.

The guard put down the receiver. "Third floor," he reported.

"Thank you," I said, and hustled Astrid over to the elevators.

We rode up to the third floor in silence. The doors opened onto a small reception area furnished with beige armchairs and rubber plants. On the wall behind the long Danish-style wooden reception desk the name Laramee, Buford & Young had been spelled out in big block letters.

Astrid and I marched over to the reception desk.

"May I help you?" asked the young woman.

"I'm Jacqueline Olsen and this is Dr. Gerte Theilen. Dr. Theilen is visiting from Germany. We have an appointment with Mr. Laramee."

The receptionist blinked at us and began shuffling papers nervously in front of her. That's what a surprise visit from the parent company will do.

"Uh—" said the receptionist and hit a button on the console in front of her.

A few moments later, the door to the inner offices opened and a second young woman came out. She had on a black pantsuit with a black shell. Her short black hair had been slicked back with Vaseline.

"May I help you?" she began hesitantly, looking from one of us to the other.

"We have an appointment with Mr. Laramee."

"I'm terribly sorry, there must be some mistake. Mr. Laramee is out to lunch."

Score one for the good guys. "Out to lunch?" I repeated. "Didn't you get our fax?"

"I'm sure he—uh, we—did. Perhaps there was an error. If you'll just let me check—"

We were wasting time. I put on my best trader face. "I don't think you understand," I said coldly. "We're from—"

"*Neem me niet kwalijk*," interrupted Astrid.

I coughed. "Uh—*nein*," I said.

"*Neem me niet kwalijk dat ik in de rede val.*"

"What's she saying?" asked the woman.

"This is Dr. Theilen," I said. "She's a senior vice president of Begelmann AG." I had been lucky here. Begelmann AG was probably one of two companies in all of Germany who had a woman as a senior vice president.

"I am so pleased to make your acquaintance," said Astrid, coming forward and shaking the woman's hand. "What is your name, please?"

"Umm, I'm Chloe Zuflack, Mr. Laramee's secretary—"

"Chloe, very good." Astrid beamed at her. "We go wait in Mr. Laramee's office for him now." She pushed her way through the inner door. I followed quickly.

"Uh—" Chloe ran after us.

"Here it is, no?" said Astrid, heading right for the corner office. She walked in, put her briefcase down on the desk and snapped it open. "It is just as well he is out," she said to me. "Now we can get some work done. Chloe, you will see that we are not disturbed, please?" she asked, turning to our guide.

"Well, uh—"

"Thank you, Chloe. I like it quiet when I am making out my reports. I'm sure you understand. So, please, will you hold my phone calls? Thank you so much."

"Uh—sure—"

"*Ja*, and Chloe," Astrid added, "I just remember. I change my plans, I must fly to Singapore after this. Would you please call Lufthansa and find out when the flights leave tomorrow? Also, I'll need a car in Singapore. Maybe you could arrange this for me also?"

"Uh—sure—"

"And make sure I get a special meal on the flight, *ja?* Vegetarian."

"Uh, *ja*—I mean, sure—"

"Oh, and the car should be a Mercedes. With a driver, please."

"Uh, sure—"

"*Ja,*" Astrid beamed at Chloe again as she led her out the door. "Such a big help, Chloe. *Danke schön,*" and Astrid stepped back inside the office quickly and closed the door behind her. "That ought to keep her busy for a while," she whispered to me.

"Astrid. You were wonderful," I breathed.

"Poof." Astrid waved a hand. "Now we get started."

I went immediately to Phillip's desk and started pulling open drawers. "I hope he keeps his files in his office," I whispered nervously. "If they are outside somewhere . . ."

"What are you looking for?" Astrid came up behind me. "Maybe I can help."

"Thanks, but I don't think so," I said as I shuffled through papers. "I'm looking for interim financial reports, statements of advances and sales on specific books. I went to the library, but there was nothing on Laramee, Buford since they were bought by Begelmann. Begelmann is a privately held company, so they don't have to file public financial statements, and I need to know the details of Laramee, Buford's current financial position."

"All this would be on the computer, *ja?*" Astrid asked.

"Well, yes, but—" I closed one drawer and threw open another, "I don't know his system, he's probably got a password . . ."

But Astrid had already seated herself in front of Phillip's computer and turned it on. "Maybe we give it a try anyway," she suggested.

I peered over her shoulder as the machine whined and blinked. There was a series of green fluorescent numbers and then the screen blinked:

PSSWRD:

I grimaced. "See, that's what I was afraid of," I said. "I don't know Phillip well enough to guess his password." I looked at my watch. "And it's already a quarter to two. In less than an hour people are going to come straggling back in here and we'll have someone more formidable to deal with than Chloe. We don't have the time to—"

Astrid typed: *LOGOFF SM*, then hit the F5 key.

"First we get out of this loop," she explained.

C> flashed the machine.

DIAG X M 0 PASS, typed Astrid.

SEARCHING, replied the machine. Then, after a few seconds: *AUTHORIZATION?*

PASS OVER D0Q, typed Astrid.

The screen went blank.

"What are you doing?" I demanded.

GOOD AFTERNOON, MR. LARAMEE, flashed the computer. *PLEASE ENTER YOUR COMMAND.*

"I'm just bypassing the password subroutine," Astrid explained.

"Bypassing the . . ." I blinked at her. "Astrid, what did you do before you had Maurits?" I asked.

"I ran a software engineering group at GE International," reported Astrid. "That's how I met Jann."

"I—I didn't know," I stammered.

"How could you?" Astrid answered calmly.

"But, Astrid. It's such a great skill. Aren't you—aren't you afraid to lose it? By not working, I mean. Aren't you afraid it will all pass you by?"

"Poof," said Astrid. "Only in America do they think that taking a few years off to have a child harms a person's career. In Holland, it is expected. Men do it, too."

"Really," I said.

"Really," she said and typed *MENU* into the computer.

MENU: ACCOUNTING
FINANCE
SALES
CURRENT LIST
BACKLIST

said the computer.

I stared at the screen. "Astrid! That's it. You're in." I pulled up a chair beside her. "Let's look at accounting," I said.

Astrid set the pointer to the *A* of *ACCOUNTING* and hit enter.

ACCOUNTING: PROFIT AND LOSS
CASH FLOW
BALANCE SHEET
QUARTERLIES

said the computer.

"What now, please?" asked Astrid.

"Cash flow," I said quickly.

CASH FLOW: DEC
MARCH
SEPT

"All three," I ordered. The December cash flow statement appeared on the screen. "Umm," I said. "Thanks. Can we get March now, please?"

"Maybe you like them on a split screen?" Astrid suggested.

There was a knock on the door. We both jumped. Astrid strode briskly to the door, opened it narrowly and stuck her head out, shielding both me and the computer from the outside.

"*Ja*, Chloe?" I heard her say.

Chloe's voice came faintly through the door. "I got the list of Lufthansa flights," I heard her say.

"Very good. *Danke*," said Astrid, and started to close the door.

"But about the car—in Mercedes they only have a two-seater. Will that be all right or should I—"

"Try someplace else," said Astrid. "*Danke*," she said again, and tried to close the door.

"Okay." Chloe apparently started to leave but then turned back. "Oh, and I called Mr. Laramee at the restaurant and told him you were here. He said to tell you he's on his way . . ."

"Very efficient, Chloe."

"He said to ask you if you want anything. You know, coffee, lunch . . ."

"No, Chloe."

"You sure? It's no problem."

"That will be all, Chloe," said Astrid firmly and closed the door. "We'd better go," she said nervously, coming back to the computer.

"Soon. Can we print this?"

"Certainly." Astrid turned on Phillip's printer.

"Can we look at something else while it's printing?"

"Of course . . ."

"Balance sheet," I said firmly. "Loan agreement."

Astrid typed, I read. "Print," I said. "Print. Print."

Phillip's machine printed.

"Elizabeth, it's been longer than you think," Astrid warned. "We'd better go."

"Midday traffic. We've still got time," I assured her. "Sales of top ten performers. Projected sales. Losses due to underper-formance. P and L. Print. Print."

The machine printed.

"Elizabeth . . ."

"Interoffice memoranda," I interrupted. "List of authors. List of agents. Print. Print."

"Elizabeth!"

The last page slid through the printer. I grabbed the stack and thrust it into my briefcase. "Go!" I said.

Astrid and I rushed to the office door and then stopped, frozen. Through the wood we could hear the sound of foot-steps coming purposefully toward us.

I looked around for someplace to hide. There was nowhere.

The footsteps grew louder.

I grabbed Astrid and pushed her to the side of the door so that when it opened we would be partially hidden, even though I knew it was futile.

The footsteps were right on top of us.

As one, Astrid and I held our breath.

The footsteps continued past the door without stopping and receded down the hallway.

Astrid and I let out our breath. "That was close," she whis-pered.

"Too close. Let's get out of here," I said and opened the door.

The hallway was empty. We slid down noiselessly. Chloe was on the phone in the office next door. We tried sneaking by. She looked up.

"Hey! Where are you going?"

Astrid attempted a smile. "We'll be right back," she promised, hurrying ahead.

Chloe put down the phone and came out into the hall. "But Mr. Laramee is on his way up," she called to our retreating backs.

"*Danke schön*, Chloe," said Astrid over her shoulder as we all but ran to the reception area. I pressed the down arrow for the elevator and hugged my briefcase to my chest. "Hurry, hurry," I murmured.

The down arrow beeped. So did the up arrow. The door to the elevator on the right slid open. It was empty. I grabbed Astrid and pulled her inside just as the door to the elevator on the left started to open. I hit the Lobby and Close Door buttons, pressed myself up against the wall of the elevator and watched as Phillip got out of the other elevator. I saw him look at the receptionist, who pointed behind him, at us. He whirled around just as the door closed.

"I don't think he saw us," I said to Astrid. "Do you?"

"I think he saw me."

"But he doesn't know you, so that's okay."

"I guess so," said Astrid. She sounded unconvinced.

The elevator stopped at the second floor and a messenger got on. Astrid and I looked at each other, and got off. We found ourselves in another reception area, this time with the name Kirby, Young Associates in block letters behind the desk.

"May I help you?" asked the receptionist.

"Uh—is this the lobby?" I asked.

"You got off too soon," the receptionist informed us. "It's one floor down." She glanced at the elevators. "If you like, you can take the stairs," she volunteered, pointing to the left. "This time of day the elevators can be a little slow. The end of the lunch hour, you know."

"Thanks," we said, and took the stairs.

I peeked out when we got to the bottom. A large crowd was

gathered around the elevator bank. One of the guards had left the desk and was trying to push his way through.

"What's happening?"

"I think they're looking for us," I whispered.

"Maybe we should go back upstairs," Astrid whispered back.

"No, I don't think so. There's a big crowd now. People are coming back from lunch." I peered out again. The stairwell was between the front door and the elevator. "The guard's not looking this way," I reported. "Let's just slip out and take our chances."

"If you think so," said Astrid doubtfully.

I opened the door just enough for Astrid and I to slide out. I tried to close it quietly, but it was one of those heavy fire doors and I couldn't hold on. It kind of banged shut. The guard's head whipped around.

"Hey, you two!" he called.

"Go!" I pushed Astrid ahead of me and we ran for the front doors. I could hear the guard coming after us. "Hey!" he called.

We pushed through the crowd coming in and made it out to the street. "Take a right," I hissed in Astrid's ear. "Cross the street. Take a left." The guard had followed us out into the street. I could see him out of the corner of my eye, debating how far to follow us. We slid in and out among the people in the street.

"Where are we going?" Astrid gasped beside me.

"Just follow me. Don't run now. Just walk fast like everybody else. Hurry, hurry."

We were on Fifth Avenue during the shopping hours. It was very crowded. "In here," I said and pushed Astrid through another revolving door. "This way." I led her through the crowds to the escalator. "Stay with me." We got off. "Take a right. Another right. Through these doors. Relax. We're in.

208 • NANCY GOLDSTONE

We lost them," I said and collapsed into a chair in the Ladies Lounge at Saks.

The ride home from New York was uneventful. We'd taken Astrid's Subaru, and she drove while I studied the papers we'd stolen.

When we got to my house I gathered up my belongings and got out of the car. Then I turned back. "Astrid," I began. "I don't know how to thank—"

"Poof, forget it," she said, waving a hand as she backed out. "It was great fun, no? Maybe we do it again tomorrow."

I laughed and walked into the house. Rose met me at the door with Emily in her arms.

"How was she?" I asked, snuggling my face against my child's.

"A perfect angel, as always," Rose reported.

"Did she eat?"

"Oh, yes, she did very well," said Rose. "Let me see. She had some peas and a glass of milk and a whole big bowl of Cheerios and . . ."

"Thank you, Rose."

"Well, I'd best be going." Rose shrugged into her coat. "Oh, yes," she said, turning at the doorway. "There's a message for you on your machine."

After Rose's truck had rumbled out of the driveway I went over to the phone and hit the Play button on the message recorder, fully expecting to hear Adam telling me what time he'd be off work. Instead, Pat's voice came floating toward me.

"Elizabeth, where are you? I must speak with you. The ballistics report came back. It's a positive ID with the gun that killed Howard.

"Elizabeth, they want to charge you. I put them off, but there's only so much I can do. I told them I'd bring you in myself, but something has come up. You must go to police headquarters. Don't worry, I'll be there soon.

"Elizabeth, do you understand? You must go turn yourself in. I can't find you anywhere, I've looked all over town. Where are you?"

Chapter

"What are you doing, Elizabeth?" asked Detective Fineburg. "You know better than to bring her here. This is no place for a child."

I tightened my hold on both Emily and my briefcase. "I want to see my lawyer," I insisted.

"Here," said the detective, and his voice was almost kind. "Give her to me. I'll see that she's—"

"No! She stays with me. Whatever you have to say, you say to both of us. And to Pat. I—where is she? I want to see my lawyer."

"We're looking for her. We can't find her. She's just—"

The door to the interrogation room opened and in walked Pat, Chief Rudge and a teenage girl wearing shorts who looked vaguely familiar.

"Pat!" I gasped, angling the briefcase in her direction. "Pat! I have to talk to you."

Pat came quickly to my side. "Shh," she said quietly. "Don't worry. Just let me handle this."

"But, Pat! I've got . . ."

But Pat wasn't listening. "Chief Rudge," she was saying. "Detective Fineburg. You asked my client to come in. I believe you intended to charge her with the murder of Howard Hack. Have you done so already?"

"No," said Detective Fineburg slowly. "We haven't. We were waiting for you. We—"

"Good," interrupted Pat. "Then we won't have to go before the judge. We can keep this all nice and quiet right here."

"Keep *what* all nice and quiet?" asked Detective Fineburg.

"Whitney," said Pat, leaving my side to go to the teenager. "This is Detective Fineburg. And you already know Chief Rudge, don't you?"

"Oh, yes," said the teenager. "He came to our school and gave a talk about drugs. Well, not *about* drugs, about not *doing* drugs. Also about AIDS and how you have to wear a condom, I mean, how the boy has to wear a condom . . ."

"Yes, yes," broke in Chief Rudge.

"Chief, Detective Fineburg, this is Whitney Hurley," said Pat.

The name was somehow familiar, as was her figure. The short, curly blonde hair like Little Orphan Annie. The Lenox High soccer jacket that said Mike on it, the thin legs in the long gym shorts and sneakers . . . who else had I seen wearing shorts in November?

"As she has already told you, Whitney Hurley is a high school student right here in Lenox," Pat continued. "To make a little money for college she sometimes baby-sits for—"

Of course! Now it was coming back to me—

"Margaux Chase," Pat finished firmly. "In fact, she was baby-sitting the Chase boys on the night in question. She has come forward of her own volition to give evidence. I think you will find what she has to say extremely interesting."

"Is that true?" asked the chief, turning to Whitney. "Did you baby-sit for Margaux Chase?"

Whitney nodded. "Oh, yes, I have a regular Saturday night job with her," she said. Then she paused. "Unless, of course, something important comes up like a dance or a party, or if I have a test on Monday or a biology lab report or—"

Detective Fineburg broke in. "Let's put it this way. *Were* you baby-sitting for Margaux Chase on Saturday, October thirty-first, the night of her Halloween party?"

"Uh, yes," said Whitney.

"Sit down," said Detective Fineburg.

Whitney pulled out a chair at the head of the conference table. Detective Fineburg took the seat immediately to her left and Chief Rudge the one to her right. Both men opened notebooks and the chief hit the Record button on the tape recorder.

"Okay, Whitney," said Detective Fineburg. "Let's talk about the night of the party. I want you to tell me everything you remember about that night. This is important, so if you need it, you can take a few moments to collect your thoughts."

Whitney nodded solemnly.

"All right. Let's begin. What time did you get to Margaux's house that night?"

Whitney squinted a little. "Five-thirty—no, five forty-five. I remember she wanted me there at five-thirty but I was running a little late because it was Halloween and I wanted to do a *little* trick-or-treating before I got there. I mean, I was already giving up the whole night, you know, and my friend Janice was having a party and everything but I couldn't go of course because Mrs. Chase said this was so important and she was going to pay me a lot of money and anyway I'd gone trick-or-treating the night before in Pittsfield—they do it on a different day than Lenox, you know, so I thought okay but—"

"So you got there at five forty-five, fine," interrupted the detective. "What did you do when you got there?"

"Umm, well, I sat with the two boys—Alden and Tolin, Alden's the younger one, he's really cute, Tolin is a little more work, you've got to watch him all the time—anyway, I sat with them while they had their dinner. There were a lot of people there—in the kitchen, you know, and in the dining room running around getting things ready for the party so Mrs. Chase said as soon as they'd finished I should take them upstairs to their room."

"Where, exactly, is the boys' room located?" asked the detective.

"Umm, upstairs all the way down the hall. Well, actually, they have two staircases so if you took the back staircase it wouldn't be down the hall, it would be the room to your right. Actually, they have two connecting rooms, one to play in and one to sleep in."

Detective Fineburg took out a piece of paper. He drew a diagram of the second floor of Margaux's house. "Show me the two rooms the boys use," he said, handing Whitney a ballpoint pen.

Whitney took the pen and very delicately checked two boxes on the diagram.

"Okay," said the detective. "So you took the boys upstairs after dinner. What then?"

"Well, Mrs. Chase said I should keep them in their rooms for the rest of the night and that both of them needed baths and that they should go to sleep around eight-thirty."

"Did she say anything else?" inquired the detective.

Whitney thought. "Umm, she said if I needed to keep them quiet they could watch *Aladdin*, but only after their bath."

"No," said the detective, "I meant, was that the extent of your duties?"

"Huh?" said Whitney.

"Did she give you anything else to do? Or were you just

supposed to put the children to bed and then go home yourself?"

"Oh," said Whitney. "No, I was supposed to stay the whole night, or, umm, until the party was over, just in case they didn't go to sleep on time, or they needed something in the night. You know, sometimes Alden wakes up in the night and needs a bottle or Tolin needs to go to the bathroom—"

"Okay," interrupted the detective. "So you put the children to bed at eight-thirty—"

"Well, it wasn't *exactly* eight-thirty. Tolin wanted to stay up and see the end of *Aladdin*."

"Okay, what time *did* you put them to bed?"

Whitney considered. "About twenty to nine," she said.

Detective Fineburg looked at her. "Whitney, how is it that you remember with such accuracy the precise time at which events occurred over three weeks ago?"

"Huh?" said Whitney.

"How do you remember the exact time you put the kids to bed that night?"

"Oh," said Whitney. "Well, see, it was my birthday the week before—October twenty-sixth—"

"Happy birthday," said the chief.

"Thank you."

"How old were you?" asked the detective.

"Sixteen."

"So, what does your sixteenth birthday have to do with remembering what time the kids went to bed?" Detective Fineburg asked.

"Well, my friend Mike—he's not *exactly* my boyfriend but he's like, a good friend, you know? He got me a watch for my birthday." Whitney held up her arm proudly. A gold-plated Seiko watch gleamed dully from her wrist. "Anyway, I wanted to make sure that the watch was working okay, so I kept checking it, because Mike said if it didn't work exactly right he wanted to take it back to the place where he bought it and maybe get me a necklace or something instead, but I said no, I really loved the watch—so, anyway, I kept looking at it because I knew I wanted to call Janice before her party started at nine to tell her to tell Mike not to—"

"*Was* the watch working properly?" interrupted the detective.

"Oh, yes, it keeps perfect time. Mike said it was because he paid extra—"

"Fine," said Detective Fineburg. "It is precisely eight-forty. The kids are in bed. What did you do? The party must have started by this time. Did you go downstairs?"

"Oh, no. Mrs. Chase didn't want me at her party. She said I should stay in the playroom. She told me I could watch TV or even a video. She said if I needed anything—you know, like something to eat or drink—I should use the back staircase and just get whatever it was out of the kitchen. The back staircase leads right to the kitchen," Whitney explained.

"Okay," said Detective Fineburg. "You're in the playroom. The children are asleep. What did you do?"

"Well—" Whitney pulled at her curls thoughtfully. "I talked to Janice for a while, but she had to go because her party started, and then I read *The Lord of the Flies* for English class."

There was a pause.

"That's it?" the detective said.

"Umm, yeah. *The Lord of the Flies* is a pretty long book," Whitney supplied.

"Well, it must have been pretty noisy for reading. Couldn't you hear the party going on downstairs?"

"Umm, well, actually no." Whitney looked embarrassed. "I kinda had the TV on too, you see. See, Mrs. Chase gets HBO and Showtime and Cinemax and VH1, which we don't get at home, so I kinda watched *The Vanishing* and *Dead Poets Society* while I waited for *Saturday Night Live* to come on. I always watch *Saturday Night Live*," she explained.

"So you sat in the playroom and watched TV—"

"No, I read my English assignment—"

"—and read your English assignment," Detective Fineburg agreed hastily. "Did you hear anything?"

"No."

"Did you see anyone during that time?"

"No—at least, not until I went to get the bottle—"

"When did that happen?"

"Well—" Whitney pursed her lips. "It was right around twelve-thirty, because I was on the phone with Mike and he has an absolute curfew of twelve-thirty—his folks are *real* strict about it—and he was still at Janice's party and I was telling him he was going to catch it when all of a sudden Alden started to cry."

"So what did you do?" asked the detective.

"Well, I put down the phone and I went to pick up Alden and I kind of hugged him for a while and then I brought him back into the playroom with me and got back on the phone with Mike and told him I had to go now and that he'd better get home fast and to call me when he got home and then I hung up with him and went down the back stairs to get Alden his bottle. It's in the kitchen," she explained.

"Did you see anyone when you went downstairs?" pursued the detective.

"No—but I did see someone when I was coming back," said Whitney.

"Who?" asked the detective.

"Why—her," said Whitney, and pointed at me.

Everyone's head whipped around.

"Me?" I stammered.

"Mrs. Hack?" Detective Fineburg repeated. "Are you sure?"

"Uh-huh," Whitney nodded. "Her and this other lady. You were wearing fishnets and shorts," she reminded me.

"The other lady," said Detective Fineburg. "You said there was another lady there, too. What did she look like?"

Whitney considered. "I only saw her back. She was coming out of one of the rooms and she and Mrs. Hack met in the hall. She was wearing a shiny kind of dress and she had this little cap on her head—"

"A flapper outfit?" asked the detective.

"Huh?" said Whitney.

"You know, a nineteen-twenties kind of outfit? A flapper?"

"Nineteen-twenties?" Whitney repeated. "You mean, like, before Vietnam?"

"Forget it," said the detective. "The costume was shiny. Was it long or short, do you remember?"

"Umm, around the knee, I think," said Whitney.

"What happened next?"

"Well, the other lady kind of stopped and looked at Mrs. Hack and then she walked down the stairs. The *front* stairs," Whitney corrected herself.

"Did you happen to see what Mrs. Hack did?" asked the detective, studying his ballpoint.

I held my breath.

"Uh-huh. Mrs. Hack waited a few moments and then she went downstairs, too," said Whitney.

"The front stairs?" asked the detective.

"Yes. The front stairs," said Whitney.

I let out my breath.

"What happened then?" asked the detective.

"Well, umm, I went back into the playroom and started to give Alden the bottle but he had already fallen back asleep, so I put him to bed and then I started to go back down the stairs to return the bottle to the kitchen—"

"The back stairs?"

"Yes, the back stairs, and that's when I saw *him*," said Whitney.

"Him? Him who?" asked the detective.

"You know, the guy that got killed."

"Howard Hack?" asked the detective. "You saw Howard Hack?"

"Uh-huh," said Whitney. "Well, actually, I just saw his head. He was sticking his head out of a door."

"Then how do you know it was Howard Hack?" demanded Detective Fineburg.

"I saw his picture in the newspaper," said Whitney. "He's kind of cute, for an old guy I mean," she added hastily.

"You saw Howard Hack stick his head out of a doorway? What was he doing?"

"He was talking to a lady on the landing," reported Whitney.

The room went completely still.

"Could you see her?"

"Kind of."

"Did you know her?"

I held my breath again.

"No."

"What did she look like?'

Whitney frowned. "I don't know. It was kind of hard to see. She had on a long dress."

"A long dress? Was it Mrs. Chase?"

"I don't know," said Whitney. "I don't think so."

"What color hair did she have?"

"I don't remember."

"Was she wearing a hat or a headpiece?"

"I don't know. I was kind of distracted. You see, I heard the phone ringing and I knew it was Mike calling me so I went right back inside the playroom because I wanted to find out if he'd gotten in trouble on account of getting home late because sometimes they ground him for that and we were supposed to go to a concert together the next weekend and—"

"So, Whitney, just to confirm, you saw Mr. Hack alive and talking to another woman *after* you saw Mrs. Hack leave?" Pat broke in.

"I'll ask the questions, if you don't mind, Ms. LaFountain," said the detective.

"I'm sorry, Detective Fineburg. I just wanted to make sure we all understood the implications of Whitney's testimony," said Pat.

"I'd like to *get* all of Whitney's testimony first, if you don't mind," the detective retorted. He turned back to Whitney. "You said Howard Hack was calling to this woman in the long dress on the landing. Did you hear what he was saying?"

"Umm, well—"

"If you can remember anything at all, I'm sure it will be helpful," the chief broke in.

"Well, I'm not *sure* but I *think* he said '. . . and a Diet Pepsi,'" said Whitney. "Of course, I could have heard wrong. It could have been 'and a quiet bepsi,' or something."

"A quiet bepsi?" repeated the chief. "What's that supposed to mean?"

"I don't know," said Whitney. "I'm only saying it *could* have been—"

"Yes, yes," Detective Fineburg cut in. "So you saw Howard Hack speaking to a woman—"

"—other than Elizabeth Hack," Pat interceded smoothly.

Detective Fineburg glared at her. "Other than Elizabeth Hack—at about what time?"

"Ten to one. I know because that's when Mike called."

"Ten to one. What happened then?"

"Then I talked to Mike for a while and—"

"Did you hear anything else?"

"Like what?" asked Whitney.

"Like—like—" the detective floundered.

"You mean, like a shot?" asked Whitney.

"Did you hear a shot?"

"No," said Whitney. "Between talking to Mike and the end of *Saturday Night Live* I didn't hear anything outside."

"Then why did you guess a shot?" asked the chief.

"Well, somebody shot him, didn't they? That's what it said in the paper and on the news and everything," said Whitney.

"So you didn't hear anything else," said the detective.

"No," said Whitney.

"And you didn't see Mr. Hack again?"

"No."

"Or this other lady in the long dress?"

"No."

"Whitney," said the detective slowly, "why didn't you tell all this to the police when they asked you that night?"

"Umm, well, I guess because nobody asked me," said Whitney.

"Nobody asked you?" the detective repeated. "I don't understand. I thought everyone in the house was interrogated at the time," he said, looking at the chief.

The chief coughed.

Whitney shrugged. "I heard all the running around, of course, but nobody came to get me," she volunteered. "So, you know, I just stayed in the playroom."

"But the next morning, Whitney," Chief Rudge broke in. "You said you knew about the murder. Didn't you tell your mother or father about it? Didn't you think to come to the police with what you knew?"

"The next morning?" Whitney repeated. "The next morning was Sunday. Sunday mornings I have soccer practice. And afterward my mom took me to the mall in Springfield because there was a dance coming up and I still didn't have shoes to match my dress and we'd already looked in Pittsfield and everything and it was the only day my mom had to take me—"

"Thank you, Whitney," Detective Fineburg cut in hastily.

"Now that you *are* speaking to us, do you have anything to add to what you've already told us?"

"Umm, I don't *think* so," said Whitney.

"In that case, would you mind waiting out in the hall for a moment?"

"Umm, my mom and dad are here waiting for me. Could I—"

"Of course," said Detective Fineburg. "Chief Rudge, would you please take Whitney out to where her parents are and explain that we will need to have her sign a written statement?"

"Of course," said the chief, pushing back his chair. "Come on, Whitney."

Pat stood up. "Thank you, Whitney," she said, "for coming forward with your testimony. You've been very helpful."

"Oh, uh, sure," said Whitney.

We waited silently until the door had closed behind Whitney and the chief. Then Pat turned like a cat upon Detective Fineburg. "Well, Detective?"

Detective Fineburg tapped his ballpoint slowly against his notebook. "I'm not sure how much this changes things," he said finally. "All I have is testimony which confirms that Mrs. Hack was in the vicinity—"

"—and left that vicinity," interjected Pat. "While the victim was still alive."

"She could have come back."

"There is no evidence of that. There is, however, evidence of someone else being there."

"There is still the issue of the gun," said Detective Fineburg. "She could have wiped down and thrown away the gun so as not to implicate herself."

"It could easily have been planted. Like a lot of other people in town, Elizabeth leaves her doors unlocked."

"Then why did she throw it away?"

"For the reason she told you. She was scared," said Pat. "You have been trying to implicate her."

"For good reason."

"Until right now," Pat rejoined. "Now it looks as though it might be worthwhile trying to implicate somebody else. Like a woman in a long dress."

Detective Fineburg was silent.

"You don't have enough," argued Pat. "You know you don't."

After a long moment, Detective Fineburg closed his notebook. "You're free to go, Mrs. Hack," he said, without looking up.

"Is that it?" I asked Pat later, Emily asleep on my shoulder, outside in the parking lot.

She nodded.

"They're not going to charge me? You're sure?" I pressed.

"They're not going to charge you. As things stand, they've got no case. It doesn't matter if they suspect you did it, if they believe you did it, if they're convinced down to their toenails that you did it. Without a case they cannot charge you. Period. And if they can't charge you, from a legal point of view you are innocent."

"Oh, Pat, that's—" I stopped. Something in her answer had struck me. "What do you mean, 'as things stand'?" I asked.

"Well, obviously, if new evidence is uncovered implicating you—"

"Like what?" I interrupted.

Pat shrugged. "Oh, I don't know, it could be anything. Someone comes forward and says you didn't really leave the party when you said you did, or that you did leave the party but came back again in time to do it, or even an eyewitness that they missed—like Whitney—who heard the shot and saw you leave the room—" She saw my face. "But, of course, none of that's going to happen," she added, giving my arm a little squeeze. "I mean, the only way something like that would happen is if you really did it, right? And of course you didn't."

"Of course I didn't," I repeated mechanically.

"So you're perfectly in the clear. Don't give it another thought," she said.

I blinked at her, then roused myself to smile. "Thanks for all you've done," I said, giving her a big hug. "I don't know what I would have done without you."

Pat smiled. "Don't thank me. Thank Didi. It was she who found Whitney."

I walked Pat to her car, watched her get in and turn on the ignition, and smiled and waved as she drove away. But as soon as she was out of sight, my smile faded.

There was another way for incriminating evidence to show up, a way with which I was already too familiar, a way Pat had failed to mention. It can be put there by somebody else—someone with a vested interest in implicating you. Someone like the real murderer. So I wasn't perfectly safe, not yet.

But I am going to be, I thought grimly, hugging Emily tightly and eyeing my briefcase, the precious documents inside still undisturbed. Oh, yes, I am going to be.

18

"Ah, yes," said the maître d'. "Ms. Halperin. Mr. Laramee is waiting for you. May I show you to the table?"

"Elizabeth!" Phillip stood up. "You look fabulous. Being cleared of suspicion in a murder case obviously agrees with you. By the way, I saw the piece on ABC last night. How did you get them to agree to air a retraction?"

"I had nothing to do with it," I replied. "It must have been in the interest of fairness."

"Yes. Broadcast journalism is noted for its commitment to fairness," Phillip observed.

He held the chair for me. The maître d' waited until I was comfortably settled, then handed me a menu. A waiter filled my water glass. Another asked if I'd like a cocktail.

"Let's order a bottle of wine," I said.

"No," said Phillip, resuming his seat. "I think champagne is in order." He looked from the wine list to the waiter. "Number four, please, Henri."

"Very good, Mr. Laramee," said Henri.

"Of course, Henri. If it weren't very good I wouldn't order it," said Phillip.

All the waiters disappeared and we were left alone at the table.

Phillip leaned forward ever so slightly. "All right, Elizabeth," he said softly. "What shall we talk about today?"

"Let's talk about books," I said.

"Wonderful!" said Phillip. "I love to talk about books. Is there any book in particular you would like to discuss?"

"Well, actually," I said, "it's not really a book yet. It's more like the idea for a book."

"You have an idea for a book?"

"Yes. As it happens I do. It's a murder mystery. Would you care to hear the plot?"

"Oh, absolutely," said Phillip. "I love a good murder mystery. Ah, but here's the champagne."

Henri displayed a bottle of Veuve Cliquot, silver label. Phillip nodded. Henri went through the uncorking ceremony with his usual aplomb and, when our glasses had been filled, put the bottle on ice and retired discreetly.

Phillip lifted his glass. "Do you have a particular toast in mind as well?"

"Yes, I do." I smiled. "To us."

"Well, that sounds promising," said Phillip.

"Let's see if you still feel that way after I give you my plot summary," I said.

Phillip nodded, sipped and sat back to listen. "Fire away," he said. "That's publisher talk."

"It's about a writer. A writer who receives a very large advance on a novel and then gets bumped off on the eve of publication. Let's call him Howard, shall we? For simplicity's sake."

"An interesting premise," agreed Phillip. "Go on."

"The murderer leaves a note with the body. It's a poem by Blake. *The Garden of Love*. Since Howard was a known womanizer, this makes it look as though the motive is passion."

"Better and better. Sex sells, you know," noted Phillip.

"But the police aren't sure the poem isn't just misdirection. They suspect the writer's estranged wife—we'll call her Elizabeth—who inherits the large advance and the royalties from the sale of the book. They believe the motive is money, not sex. And you know something? The police are right."

"They're right about Elizabeth?" asked Phillip.

"No. But they're right about the motive. The motive was money."

"But who, outside of Elizabeth, profited by the murder of the writer . . . Howard, wasn't it?" asked Phillip.

"I'm getting to that," I said. "You see, you have to know the book business to get it. That's why Howard was killed way out in the country. The murderer knew—or hoped, at any rate—that the investigation would be left in the hands of local small-town cops, who couldn't be expected to understand the ins and outs of publishing. Even a state detective would have trouble figuring it out, not being familiar with book contracts and the accounts of publishing companies and the like."

"So if the police don't get it, then—" Phillip began.

"When suspicion falls on Elizabeth, she is forced to try to solve the mystery herself. At first, she is fooled by the Blake poem and by her own bias against one of Howard's past lovers. But then she reads Howard's book—*Passion Palace*, it's called—and she figures it out. But to prove it, she has to break into the publisher's computer."

"Hmm," said Phillip. "This wouldn't have anything to do with the unannounced visit you made to my office last week with that rather Teutonic—"

"She's Dutch."

"Whatever. By the way, the next time you see her, you might tell her that there is still a Mercedes waiting for her at the airport in Singapore."

"Shall we get back to my plot outline?"

"By all means."

"Elizabeth has an interesting visit," I admitted, taking out my briefcase. "She takes the liberty of copying some information off of the publisher's computer, but then she finds, thanks to a high school baby-sitter in Lenox, that she doesn't have to show it to the police. At least for the moment. So she thinks, well, she'll show it to you."

"To me?" said Phillip.

"Well, you are Howard's publisher, aren't you?"

"Okay," said Phillip. "So Elizabeth shows me my own accounts. That's great. I love looking at my own accounts."

"I find that rather surprising, Phillip. Your accounts weren't in particularly good shape. Until *Passion Palace*, that is. *Passion Palace* is going to make you a rather substantial amount of money. But then, it had to, didn't it?"

"It was helpful," Phillip admitted.

"I read it, you know. *Passion Palace*. All the way through. From beginning to end."

"Really. What possibly could have possessed you to take on such an odious chore?"

"It was the strangest thing, Phillip. There I was, sitting in the living room of a woman I know, whose taste in literature generally runs to Sue Grafton or Dick Francis—"

"I certainly wish we had one of them," Phillip sighed, taking another sip of champagne.

"Oh, but Phillip, you don't need them," I assured him. "Because there on her coffee table was *Passion Palace*."

"Really!" Phillip looked up and beamed.

"Of course she hadn't read it," I continued.

"Well, nobody *read* it," Phillip murmured.

"Exactly what I thought." I turned to him. "And why has nobody read it, Phillip?"

"Well, Elizabeth, the reason for that, I am embarrassed to say, is rather simple."

"Yes?"

"The book is utterly dreadful," said Phillip. "No, dreadful is the wrong word." Phillip thought for a moment, then brightened. "Execrable. *That's* the right word."

"Exactly what I thought." I paused. "Phillip, I have a literary question for you."

"My specialty. Fire away."

"Hypothetically speaking, how many copies do you think *Passion Palace* would have sold if its author had not been so fortuitously and sensationally murdered?"

"Are we including his close friends and immediate family?" asked Phillip.

"Howard didn't have much immediate family," I said.

"Any little bit would have helped," said Phillip.

"Exactly what I thought."

"You may have a flair for publishing, Elizabeth," Phillip noted.

"But here's what I want to know," I continued. "Did you plan the whole thing *before* you bought the book?"

"In retrospect, I wish I had been clever enough to think of it. But no, this was an idea born strictly of necessity."

"So you gave Howard his contract in good faith. You really believed *Passion Palace* was going to be a great book."

"It was hard to tell. I hadn't seen any of it," said Phillip.

"You mean you paid a million dollars for a book you hadn't seen?"

"Oh, there's nothing unusual about that," Phillip assured me. "Happens all the time."

"But after he turned in the book," I persisted. "The

advance was payable upon delivery of the manuscript. Why did you still pay him the money after you'd seen the book?"

"Well, what can I tell you? We were caught. We'd made such a hoopla over him in the first place that we couldn't very well change our minds in the middle. And then, I had nothing to replace him with and some very stern Germanic corporate types in suits—you should meet the *real* Dr. Theilen—worrying about interest payments and rates of return and the like peering over my shoulder all the time and second-guessing all of my efforts. I tell you, the biggest mistake I ever made was getting involved with Begelmann. Of course, I didn't have much choice about that at the time, either, but—I've always said art has no business getting mixed up with commerce. You see the results," he added virtuously and took a sip of champagne.

"So you really had two problems," I said. "Getting out of Howard's contract *and* coming up with a bestseller at the same time."

"Exactly. And the only way to do it was to work with the existing manuscript, pathetic as it was," said Phillip.

"But what made you think of killing him?" I asked.

"Oh, killing him was the easy part. Making it all look sexy, that was hard," said Phillip. "We had to make it look like a lover was involved, not only for the publicity, but to deflect suspicion from ourselves. Luckily, Howard's physical appearance and personal life were helpful. But, of course, we knew that when we signed him on," he added.

"So that's why you left the note with the Blake poem."

"Oh, yes, you can't be too obvious where the police are concerned ... Besides, not only did it help establish unrequited passion as a motive, it gave a touch of class to the proceedings. Remember, we were pitching Howard as literary," noted Phillip.

"And that did it," I said.

"Yes, if I do say so myself, it worked beautifully. As it turned out, there were any number of women who fit the role of betrayed lover."

"But you chose to implicate me."

"Elizabeth, how can you think such a thing? You know how much I enjoy your company. No, when we planned this we had no set suspect in mind. We intended just to wait and see who naturally rose to the forefront. Imagine my unhappiness when it turned out to be you and not, say, Holly Ivy." He shrugged. "I really had no choice. We had to have a murderer, not only for our own safety, but to keep up sales. At first, we thought that saying that the solution lay within the book would be enough, but nobody got it, so we had to go farther. Literature is so competitive," he sighed.

"So you had the gun planted at my house," I said.

"It was unavoidable. We needed that little extra push over the top." Phillip shrugged. "But I want to assure you," he said quickly, "that my offer at the end of our first lunch was genuine. I was quite sure that the gun had been safely tucked into your house by then."

"I can't express to you how flattered I feel."

"No need to thank me. No one was more thrilled than I that you succeeded in wiggling out of it. Now everyone is happy."

"Except Howard."

"On the contrary. Howard got precisely what he always wanted. This way, he will attain a place in American letters which he could never have hoped to achieve on merit."

"Tell me, Phillip," I said, leaning forward, "what prevents me from getting up right now and taking everything I know to the police?"

"And leaving the champagne?"

"After the champagne," I acknowledged.

"I wish you wouldn't do that," said Phillip. "I'm sure we

can work out something much more interesting. Besides," he said, with a glance at the papers from my briefcase, "those are hardly admissible in court."

"Just because they're not admissible in court doesn't mean they're not useful," I pointed out. "I might show them to the police, for example. It would make them so happy to finally have the identity of the killer and the real motive." I took another sip of champagne. "I'm told the police are quite adept at constructing a case once they already know who did it and why."

Phillip paused and thought this over. "It is possible that they just might be capable of that, yes," he admitted.

"And then there's always the press," I continued. "They might be interested in the story, don't you think?"

"Ah, yes, the press," Phillip agreed.

"And then, of course, the police will see it . . ."

"Do the police read these days?" asked Phillip.

"They can always catch it on the evening news."

"Ah, yes."

"But then, these alternatives are strictly hypothetical," I assured him. "I would never consider taking such action unless something unfortunate happened to me," I added.

"Dear Elizabeth. Why would anything happen to you?" asked Phillip.

"There is precedent, Phillip."

"Elizabeth, you do me a disservice. Actually, I want nothing more than that we should all work together. Ah! And along those lines, I took the liberty of inviting someone else to our little party, and here she is."

Phillip rose, arm extended. I turned to look at an older woman with hennaed hair wearing a tasteful black suit being escorted to the table.

"Francine," he said, drawing her close and giving her a quick peck on the cheek. "Glad you could make it."

"Am I on time?" Francine asked.

"Perfectly. Elizabeth and I have just gotten through the preliminaries."

"Elizabeth," Francine Weezle said with a smile. "So nice to see you again."

"Francine," I said, and shook her hand.

Francine plopped herself into the chair next to me. "Well," she said, putting down her handbag and leaning forward. "How far have we gotten?"

"As far as the champagne," said Phillip.

"That far," said Francine. She turned to me. "I hope you haven't agreed to anything yet," she said.

"Not yet."

"Actually, Francine," Phillip broke in, "I was just getting around to it."

"Well, go ahead, then," said Francine, as Henri brought a third champagne glass.

"Yes," I said to Phillip. "Please. Go ahead."

Phillip smiled. "Well, I must say, Elizabeth, that when I received your phone call asking me to lunch—after your clandestine visit to my office—I had a pretty good idea what it was you wanted to talk about. And I thought it wouldn't hurt to come prepared. So Francine and I put our heads together to see if we couldn't offer you a deal that would be satisfactory to all of us. Francine being involved as well," Phillip added.

"I guess pulling the trigger does sort of involve a person," I agreed.

"Exactly. And what we thought was, why should this have to be acrimonious? After all, you've been cleared. Why make life difficult for others if there is not an overriding need to do so?"

"An interesting moral quandary."

"Isn't it?"

"So what do you propose?"

"It's very simple. I'm always in the market for a new book and now, as you yourself pointed out, you've got one. I think I can offer you quite good terms, considering that you've never been published before, that is," said Phillip.

"Are you actually suggesting that I write a book about Howard's murder?" I asked.

"No. I'm suggesting you write the book you just pitched. A nice, light comic mystery about a writer who is—how did you put it?—oh, yes, bumped off. I think I can offer you—"

"What makes you think I want to write a book?" I interrupted.

"Oh, come on, Elizabeth. Everybody wants to write a book. Taxicab drivers want to write a book. College professors. Rabbis. Besides, you wear it. Why do you think you married Howard in the first place?" asked Francine.

"You yourself brought it up," Phillip reminded me. "Of course, you don't have to—"

"But I don't know why you wouldn't want to use something with such obvious commercial possibilities—" started Francine.

"I would be willing to go as high as ten thousand," said Phillip.

"We won't do it for less than twenty," said Francine.

"We?" I asked. "Who is we?"

"Why, I am," she said with some surprise. "Why do you think I'm here? If you want some other representation, of course you're welcome to find someone, but really, don't you think it's best to keep this particular project among ourselves? Involving other people gets so messy," she said with distaste, stealing a glance at my briefcase.

"But what makes you think I'm good enough to write such a book?" I wanted to know.

234 • NANCY GOLDSTONE

"You couldn't do worse than Howard," observed Phillip.

"Yes, but look what happened to him."

"All the more incentive to do a good job," Phillip rejoined. He lifted his glass. "Have we got a deal?"

"Everything work out all right in the city?" Rose rasped later that afternoon.

"Yes, thank you, Rose. Everything all right here?" I replied.

"Oh, yes." Rose heaved herself to her feet. "If you don't mind, I'll just be going," she said, collecting her handbag and hat. "The truck needs a new carburetor. Damn thing breaks every ten years."

"Umm, Rose," I said, following her to the front door. "Two weeks ago, when I went into the city for lunch, did anyone come to the door?"

Rose looked up at me. "Well, let's see. Two weeks ago—"

"It was a Wednesday," I reminded her. "I went into New York for lunch. Did anyone come to the door while I was out?"

"Well, let me see, I believe there *was* someone . . . Oh, yes, of course. That older woman."

"Older?" I repeated. Rose was seventy-two. "How much older?"

"Aw, she must have been in her fifties," said Rose. "But she was one of those who tries to hide it. Had her hair dyed this red color. Sort of like the color the bottom of the chassis turns after a winter when I didn't bother to rustproof it. I can't ever tell if it's worth it to try to keep up with the snow and the ice and the salt or just wait until the whole blamed thing's over—"

"She came to the door? What did she want?"

"Who?"

"The woman with the red hair."

"Oh! Let me see." Rose squinted a little. "Oh, yes. She asked for you."

"What did you say?" I asked.

"I said you weren't there right then and I didn't expect you back until later."

"Then what happened?"

"She asked in that case, could she please use the bathroom," Rose reported.

"Did you let her?"

"We-ell, she had to go pretty bad. You could tell by the way she was sort of clutching her handbag. Older people, you know, can have trouble that way. Why, my first cousin had that kind of trouble. Couldn't pass a john without contributing to save his life. The doctors had some fancy name for it—I can't remember what they called it—"

"Thank you, Rose," I said, and opened the door.

"There wasn't anything wrong with that, was there?" Rose demanded from the front step. "I mean, when you got to go, you got to—"

"It's fine. Thank you, Rose," I said. "I just wanted to know."

"Well, as long as you're satisfied. Good night, my darling," she trilled to Emily and waddled down the steps.

I watched Rose go, then picked up Emily and walked slowly up the stairs to my office. On a hunch, I shoved Howard's disk once more into my computer.

SEARCH FOR . . . ? asked the computer.

F-R-A-N-C-I-N-E, I typed.

FRANCINE

I met Francine one cold winter's evening at Margaux's. Margaux had asked her up specifically to meet me. She thought Francine might be helpful in placing *Genius Tortured*. Even before the entree was served, I was aware that Francine didn't mind being helpful in other ways as well. I was amenable to this. In my experience, older women are underrated as lovers. Not only are they surprisingly inventive, they're so *grateful*.

Once Francine had agreed, in a manner of speaking, to take me on, events spiraled forward at an alarming pace. She proved herself to be both efficient and highly ambitious. Before I had even had a chance to complete it, my book was sold for a large sum of money—deservedly so, of course, but still. Francine was ardent the day I signed the contract. I remember being flattered by her regard for me.

But then, almost immediately upon my delivering the finished manuscript, I sensed a change in our relations and grew apprehensive. The publisher demanded alterations: I, of course, refused. Great artists do not give in to petty commercial concerns, I told Francine, who, to my complete surprise, immediately flew into a violent rage. I won't recount here the vile expletives she used, nor the contempt she showed for my art. Suffice to say that I was stunned by her reaction. It seemed as though she were capable of anything. I had heard, of course (as who had not?), the rumors that she had killed her first husband in order to gain control of her literary agency, but I had always put it down in the past to the work of envious competitors. Now, after a few more sessions with her—during the last of which she tried to bully me into changing the title to *Passion Palace* or some such ridiculous verbiage—I was not so sure. It was a relief, after all, when she called up, in the friendliest way possible, to ask if I intended to go to Margaux's Halloween party, and, if so, could I schedule her a private moment upstairs later in the evening.

I looked at Emily.

"Well," I said. "So that's that. The last piece of the puzzle. The End. Finis," and turned off the machine.

Chapter

19

"Oh, Elizabeth, this is so nice," sighed Didi, lifting her wine glass and taking a small sip.

"Really," Pat agreed. "We don't do this enough. You know, get together just as friends without the kids."

"*Ja*," said Astrid. "And maybe next time we won't have to wait for Elizabeth to almost go to jail in order to think of it."

We all laughed and clinked our glasses. We were sitting at the Church Street Cafe at the big table by the window.

"You all saved my life," I said. "The least I can do is buy you dinner."

"Nonsense," Didi chided. "What are friends for?"

"Well," I said, "if friends are for stepping in and saving the day, you win the prize. I still don't understand how you came up with Whitney."

"It was easy," said Didi. "The children. Whenever *I* give a party, Samantha's in and out of bed the whole night trying to wheedle her way down to the dessert table and Sean invariably picks that evening to throw up his rice cereal. But halfway through Margaux's party I realized that not only hadn't I seen or heard either Tolin or Alden the whole evening, Margaux had not once been called away from her post to play mommy. I remembered thinking how she must have hired a baby-sitter to stay upstairs with the children, and how clever she'd been to have thought of it. Then, after I realized that Howard had been killed upstairs, I thought the baby-sitter might have seen or heard something. But when I asked Cousin John about it he just said, 'What baby-sitter?' and then I knew the police had missed something."

"Did Margaux give you her name right off or did you have to pry it out of her?" I asked, taking a sip of my wine.

Didi turned to me seriously. "You know, Elizabeth, I think we've been wrong about Margaux. She was just as sweet and helpful as she could be."

"Ha," I snorted.

"No, really. Not only did she give me Whitney's name, she drove over with me to her house to question her. And when she heard what she had to say she called Chief Rudge at once and told him he was wrong about you and that they'd better come and listen to Whitney's story." Didi nibbled a carrot stick. "You know what it is about Margaux?" she said. "I think she's lonely. That big house and all that money—people just naturally shy away from her. That's why she wanted to join the play group in the first place. And now that she's going out with that reporter she's so much nicer to be around any—"

"Reporter?" I demanded. "Did you say that Margaux is going out with a reporter?"

"Why, yes, quite an important one, too, I think. He just got a new job with Peter Jennings. Let me see if I can remember his name—" Didi paused. "Derman, Berman—"

"Sherman Forrest," I supplied.

"Why, yes, that's it. How did you know?"

"Lucky guess," I offered, and drank.

"Oh. Yes. Well, anyway, she actually felt terrible about you. You see, she honestly believed you did it, so she had been feeding Herman—"

"Sherman."

"—whatever, information about you and about the crime to help him advance his career. As soon as she realized she was wrong, she told everybody. She's the one who made him publish that retraction on the evening news last week."

"Talk about somebody's being wrong about someone," Pat broke in, "I might as well own up about Caitlin."

"Caitlin? Who is Caitlin?" asked Astrid.

"She was Howard's attorney," Pat explained. "She was handling the estate for Elizabeth."

"You suspected Caitlin?" I asked. "But she wasn't even at the party."

"Well—" Pat drawled, "I wasn't so sure about that. She might have been."

"Pat! Not really," I said.

"Yes, really. I'll tell you what made me think of it. That first time when I spoke to her. She pulled all this cleanse your soul stuff with me over the phone." Pat sniffed. "What a phony! That woman didn't know wheat germ from witch hazel. Told me she'd learned all about it at the Living Alternatives Institute in Sheffield the weekend of the murder. That's when I thought, hmm, Sheffield's not so very far from Lenox. So I called some people I knew at Living Alternatives and I found out that, sure enough, Caitlin had been down there for the weekend but that she'd spent part of Saturday night off institute grounds. Called for her car about eleven-thirty and didn't pull in again until nearly two. Plenty of time, in my opinion, to get herself to Margaux's party, pull the trigger and get back to the Institute in time for the breakfast soul-searching.

"But I didn't have a motive," Pat continued. "Just this

hunch. So I thought, well, just keep your eyes open. And then the papers arrived and I thought yes! I've got her."

"What papers?" asked Astrid.

"Copies of Howard's last will and testament—both of them—and an outline of the estate. Everything was in order except—"

"The Locomoro Land Trust," I said.

Pat turned to me. "So you knew," she said. "Why didn't you say something?"

I shook my head. "I'm just guessing."

Pat threw me a look. "Some guess," she said.

"What, if I may ask," asked Didi, "is the Locomoro Land Trust?"

"It was a speculative investment that Caitlin's law firm got involved with at the end of the eighties, right before real estate prices crashed. They lost a lot of money on it, almost enough to put the partnership out of business. In cases like that it is always a temptation to substitute your client's money for your own, especially when your client is unsophisticated about finance. That's why the law firm branched out into artists and authors in the first place. Generally people like that know very little about money." She turned to me. "Holly Ivy is one of their clients, did you know that? For a while I suspected her, too."

I shook my head. "She couldn't have done it. I would have heard the shot."

"She could have come back."

I stared at her. "I never thought of that."

"You should have," said Pat. "I did."

"I saw her going in to see Caitlin one day soon after Howard's death, but I thought she was trying to steal his notes," I explained.

Pat laughed. "She probably was. She hired Caitlin just after Howard died to try to get what she could out of the estate.

Instead, Caitlin got what *she* could out of Holly. I'm sure she fell all over herself signing Holly up for the Locomoro Land Trust."

"Couldn't have happened to a nicer couple," I said.

Astrid broke in. "But what has this to do with Elizabeth?"

Pat turned back to her. "Caitlin was intending to put Howard into Locomoro—and thereby take herself out of it— but the terms of his new will were such that she couldn't," she explained. "I think she thought she'd have a better chance with Elizabeth."

"But Elizabeth knows about money," protested Astrid.

"Yes, but I think Caitlin thought she could slip it by her because she stays home with Emily. I think she thought Elizabeth wouldn't be paying attention," said Pat.

"Humph," I snorted, this time with dignity.

"You mean, she had a motive?" asked Didi. "Maybe she did do it after all."

Pat shook her head. "I hired a detective and had her whereabouts traced the night of the murder. She spent the whole time between eleven-thirty and two drinking double martinis at Railroad Street."

"No!" I exclaimed.

"I told you she was a phony," sniffed Pat again.

"Pat," I said. "You spent your own money. Let me—"

"Forget it," she said with a wave of her hand. "It's already paid for itself. You're not going to believe this, but Detective Fineburg was so impressed with my work that he's going to talk to the DA about me. He said there's an assistant DA position opening up."

"Pat, that's terrific!" we all said at once.

Didi played with her salad fork. "Well, what I want to know is, if it wasn't this one and it wasn't that one—just who was it?"

Astrid turned to me eagerly. "Elizabeth, what about those papers we—"

"Dessert!" I said brightly, signaling to the waitress. "Would anyone like dessert?"

"I'd like something." Astrid accepted a menu. "But what about—" she persisted.

"Didi? What will you have?" I asked.

"Oh, nothing for me," said Didi.

I looked at her closely. "Why, Didi, you've lost some weight," I said. "Quite a bit of weight."

"Ten pounds," said Didi, struggling to keep the pride from her voice and not succeeding.

"Ten pounds! Congratulations!" I said, giving her a hug. "You must really have been working at it."

"Well, actually, I owe it all to you, Elizabeth," said Didi. "It was having to get up early all those mornings to go to the gym to snoop around Cousin John. Kind of got me in the habit of working out again."

"*Ja*, well, I'm going to have the mocha torte with the home-made hazelnut ice cream and fudge sauce," Astrid announced. She looked at us slyly. "With a side order of pickles."

We all looked at her.

"Astrid," I said. "No—

"Astrid," said Didi. "You're not—"

"Astrid," said Pat. "Are you saying—"

Astrid smiled and patted her stomach. "How do you say it? In for a penny, in for twenty-five pounds?"

In the crush of hugs and congratulations that followed I heard Didi sigh, "This is all so nice. Imagine all this coming from a murder case!"

"Not all of it," said Astrid.

"You know what I mean. How peculiar that we still don't know who did it."

"I guess this is one of those cases that will never be solved," I said, calling for the check.

Epilogue

I wish I could tell you that I reconsidered, rose up in righteous indignation, spurned Phillip's and Francine's deal and took everything I knew to the police. At the very least, I wish I could tell you that although I didn't exactly turn in Howard's killers, I didn't work with them, either. I wish I could tell you . . . but why waste time? In the movies, the heroine may turn down a book contract by a major publisher on principle, but hey, this isn't the movies.

I also kind of wish I could tell you that it didn't work out, but, unfortunately (or fortunately, depending on your point of view), it did. In fact, it worked out extremely well. My book got reviewed in all the major papers, something of a feat, Phillip assures me, for this kind of a book. It didn't make the bestsellers list, but it did well enough for Francine to negotiate another, larger advance on the next one. Francine, by the way, has turned out to be an excellent agent. She even got me optioned for the movies.

As I was telling Adam just the other day, it really is amazing how my life has turned around since the day I started that play group. I must start thinking about organizing a new one. Adam said he thought that was a good idea but that I should probably wait until we actually have a baby.

Emily is growing up, of course. Someday I'm sure I will explain all this to her. How it was all necessary. How, sometimes, you have to do things that are . . . you know, not exactly . . .

Well, she'll understand.